LET ME HEAR A RHYME

TIFFANY D. JACKSON

WITH LYRICS BY
MALIK "MALIK-16" SHARIF

KATHERINE TEGEN BOOKS
An Imprint of HarperCollins Publishers

Katherine Tegen Books is an imprint of HarperCollins Publishers.

Let Me Hear a Rhyme

Library of Congress Control Number: 2018968472
ISBN 978-0-06-284032-5

Typography by Erin Fitzsimmons
19 20 21 22 23   PC/LSCH   10 9 8 7 6 5 4 3 2 1
❖
First Edition

For my cousin Sherrill Lavonne Bryant,
who introduced me to hip-hop, bamboo earrings,
Martin, Yo-Yo, En Vogue, and Jodeci.

For the hustler in front of my auntie's building,
who taught me how to move in a room full of vultures.

For Brooklyn, home no matter where I go.

1
Quadir

You've probably seen this scene before:

Ladies in black church dresses, old men in gray suits, and hood kids in white tees with some blurry picture printed on the front under the spray-painted letters *RIP*. Pastor in the corner eating lemon cake, grandmas in their regal crowns waving church fans, while aunties swim around, refilling plates, sneaking sips of Henny stashed in their purse.

My best friend, Steph, smiles at me from his cousin Roger's T-shirt. Roger lives in Queens, so Steph never saw him much. We Brooklyn kids don't travel to other boroughs like that. I mean, why would we?

Deadass, it's gotta be close to a hundred people stuffed in

this tiny-ass apartment, and them Sternos heating up lunch is making this place feel like we sitting inside a radiator. I don't recognize half the grown-ups walking around with long faces. They must be friends of Steph's mom. Or his pops.

I thought I'd see some reporters and cameramen at the church. For the past few days, I flipped through channels waiting to see Steph's photo cross the screen, but everyone was still busy talking about President Clinton hooking up with that intern. Like, damn, don't murders make the news no more? Don't they know who Steph was? I mean, yeah, folks die every day. But it's not every day you lose your main man.

Guess I'mma have to be the reporter and tell his story. What Ms. Greene in history class call it? Oral history, black storytelling, or something like that. Bet a real reporter would set up the scene better than I did. Probably something like:

Headline: Funeral Held for Slain Teen
On Saturday, roughly a hundred friends and family filled the victim's home in Brevoort, the notorious housing projects in the heart of Bedford-Stuyvesant, to celebrate the life of Stephon Davis, Jr.
Suspect still at large.

"Heard she almost requested a closed casket," someone whispers, but doing a shit job of it. "Poor thing, just been through so much."

"She" being Ms. Davis, Steph's mom, sitting across the room in the beat-up tan recliner Steph used to play in until he broke the handle and now nobody can recline like they supposed to. Her eyes stay locked on the green carpet, not caring if everyone tracks dirt across it. My mom made us take our shoes off at the door.

Jarrell is sitting next to me with a hole in his sock. He got that same look in his eye, like he's real far away, leaning on the love-seat arm, his thick fist smashing into his baby-fat cheek. This is the same rusty-color love seat all three of us used to chill on when we watched Knicks games, 'cause Rell thought it'd bring us good luck. Ain't never seen him look so sad. Not even when the Knicks lost in the playoffs and he owed Big Rob two hundred dollars. I know that's a wack comparison. But if you saw the way Jarrell carried on for a week, you'd understand.

Ms. Viv from apartment 6C stops in front of us, smiling. "You two okay? Can I get you anything?"

I shake my head real slow. "No thank you."

When Jarrell doesn't answer, I jab him with my elbow and he wakes up.

"Oh. Nah, I'm good. Thanks."

Ms. Viv sighs, heading for the kitchen, and I check on Ms. Davis again. Carl is curled up in her lap, eyes ping-ponging at everyone walking by. Poor homie, he's probably real confused. First, his big brother dies, now he has all these strangers up in his house. I don't know what I would've been thinking as a six-year-old. Ms. Davis rocks him back and forth, squeezing him like a pillow to her chest.

I could use a hug like that. Which reminds me, where's

Veronica? She said she'd stop by, and she knew what time the service ended. She get lost coming downstairs?

"Damn, it's hot up in here," Jarrell grumbles, tugging at the tie choking his neck. He can't take it off 'cause his moms is in the room, watching us like the Feds. One thing about Ms. Mullen, she don't play no games. Don't matter if you her child or not, she'll set you straight in a minute. Jarrell looks like the male version of her. Both got glowing dark skin, bowlegged, got deep wheezy voices, breathing mad hard like Darth Vader. Both got some weight on their bones, but while Ms. Mullen has all the fellas breaking their necks when she walks by, Jarrell's FUBU sweaters be looking extra-small.

I check on Ms. Davis again . . . and Jasmine sitting next to her. I almost didn't recognize her. I'm used to seeing her two Afro puffs and baggy jeans. Only seen her hair straight on picture day, and can't remember the last time I saw her in a dress.

She glances at me, her eyes real glassy like she's about to cry. And I can't look away.

She looks so much like Steph.

"Yo, I just can't believe he's gone," Jarrell says.

I blink at him, wondering if he caught me staring all hard. But his eyes were still glued to the rug.

"Yeah," I mumble. "It was mad crazy seeing him in that box."

He shakes his head. "Damn. He's really gone, though. I mean, they just offed him . . . just like that."

"Yo, chill, Rell. I don't even wanna think about that. Not here. Not now."

"You right. My bad, son."

Mourners line up to pay respect to Ms. Davis, and Jasmine walks out the room. Wish I knew what to say to her. Steph always had a way to cheer her up.

"I heard Steph's mom took it pretty hard. Jada said she could hear her screaming from her building."

"Yeah. But she did aight during the funeral, though."

Jarrell tugs at his collar. "I need a new suit. This shit is mad tight."

I chuckle. "Or you could chill with the McDonald's."

Jarrell sucks his teeth. "Man, I've been in mourning. Stop clocking my mouth."

As much fun as it is snapping on Jarrell, all I really wanna do is go home, lie in my room, turn up the radio, and read every magazine I ever saved cover to cover just to clear my head. This ain't how I planned to end summer, held up in the house, mad depressed.

Last night, they played Puff Daddy's "I'll Be Missing You" at least five times. That tribute to Big never made me cry before, but I sure lost a few tears thinking about Steph.

"We were supposed to go to Coney Island today," I mumble.

That's what Steph wanted to do. Tradition. Last Friday of summer break, we head to the beach, check out the shorties, then stay for the fireworks. Now we chilling at a funeral.

Biggie Smalls was right. Things done changed.

2
Jasmine

I always know when I'm about to faint.

First, all the muscles melt off my bones and slide down to my feet. Next, the room spins slow. Then, my knees stop working. Last, with all ninety-five pounds of muscle on the floor in a heap by my ankles, someone ties my shoelaces together, I take a step and fall flat on my face.

I overheat easy. Always have. Steph used to say if white folks ever send us back to Africa I wouldn't last a day.

My knees just started to feel numb when I escape all the eager eyes in our living room. Everyone's watching, waiting to see if Mom, Carl, and I will crack so they can open us up and see our insides. The hood is filled with nosy people, sucking up all the air, standing in the buffet line snaking out of our kitchen. How could anyone eat after seeing a body lying in a casket?

And not just any old body. Steph's body.

"First her husband, now her son. Poor thing," someone says, like they don't know how to whisper.

"Poor child, they were like twins."

"Mm-hmm. Lost a brother, but gained an angel."

Mom squeezes Carl tight with one hand, clinging to the back of my cardigan with the other. But just the simple touch has my body hitting a thousand degrees.

I don't want an angel. I want my brother back.

I rush out the room, in search of air that's not mixed with perfume, pity, and fried chicken.

Sweating through the stockings Mom made me wear under the dress that I can't stand, I bust into Steph's room and throw open the window. The relief is like sticking your face in the freezer. After spending two hours fighting with Mom's hot comb last night, my hair is already frizzing. Of course. There could be a drop of rain two states away and my hair would peep it and shrink up. I wanted to wear it in my regular puffs, but Mom made a big deal about straightening it for the funeral, and I didn't have the courage to argue with her. She doesn't like me rocking my hair natural. She's old-school. She still believes in blue flames and blue grease to straighten hair when all the other girls are using flat irons.

At least she didn't say nothing about my medallion. It's round, leather, with a cutout shape of Africa, stitched with red, green, and gold thread. It used to belong to Daddy. He wore it everywhere.

Déjà vu.

I hid in here during Daddy's funeral too. Except Steph was already in here, recording songs off the radio to make a new mixtape. He had this technique that made his tapes sound real professional. You have to listen close, one finger on the Record button, the other on the Play, half pushed down. Then when the first beat of the song he wants comes on, he'd push both buttons down real fast and it made for a smooth transition on the cassette tape. Last February, he gave Mom an R&B mixtape for Valentine's Day, and she thought he'd paid big money to have it done.

Lady of Rage stares down at me with that "Don't even try it" expression as tears rain on my dress. Would she be crying like this? I remember when I put that poster up for Steph. All he had were pictures of brothas, but ladies rap too. And no, not some models/side chicks pretending they know how to spit, rapping about all the clothes, sex, and money they get. I'm talking lyrical geniuses. Independent and strong. Everything I want to be.

"What up, Jazz?"

Quadir stands in the doorframe, squirming, looking unsure of whether it's safe to take another step.

"Uh . . . what up?" I say, sniffing back tears and quickly wipe my face dry. Dag, I don't want anyone seeing me like this. Especially Steph's friends.

"You okay? I was just . . . whoa." He gapes at the walls.

Mom used to say Steph's room looked like a magazine threw up all over the place with every artist you could ever think of: Biggie, Puff Daddy, the Lox, Mase, Method Man, Capone-N-Noreaga, Jay-Z, Big Pun. One side of the room dedicated to *The Source* magazine, *Rap Pages*, and *Vibe*. The other, movie posters: *Scarface*, *Coming to America*, *Boomerang*. You'd never know the walls were painted blue underneath his shrine to hip-hop, his first love.

Quadir gawks like he's walking into a museum. We lock eyes for a brief moment before Jarrell pushes past him.

"Yo, son. You think you a ghost or something and I can just walk through you? Move out the . . . whoa." Jarrell spins around, letting out a small chuckle. "Damn, look at all this shit!"

He grabs the basketball propped up next to Steph's bed, tossing it in the air.

On the desk is a three-disc-changer stereo with detachable speakers, covered in old fruity scratch-and-sniff stickers, so worn down the colors are faded white. Steph begged for almost a year for that thing, drove Daddy crazy over it. Daddy found one at a pawnshop, slightly damaged (one of the CD slots doesn't work) but for Steph, it was love at first sight. He almost cried when Daddy walked in with it. Stacked around the stereo were cassette tapes and CDs. Dozens of them. Some named, some left blank.

"No wonder he never let us up in here." Jarrell laughs, snatching a tape off one of the piles, and reads the label. "'The Build, Volume 1.' Yo, this fool was serious."

9

"You know how he is . . . was about his music," I say, feeling the need to defend Steph. He wouldn't want nobody touching his stuff, but I'm too numb to stop them.

"How you holding up?" Quadir asks. He's always been friendly, in a quiet, shy type of way.

"I'm straight," I lie, adjusting my posture. Just because Steph is gone don't mean I'm some weak girl who needs to be babied. "How you two doing?"

Quadir glances at Rell, combing through tapes. "We aight. Sorry about Steph. We know you two were close."

I swallow back the rising tears. "Not as close as you three."

"Aye, Quady, come look at this," Jarrell says.

"Yo, quit messing with the man's shit. It's why he never wanted us in here in the first place."

Jarrell blows him off with a wave of his hand.

"Check it," he says, flipping through the pages of a black-and-white composition notebook. "Look at this. All this fool ever did was write rhymes."

Quadir reads over Rell's shoulder. "He didn't even need to. He was better off the dome anyways."

"Yeah. Remember, when he called that dude 'a player who got burnt up and strung up 'cause he hit that broad up?' With his girl standing right there? Son, I was *dying* that day."

Rell cackles and Quadir can't help but snicker with him.

"Damn, that kid was good."

Quadir sighs. "Yeah. He was."

Their laughter slowly dies down and they both glance at me, like they forgot I was in the room. Yes, y'all, we're *still* at the repast for my brother.

Rell clears his throat. "Let's see what this fool was listening to."

He presses Play on the stereo, and the cassette tape hisses before Steph's voice fills the room.

"Oh shit, this must've been those tracks he was working on."

"Didn't he say he was going to a studio the night before he . . . died?"

Wait, Steph was in a studio? Like a real one?

Jarrell presses stop and ejects the tape before turning to me. "Yo, Jazz, you think I can have this?"

Quadir watches me. Is he waiting for me to crack too? Bet they expecting it, but I ain't giving them the satisfaction.

"Sure. It's not like anyone else is gonna listen to it," I say with a shrug as the little girl inside me says in a small voice, "Anyone except me."

3
JARRELL

Whenever we chill on the corner, we got to play our positions: me, posted up against the wall; Quady sitting on milk crates; and Steph leaning against the lamppost outside Habibi's bodega. Homie loves Quady 'cause he got a Muslim name even though he ain't Muslim. Can't stand me 'cause I mess up his name all the time. Not my fault I can't roll my r's and shit, but they halal food be the truth.

The spot Steph would've been standing in is looking mad empty now that he's gone.

My pops hate them type of words: should've, would've, could've. They ain't nothing but excuses. Pops don't even live with us and I'm afraid to use them words up in our spot. He's quick to make me do twenty push-ups when I try. Probably got the place wiretapped or something.

He's right, though. There ain't no excuse for Steph not being here with us. Somebody killed him for no reason.

"Damn, it's hot out here," I say, and gulp down another ninety-nine-cent Arizona Iced Tea. "Hotter than it was up in Steph's crib."

After we rapped with Jazz real quick, we took to-go plates of Mummy's jerk chicken, rice and peas, and cabbage, then bounced. I didn't want to be up in there with all them sad people and pictures of Steph staring at us. I'm sad enough as it is. Quady is too. He don't have to say it. It's all over his face, living in his voice.

"Yo, you think he knew what was about to go down?" Quady says, glancing at Steph's spot on the corner.

"Nah, son. No way."

I loosen my tie, my collar wet with sweat. These church clothes be killing me. Don't get it twisted. I still look fly, and no one in the hood have these black gator dress shoes. But I had to pop a pant button open just to finish my plate. Yeah, I could've stopped eating, but when Mummy gets busy in the kitchen you never let her food go to waste. I mean, I guess I can't really call them church clothes since we only roll up in there for holidays. Now they got a new name: funeral clothes.

Never thought my first funeral would be for someone I really knew like that. I thought it would be a random kid from school or some great-aunt back in Jamaica. Not my main man hundred grand. I used to wonder what Peter Parker felt when

Uncle Ben was killed in *Spider-Man*. How it felt to lose someone you looked up to, someone you cared about. Now I know.

The shit aches, and the thoughts are giving me ruthless bubble guts. Or it could've been that Cap'n Crunch.

A gold Lexus stops at the light, its tinted windows halfway down, blasting "Can I Get A . . ." by Jay-Z with Ja Rule and this new chick Amil. The bass thumps through my chest and I'm not even in the car. They keep it up and they gonna blow out their speakers by Halloween.

Two cats stare at us, their seats leaning like they about to take a nap. We stare back. You never know what a dude is holding, so you gotta stay ready so you ain't got to get ready, feel me? And the way they did Steph . . . I don't trust nobody out here in 'Do-or-Die Bed-Stuy,' and neither should you.

Once the light turns green, they roll off and I take a breath.

After a while Quady says, "That's that new Jigga Funk Flex dropped last week." Music is our thang and I'm happy to change the subject.

"Yeah. What'd you think?"

Quady shrugs, rubbing his arm. "It's aight." He stops to think for a second. "Steph would've murdered that beat, though."

Can't argue with that. You gave that fool Steph a hot beat, and he'd smash it to smithereens with the quickness. I palm his tape in my pocket, rubbing my finger against the grooves.

"I just can't get over that part," Quady says.

"What part?"

"The part about him being dead and all that niceness

going into the ground. It's blowing my mind! Yo, deadass, he would've been one of the hottest emcees to come out of Brooklyn. He should've *been* signed."

More should've, would've, could'ves.

"And I'm not saying that 'cause he was my man; it's just facts," he continues, and starts pacing. "He had shit wayyyy better than anyone you heard on Def Jam, Death Row, or even Bad Boy."

"Yo man, you right! This is some bullshit," I say, slamming my empty can on the ground. "I could've been kicking it with some shorties on a tour bus right now."

Quadir gives me a look then starts snickering.

"What, son? What you laughing at?"

He waves me off. "Nothing, man. Nothing."

"What you saying with that laugh? You saying I'm fat? You saying I can't bag no shorties?"

"I didn't say that, you did," he chuckles.

"Man, get out of here," I laugh, patting my belly. "The ladies love rubbing the Buddha. You know Biggie was getting all the ladies too. So was Heavy D. Big boys like me be smooth as fuck and snatch yo' girl when you ain't looking."

Quady frowns. "Yo, did you just fart?"

I gulp and go serious. "Aight. You know what? I ain't even gonna lie to you. I did."

He howls, and that light-skin pretty-boy face of his turns red. Quady got the complexion of a waffle. He acts tough, but that fool is soft, soaking up all the syrup he showers in.

"It ain't funny, man," I say, trying to hold back a smile. "All this death talk got my stomach leaning. Think I ate too many of Ms. Rogers's deviled eggs."

Quadir is crying real tears, he's laughing so hard, until he slowly stops, his shoulders sagging.

"Damn," he mumbles.

"What now?"

"It's . . . it's just not the same snapping on you without Steph here."

I know exactly how he feels. "Yeah. That fool was pure comedy."

A blue Toyota Camry rolls by, his chrome rims gleaming in the sun, blasting Tupac's "How Do U Want It." All the girls love that song. Funny how over a year ago, no one would be caught dead rocking to Tupac like that. During the East Coast vs. West Coast beef, we rep hard for Biggie and the whole Bad Boy family heavy. But in the end, it didn't make no sense. Tupac's gone. Biggie's gone.

Now Steph's gone.

I feel myself dipping back into sadness until I hear Dante's voice.

"Oh shit, look at Rico Suave with this here suit on!" Dante strolls down the block with a grin and dusts my shoulders off. "Looking smooth, kid!"

Dante's our age but barely taller than my baby brothers. He keeps his braids fresh, his gear tight, and his Timbs clean, so you gotta pay him mad respect.

I laugh. "What up, boy?"

We pound, dap, thumb, and snap. The handshake be

looking real complicated, but it's actually mad easy. Dante offers his hand to Quadir, and he shakes his head.

"Nah, son. I'm good."

Dante smirks. "No problem, man. Yo, sorry about Steph. Shit is crazy out here on these streets. Anyone find out what happened yet?"

Quadir and I share a quick look. Surprised Dante doesn't know. He be knowing all the hood gossip.

Quadir sighs. "Wrong place, wrong time. You know how it be."

"Yeah, man. I heard Ro Ro got murked last night."

"Which Ro Ro?"

"You know, Ro Ro, the one who played with that hood team who lived down Ralph."

"Son! That kid used to dunk on cats."

"I just played him the other day," Quadir yells. "He was supposed to go to St. John's next year. Full ride and everything."

"Well, not no more. Got murk over some girl. Swizz-cheesed his ass just like Steph, right in front of his crib."

The thought of bullet holes in Steph makes my stomach lean left.

Quadir closes his eyes and shakes his head. "Damn."

"Anyways, y'all look like you need some cheering up, and I got just the move."

He hands out orange flyers like a car salesman.

"What's this?"

"Party at E. Rocque's tonight. All the blunts and girls

with big butts you could want."

"E. Rocque's having a party? Bet! I'm there."

Quady shakes his head. "Nah, son, I'm not in the mood."

No way, man, he gotta come! Can't have him out here looking like a sad puppy. We all we got now! "Quady, it's an E. Roque party! We gotta go."

"And you know your girl Ronnie's gonna be there," Dante added.

Quady raises an eyebrow. "When you see Ronnie?"

"Just a couple minutes ago, stepping out the salon."

I roll my eyes. "So your girlfriend can get her hair done but can't come with you to your main man's funeral?"

Quady waves me off. "Whatever."

Quady always acts like he don't feel what kind of knockoff material his girl is made of.

"But for real, though, we gotta roll through. Come on, man! Steph wouldn't want us crying like this. He would've wanted us to go and live life to the fullest."

More could've, would've, should've.

"Shit, if it was one of us and he was still alive, he'd be the first one to wanna go just to take our mind off it."

"Yeah, just come," Dante adds. "Get your party on real quick and dip. Easy."

Quady hesitates then smiles.

"Aight. You right. Let's do this."

Cheesing, I dap him up. "Word, kid."

4
MARCH 18, 1997

The air was thick and electric.

A hum buzzed through the crowd blanketing sidewalks. Heads popped out of open windows, staring off into the distance. Everyone watching anxiously . . . waiting to catch a glimpse of hip-hop royalty.

Stephon Davis snorted up the electricity with a smirk. He craned his neck into the desolate street lined with blue police barricades working like dams to hold the overpacked crowd from flooding the empty space. Any moment now, the cars would roll through, and his hometown hero would make his last drive through the borough of Kings.

Steph touched the tender spaces in between the cornrows

under his knit hat with a slight wince. Jasmine always redid his hair when his mom couldn't, but she had a nasty habit of pulling too tight and twisting pieces of his scalp into his braids. A little pain is better than looking busted, he thought, and sniffed the air again.

Old ladies held candles around the makeshift memorials peppered with cards and teddy bears. Kids held up handmade posters . . .

Notorious B.I.G. Forever! Biggie Lives! We Love You Big Poppa!

Much different from the guys he passed on Fulton selling *Biggie RIP* T-shirts.

"I can't believe we skipped school for this," Quadir said behind him. "You know Ms. Reign's gonna call my moms on me."

"Fuck reading about all those dead white people," Jarrell said, squished next to him, his hoodie up. "This is *real* history happening right now!"

The temperature began to drop and the cold sank into their bones. All they could do was blow hot air into their hands and hope the March sun would peek out from behind the clouds. They hadn't come dressed for the weather. It was a spur-of-the-moment decision by Steph.

I should've brought Jasmine, Steph thought, watching a group of girls cry across the street. She needed to see that it wasn't just him with unconditional love for Biggie.

TV crews and cameramen wiggled their way between residents. On the opposite end of the block, cops gathered, patrolling in riot gear. A few people booed, their presence unwelcome.

A hushed stillness came over the crowd. The quiet felt unnatural for Brooklyn, and it made Steph edgy. He was more comfortable with the noise of hectic traffic, street sirens, and arguing neighbors. He couldn't even fall asleep without the radio on.

"Yo, where this fool at?" Jarrell said, shivering. "It's brick out here."

"You sure they gonna drive this way?" Quadir asked, bouncing on the balls of his feet.

"This is Biggie's block. He lived right over there, 226 St. James Place!"

"But we've been waiting for like two hours. The funeral gotta be over by now."

Steph started having doubts. What if they lied? What if he wasn't coming through Brooklyn like planned? That would mean he had convinced his best friends to ditch for nothing. That also meant he wouldn't have the chance to say goodbye.

"Aye! There they are!" Someone cheered.

At first only a few cops on motorcycles rounded the corner, crawling up the street, but behind them, the procession slowly followed, a caravan of limos following a black hearse, similar to what Biggie stood next to on the cover of his last album, *Life After Death*.

The block erupted with cheers. Everyone waving signs, clapping, whistling, saluting with fists held high, as girls screamed, "We love you, BIG!"

"Look! There's Faith!" Someone yelled, pointing at Big's widow in the back of one of the limos.

People peered through the tinted windows, straining to see the stars inside. One car passed, covered in beautiful wreaths, a standing spray with B.I.G. spelled out in red flowers. Tears flowed, even from the hood cats and stickup kids. They felt the impact of losing someone who had represented not only their struggle, but the life of every kid growing up in Brooklyn.

One of those kids was Steph. And as the hearse rolled by, surrounded by his best friends cheering and screaming, he raised a hand to wave and watched in silence.

The last car made a turn with a sharp finality and the block became still again. The small ripples of sadness that washed over them while they waited became giant tidal waves.

"Damn," Jarrell said. Only word to describe the feeling.

The boys instinctively started walking toward Fulton as raw emotions spilled into the streets.

"He was ours, yo!" A man cried on the corner, sniffling through his words. "He was us! He dressed like us, talked like us, looked like us. No one from Brooklyn represented us like Big. No one!"

"Yo, duke is messed up," Quady said solemnly.

"That's what it's like when you lose family," Steph said. He was familiar with the shape mourning leaves you in: bent, broken, shattered, grasping at anything that would make you feel whole again. Music healed Steph after his father died. Biggie healed Steph.

Now, they're both gone.

Then, out of nowhere, someone turned up the volume, and "Hypnotize" rumbled through speakers. . . .

Uh, Uh, Uh . . . c'mon

Biggie's voice was the lighter that set the streets on fire. Everyone started jumping, dancing, and singing. The boys grinned at one another and took off into the crowd.

Hah, sicka than your average
Poppa twist cabbage off instinct
Niggas don't think shit stink, pink gators,
My Detroit players
Timbs for my hooligans in Brooklyn

On the corner, Jarrell jumped on a dumpster with a crew of other kids, waving their hands in the air. Quadir and Steph set it off with the crowd below. They partied, singing at the top of their lungs, celebrating a dynamic life cut short on the very block he sold crack.

WOOP WOOP! In an instant, the cops descended like an army, shutting down their one moment of happiness. They ripped people off the cars they danced on, throwing men on the ground and against store windows, struggling to slap cuffs on anyone they could get their hands on.

In a panic, Steph looked up at Jarrell, unaware of the cops approaching.

"Rell! Watch out!" he screamed, but it was too late. A cop yanked at his arm and he toppled over to the ground. Another cop pressed a knee into Jarrell's back.

"Yo, get off me," Jarrell gurgled out, cheek pressed into the concrete. "I ain't do nothing!"

Pepper spray perfumed the air. Pandemonium. Women coughed, sergeants barked, and sirens blared as Biggie continued to play in the background.

"Why y'all doing this?" a young girl cried to the cops pushing at the crowd. "This is mad unnecessary! We came here to represent for Biggie. Y'all won't even let us have this!"

Steph looked to Quadir. There was only one way to save their friend. On the count of three, they bum-rushed the cop with their joint shoulders. The cop fell on his back. Quickly, Quadir helped Jarrell to his feet, doubling back.

"Yo, go! Go!" Quadir yelled, pulling Steph with him. "Run!"

Steph took off running, down Fulton Street, toward home. Wind whistled through his ears; his sneakers smacked the pavement as he ran harder, faster. Running from the cops and the new pain thumping in his chest he couldn't tell his friends about. They would look at him . . . funny. He hated having to be so strong all the time. He looked back at Quadir, hot on his tail, Jarrell trailing behind them.

They all knew where to go: straight to Habibi's.

They jogged down Marion Street to Patchen Ave, collapsing outside the corner bodega facing Brevoort.

"Yo, shit got crazy, I can't believe they tried to bust me," Jarrell wheezed. "Good looking out back there, y'all. Drinks on me!"

Jarrell grabbed three red quarter waters, a pack of sunflower seeds for Quadir, Dipsy Doodles for Steph, and chocolate Hostess cupcakes for himself.

Steph leaned against the light post, gazing at Brevoort across the street, Biggie playing out the speakers of almost every other window.

"Son, there were mad people out there," Jarrell said, leaning against the brick wall. "Even white people! So much love for Big!"

"And you saw all them cameras and reporters," Quadir added, squatting down on an empty black milk crate. "It's gonna be all over the news tonight."

Steph remained silent, lost in his own thoughts. The weight of grief settled like dust upon his skin. How could he lose the two men that shaped him? Why do the people that he love got to die? And how does he protect everyone left who's important to him?

Quadir glanced up at his friend, cocking his head to the side. He always noticed when Steph drifted too far and had to fish him back out.

"You aight, kid?"

Steph sighed. "I just can't believe he's gone. He should've never went to Cali! Should've stayed his ass right here in Brooklyn. Cats took him out on some revenge-type shit when he never did nothing to nobody."

Quadir spat out a few sunflower seeds on the concrete.

"Yo, deadass," he said, cautious of the ears around them that could brand him a traitor. "This whole East Coast–West Coast beef never made sense to me. They even said it in

Vibe—it was just a bunch of 'he said, she said' shit. And look what it cost us. Two of the best rappers alive." He shook his head. "Tupac was the man, and I was shook to listen to him 'cause cats were wildin'. Why can't I rep for Bad Boy but fuck with an artist on Death Row? Good music is good music. Point, blank, period."

"Yeah," Jarrell said, stuffing his mouth with the last cupcake. "That's like when cats go 'which one is better, DC Comics or Marvel?' Son, everyone know Marvel is the illest. *But* you gotta respect Superman. I mean, duke's an alien that can fly, carrying buildings and shit."

Steph smirked. "So Tupac's an alien?"

"He ain't from our world," Quadir said, laughing. "Duke was from the future or something."

"Word, kid. See, 'cause Superman was born on the planet Krypton, which is like light-years ahead in the future, so he got all these powers beyond our human capabilities."

His friends stared at him as if he had five heads.

"What?"

Quadir laughed. "Son, I can't believe you got us out here on the block talking about comic books like a bunch of nerds."

"Shut yo' ass up!" Jarrell snapped. "Everybody reads comic books!"

"So what you saying?" Quadir challenged. "Biggie was like Spider-Man or something?"

"Yeah! Well, except the part him being from Queens and all."

"He was one of us," Steph added with a shrug. "He looked

out for his people. He was . . . home."

The boys looked up through the trees at home, Brevoort. Towering brown buildings, a busy hub full of life.

"Yo, son, let me hear a rhyme or something," Jarrell said. "Out here all sad and shit."

Steph smiled. "Aight, set it off."

Jarrell smirked before covering his mouth, and started beatboxing, Quadir already bobbing his head.

Unh! Watch me smash it
Funny how these days,
You can't even view a casket
Of your favorite rapper
Without gettin your ass kicked
by the jakes
That's harassment, them bastards tried to chase
Ran out of breath
We ran out from death
Tried to Rodney King me
My peeps ran out like "Steph!"
Felt like my heart ran out my chest—but I'm blessed!
Tell 'em, "King Me!"
This is checkers, not chess!

But we doing this for B.I.G.
Rell compared him to Spider-Man, now I think see why,
    G . . .
'Cause it's all about them red and blues

He got caught up in that web
Had the press confused,
telling lies like the *Daily Bugle*
But ain't no J. Jonah Jameson,
Just some busters in Cali,
Lames wanna hate him.
So today we rally,
They ain't gonna stop us,
The year ninety-seven and it ain't the same without ya
So you gon' hear this on these streets all day
"Spread love is the Brooklyn way"

5
Quadir

We walk into the basement of E. Rocque's brownstone on Halsey and Malcolm X Boulevard a little after eleven. It would've been sooner, but you know the deal: first you gotta get your hair cut. Then, you gotta come up with some lie to tell your parents about where you gonna be, then you gotta follow up with that lie to make sure you're straight. As usual, I'm "sleeping over Jarrell's house" and Jarrell is "sleeping over his older brother's house" in Crown Heights.

The joint's packed with kids sipping red cups and smoking trees. The red lights got it looking like a scene straight out of Big's "One More Chance" video. Once every other month E. Rocque's parents spend the weekend down in Atlantic City and E throws the illest parties. I think her parents know and don't care, just as long as they get a cut of the five bucks she charges at the door.

I'm just happy to be out them funeral clothes and back in my jeans, Timbs, polo shirt, and durag.

We squeeze through the crowd and hold up the wall by one of the massive speakers near the DJ table.

"Oh, this party is off the hook!" Jarrell says, bopping his shoulders. "About to get a few shorties up in here."

"Just behave yourself, aight? Don't want no problems like last time."

He chuckles. "Ain't my fault shorty didn't tell me she had a man. Innocent bystander."

I shake my head and laugh. "Man, whatever."

She must have saw me from across the room with her eagle-eyes, and all heads turn as Veronica Washington marches in my direction, hips swaying, a crew of girls behind her like a pack of wolves. My back tenses up. My instincts always kick in when she stares at me like I'm dinner and she's starving.

"Thought you said you were gonna be here by ten," she snaps, her arms folding. "I've been waiting."

I inhale deep, trying to convince myself I'm just out of breath and not annoyed.

"Sorry, baby," I say, inching to kiss her cheek.

She smirks and kisses me back. "You lucky you so cute. You know how many brothas in here trying to holla at me, right?"

Ronnie could have any dude she wanted, and she reminds me of this every single day. She's the type of girl you'd see in music videos, the main chick. Got that smooth, delicious dark skin, hazel eyes, thick lips, tits, and confidence to match. I've seen grown men try to check for her in the grocery store. I can't explain how we got together, but I ain't questioning it. She fine and she mine, and that's all there is to it. But damn, it's a lot of work to keep her happy. I rather her happy than on my back. Like my Dad says: happy wife, happy life.

Yeah, I just compared us to an old married couple, that's how deep I'm in it.

"What up, Ronnie," Jarrell says over my shoulder. "I didn't see you at Steph's funeral *today*. You know 'cause your man's best friend and mine was shot, and his funeral was *today*!"

"Son, really?" I groan.

Ronnie's eyes narrow at him before turning to me, her face softening, squeezing herself closer to my chest.

"I'm sorry, baby. I . . . didn't know you wanted me there."

I didn't think I'd had to ask. I mean, I sat in the hairdresser with her for over four hours while she got that long swoop bang like Aaliyah that covers half her face. The least she could do is be there for me. I could have used the comfort.

"And you know . . . I don't do good at those things. They scare me. Thinking about it now scares me."

Them almond eyes of hers, the way they stare up at you and rip your soul out your body . . . that's why I'm with her. Yeah, I'm a little tight that she wasn't there, but I know she ain't lying. She doesn't even like reading the news or watching scary movies, everything I love.

"I know," I say with a shrug. "It's aight."

She nervously pushes her bang out her eye and reaches up on her tiptoes to kiss me with them lips that taste like the cherry gloss she stays wearing. She kisses me hard, like making a scene of it, which is weird 'cause she says she ain't into doing things in public, but I guess she got something to prove to Rell, so I'll take it. When we done kissing, she bites her lower lip.

"Anyway, you here, so . . . just forget about all that for now, aight," she says mad sexy, winking at one of her girls. "I mean, people die every day, right?"

I shake my ear, hoping I'm hearing things. Did she really throw Steph in with everybody else?

Jarrell sucks his teeth, grumbling. "It wasn't just people. It was Steph."

Ronnie winces at his name, and I pretend it doesn't bother me.

"Quady! Rell!" E. Rocque pushes her way through the crowd with a smile that lights up the dark room. "I didn't see you come in!"

"What up, E! Sick party."

Ronnie squeezes herself under my armpit, laying one palm flat on my stomach.

"I heard what happened to Steph," E says over the music. "I'm so sorry. I can't believe he's gone!"

Ronnie sort of flinches under me but still doesn't say nothing.

"Yeah, neither can we."

"Y'all want a drink? I can mix you up something!"

"Wellll," Jarrell chuckles, smoothing his eyebrows down

with his pinkies. "You know I don't turn nothing down but my collar."

E. Rocque laughs. "Be right back."

"Oh yo," Jarrell says, tapping my arm and pointing to the DJ behind the turntables. "That's my boy Cash! Let's go say what up!"

"Be right back," I whisper to Ronnie, unhooking her from my arm.

"Come back soon, okay? Don't leave me alone."

I nod and follow Jarrell through the crowd. DJ Cash is digging through his crates of records under the table, his Yankees fitted hat turned backward.

"What up, kid!"

He gives us both a dap. "What up! What up!"

"We see you doing your thang," Rell says.

"Ain't nothing. Making a little bread, keeping the people happy."

"Yo! You wanna do me a favor?"

"I got you. What's up?"

Jarrell digs in his back pocket and pulls out a CD. Steph's CD.

"Play this for me, man."

Cash takes it and chuckles. "What, you a rapper now? Shopping your demo?"

"Nah, it's my homeboy's. I just want to hear it . . . I guess."

Cash nods, noticing the pain in his voice.

"Aight, kid. No problem."

"Word. Thanks, man."

Jarrell looks at me as his face crumbles. Whoa, I've never seen him cry before. He shakes his head and rushes through the crowd toward the back.

I don't chase after him. Sometimes you need to let people just be. But the sadness came down like a hammer on top of my head. I walk back to Ronnie, who doesn't notice my change, and sip on the cup of Henny and Coke E. Rocque offers. Time to drink the pain away.

I lean against the speaker, watching the party through some sort of red filter. Everybody's smiling, happy, laughing, the room a blur. Ronnie is grinding and dancing on me hard, but I can barely feel her. The third cup of Henny ain't helping.

Suddenly, I hear Steph, the bass in his voice vibrating through the speakers pulsing on my back. For a split second, I forget, and my eyes run around the room, searching for him. Maybe it was all a dream. Maybe I didn't see him lying in that casket.

The hype of the crowd dies down a bit. They don't know him, they don't recognize his voice or music, but they're listening. They're drawn to him, and in a few short moments, they're feeling it. Arms in the air, singing the hook, bouncing to the beat. Loving it, loving him.

I sip my cup and take it all in.

6
Jasmine

There's a Lauryn Hill concert going on in our living room.

"Tell Him" bumps out the speakers over the roar of the vacuum. It's the secret track on her new solo album, *The Miseducation of Lauryn Hill*. Steph and I been hyped about it since she dropped her "Doo Wop" single earlier in the summer.

"This is about to be hot," Steph had said. He bought the CD for me at the Wiz downtown, popped it in the living room stereo, and it's been there ever since. I don't think he had the chance to listen to it.

They found his body the next day.

I hum along until the words can no longer stay in my head and start singing. Not too loud. Not as loud as I want. I want to belt the song sitting at the bottom of my belly and wear my lungs out. But I can't.

Because Mom is home.

So I keep my voice low, and it feels like I'm holding in a sneeze. I vacuum up the cookie crumbs and rice pellets from yesterday's repast, hoping if we put the house back in order, maybe we can start being normal again.

"We got enough leftovers to last us through October," Mom shouts from the kitchen, her sanctuary. "Won't have to worry about cooking much when I head back to work."

Work? Already? Steph's barely been in the ground a day. But I guess she has no choice. The bills ain't gonna pay themselves, plus I don't want to argue with her. So fragile, any word out of line could break her in two. If Steph was here, he'd know how to put a smile on her face. He's been filling in since Daddy died. Now I got both of their shoes to fill.

But I'll do it. I'd do anything to make them proud.

Carl runs into the room giggling with his toy Hess truck, driving it into the vacuum with crash sound effects.

"Watch out, pook," I say, shooing him away with a smile. He's been handling all of "this" better than the rest of us.

Mom inches out the kitchen, her eyes swollen. She hasn't really slept since it happened. She wipes down the TV stand, staring at the picture of Steph sitting on the top shelf, next to some of Daddy's books I've read—Huey P. Newton, Malcolm X, James Baldwin, and Marcus Garvey.

"Hmph. I see your hair is back in them puffs. After all them hours it took to straighten it."

Wish Mom liked my natural hair like Daddy did. Daddy had to fight her not to put a perm in it. Said it made me stand out from the rest of the weaves. I mean, why would I want to look like the people who stole us from our home, enslaved us, and murdered our ancestors? Why we worshipping white as beautiful when we were queens?

"*Chill, Sis,*" Steph would say. He ain't here but he always a second voice in my head.

"Nice of the boys to come, Jarrell and Quadir." Mom sighs, sitting on the orange sofa. "I saw them . . . coming out of Steph's room. They didn't take anything . . . did they?"

"Nah."

Mom nodded a few times. "Good. That's good."

I don't know why I lied to her. Something about the way she's been trying to track everything down. Before the funeral she had counted all the towels and washcloths in the closet. Maybe it's her way of holding on to . . . something. After losing so much.

"You know, I'm surprised no one from his job came. Did you see anyone?"

"I don't think so."

"Oh. Maybe we missed them. They must've heard by now. Seems like everyone . . . knows."

I take a deep breath. "Mom . . . do you . . . know what happened yet?"

Mom's eyes go wide and shakes her head. "Oh no no no. They're still investigating. No witnesses yet."

We both know what that means. There would be none.

"But . . . he was working up until . . . ," she says with a frown. "And . . . they probably have his last check. Think I'mma stop by there tomorrow."

"I'll take care of it, Mom."

Mom hesitates before nodding. "Alright. Just make sure they pay what they owe him. Don't let them cheat him 'cause he's . . . gone."

"I got you, Mom," I say. Something Steph would've said.

She looks at me for a long time, like she's thinking.

"Gonna pick up some extra shifts . . . try to save up some. That way, we can move."

"Move?"

"Yes. It's just . . . not safe here."

I don't want to leave home, not yet. What happened to Daddy was an accident. But Steph . . . I don't know what happened to him. And I can't leave without knowing.

She grabs her giant black purse off the recliner. "Can you put this in my room? I don't want to lose it."

"Uh, sure."

She smiles and curls up on the sofa with Carl, turning on the TV.

I slip into her room, setting her purse on the bedside table. Inside is a stack of Hallmark cards, some filled with cash. No wonder she wanted to keep tabs on it. All through the repast she kept asking for her purse. Thought we were gonna have to live with Grandma at the old-folks' home while she stayed at the crazy house. I laugh at myself and head for the door before noticing a manila envelope sitting on the dresser. I wouldn't have paid it no mind if I didn't catch *NYPD* written on a card paper clipped to the seal. Didn't she say she didn't know nothing yet?

Back in the living room, I shove the vacuum cleaner in the hall closet with a yawn.

"Tired, Mom. Think I'mma go to bed."

"Okay, baby, good night," she whispers, Carl asleep in her arms. "And, uh, Jasmine?"

"Yep."

"Ms. Greene offered to watch Carl after school, so he can play with her boys. Your afternoons will be free, so when you go tomorrow . . . maybe see if they'd hire you . . . to take your brother's place. We could . . . use the money."

I force a smile. "Okay."

I kiss her cheek and rush into my room, with the manila envelope tucked under my shirt.

Steph said he worked at Star Caribbean, on Fulton and Kingston. West Indians went there to buy and ship barrels or boxes of goods back to their peoples in the islands. He had joked about not being able to understand his boss's accent.

"He be yelling at me with all types of crazy Jamaican words. I don't know what he be saying, Jazz! Need Rell to translate!"

So I slicked back my hair in my usual two Afro puffs, slip on my uniform (baggy Guess jeans, white tee, plaid shirt, black Reeboks) and head down Fulton.

"Aye yo, Queen of Sheba! You need my comb, girl? Ha!"

I quickly cross the street without turning, recognizing the

stupid nickname some girl from school gave me the beginning of freshman year, when I started wearing my puff.

At Star Caribbean, the line stops at the door, people miserable in the stuffy heat, Mr. Vegas's "Heads High" blasting out of speakers. The place must be short staffed with Steph being . . . gone. I skip ahead to the front where a young rasta stands behind the counter, checking items off his clipboard.

"Hi! I'm . . ."

"You have to wait in line," he says in a crystal clear American accent without looking my way. Okay, maybe not a rasta. Just a brotha with dreads.

"Nah, I'm not shipping nothing. I'm here to pick up my brother's check."

He frowns and glances down at me. "What?"

"My brother, Stephon Davis. He worked here, right?"

"Stephon Davis? No one here by that name."

"Um, you sure? We called him Steph. He was here all summer. Maybe the manager knows him."

"I *am* the manager. And like I said, they ain't never been no Steph, Step, or Stephon working here. I got five guys, and they all on my payroll!"

My heart deflates. "Aight. My bad."

On the walk home, I keep replaying all the times Steph left or came home from work. All the stories he told. All the money he slipped Mom. That wasn't no pocket change. Steph was peeling off hundred-dollar bills. So if Steph wasn't working there, where did he get all that money from?

"Hey! Jazz! What's up!"

Drama waves from the corner . . . while holding Tania Stewart's hand. What's he doing with *her*?

"Um, heyyyy, Drama."

Drama's this cool brotha from around the way that's big in the underground poetry scene. I always run into him at open mics. He tilts his fatigue cap back, and the smile glowing under his freckled nose competing with the sun warms me.

"Yo, I heard about your brother. My condolences."

Tania twirls her long blond braids around her fake pinkie nail, the same way she did in second-period math. I'll admit, been crushing hard on Drama since I was thirteen, but seeing Tania snuggling up on his arm, marking her territory, makes me want to barf.

"Thanks. So, um, did you roll through the Nuyorican yesterday?"

"Nah. I was at E. Rocque's party."

"E. Rocque had a party? Why ain't anyone tell me?"

"You? Ha, nah. That ain't your scene."

"Why it ain't my *scene*?" I ask, eyes narrowing. Especially since I thought we were a part of the *same* scene.

He looks at my hair, my African medallion and shrugs. "Just . . . ain't."

Tania chuckles. "What he means is, they ain't burning incense, beating drums, and talking 'bout, 'the revolution will not be televised'!"

I give Drama a look and he gulps, cheeks turning red. Is he really going to stand for her clowning Gil Scott-Heron's legendary poem? The one I performed at the Black History

Month assembly last year? Daddy's favorite . . .

"Um. Well, later, Jazz," he says, pulling Tania across the street.

I ain't even tripping about him being with Tania. What hurts most was him assuming that I didn't belong at a *party.* Why? 'Cause I listen to Heron and rock a natural? I love good music and dancing as much as anyone!

See, Steph, even when I try, people still play me.

And I can hear him now. *"You . . . different, Jazz. Not everyone knows how to deal with different."*

I just wish being different didn't make me feel so . . . alone.

7
JaRReLL

"Damn, this weather feeling mad good," my big homie Ray
Mack says, licking closed a dutch as we chill on a bench near
the chess players. "Got me wanting to cook out or something."

Mack ain't dressed like he's ready to barbeque. He got on
the fresh Jordans, a Ralph Lauren Polo, and every piece of jewelry he owns, like he ain't afraid someone might snatch his
chains. He's good though, since no one's crazy enough to mess
with Mack.

"J-Money, you aight, kid?"

I know what he's really asking. Am I okay after losing my
best friend, but there ain't no good answer for that.

I shrug real cool like. "Yeah, I'm straight."

The B-voort courtyard is filled with kids playing double Dutch, tag, and hide-and-seek. I peep over my newspaper at my twin little brothers, tumbling around in the grass, but as soon as them ice-cream-truck tunes hit our block, I know within two seconds the boys will be up in my face.

"Rell, we want ice cream," they say in unison.

I suck my teeth. "Y'all got ice cream money? And what I tell you about talking together like that? Mad creepy, looking like the black *Shining*."

Mack chuckles. "You boys want ice cream?" He yells over his shoulder to the rest of the kids playing in the courtyard. "Y'all ALL want some ice cream? Well, come on then."

Mack strolls over to the truck with a horde of kids behind him.

"My man," he says to the driver. "Give them whatever they want. On me, yuh heard!"

The kids crowd the window, ordering ice cream sandwiches, swirl soft cones, and Strawberry Shortcake bars as Mack peels two crisp hundred-dollar bills off a stack he keeps in his Gucci clip and hands it to the driver. I can't tell you how Mack makes his money, but I can tell you he ain't without it.

Little Tamika with the pink bobo's in her hair hangs back with her jump rope.

"Aye yo, baby girl. You don't want no ice cream?" Mack asks her.

Tamika crosses her arms and stares, eyes narrowing at him.

"Tamika! Don't you hear him talking to you?" I snap. "How you gonna diss Mack like that?"

She don't flinch and keeps her distance. The way she mean-mugging, she's clearly heard more about Mack than the others and wants no parts of him.

"Nah, it's all good," he says with a smirk. "That's aight, boo-boo! You stay quiet and keep doing you. Real hustlers don't make noise."

That's Mack. He be dropping gems everywhere he go, like Beast from *X-Men*. Got quotes for days.

I laugh and go back to my paper. My love of comics started from reading the funnies every Sunday with my pops. I still read them whenever I can, but today, I'm flipping through the *Daily News,* looking to see if they mention anything about Steph.

"Hey, don't read them papers too close," Mack warns, unwrapping a King Cone. "All they do is gas up the bad shit. They never report about the good shit happening in the hood."

He hands me a Batman ice cream bar.

"I mean, look at me! Out here playing Ice Cream Santa. They ain't gonna report about that! My Old G used to do the same for me when I was a kid. We hold down our own, nah mean?"

See? That's why I fucks with Mack. He knows what it's like to be a kid growing up in Bed-Stuy. Wish Quady and Steph rocked with him too, but like Tamika, they just think he's bad business. Going off rumors, they don't know the real Mack like I do.

I fold up the newspaper and unwrap my ice cream, watching three little boys stroll by with Sonic the Hedgehog bars.

Reminds me of when we were little—Steph, Quady, and me—heading to the summer basketball clinic at the YMCA. I remember that first summer, we were playing these three cats from Marcy. Ain't no way these fools were some eight-year-olds. Homies had bass in their voice, nah mean? But Quady had the nice jump shot, Steph hit 'em with the three-pointers, and I had defense on lock.

My skills weren't that tight, but being with them made me feel like I could do anything. Be anything, y'knowwhatumsayin?

Quadir

School ain't the same without Steph.

Basketball ain't the same without Steph.

Deadass, nothing's been the same without Steph.

"You wanna shoot some hoops later?" Jarrell suggests on our walk home after school.

"Nah. I don't feel like whooping your ass today."

He unzips his book bag, grabs his Discman and the mini booklet that carries all his CDs.

"Yo, it's Friday! We gotta do *something*!"

There's a plea in his voice. Jarrell must be feeling it too. That void. It creeps up on us when we least expect it. Any other Friday we'd have something to do.

Steph's death was nothing but a paragraph in the *Daily News*: "Teen Found Dead in Housing Projects," buried somewhere after page six. Since then, I've been brainstorming new headlines for a follow-up story:

Friends Nearly Die of Boredom after Teen's Death

Slain Teen Leaves Friends Mad Confused

"Anyway, what you and Ronnie getting into this weekend?"

"Nothing. She's shopping with her moms *all* weekend for her sweet-sixteen dress."

"Oh, word? That's coming up soon, right?"

I swear, Ronnie's been planning this super sweet-sixteen bash since she was fourteen. The banquet hall's been rented since she turned fifteen. With a guest list pushing close to two hundred, everyone has to wear either pink or black to match the theme: Black Princess. Her dad drove her around the hood in his Escalade so she can personally deliver pink invitations. Open up the envelope and gold sparkles pop out. The school hallways were covered with it. She's having a seven-tiered cake, a chocolate fountain, cherry soda dispenser, fettuccine alfredo (her favorite), and two DJs. She even ordered a custom-made gold throne with her name stitched into the pink cushions.

I know all this, because she tells me about every detail, every day, nonstop.

"Yup. Gonna be the 'party of the year.'" I don't get the big deal about turning sixteen. It's just another birthday. For my sixteenth, my parents took me to Dallas BBQ in the city, then the Virgin Megastore, where I bought five CDs.

"Mad kids been talking about it. She's inviting everybody!"

That's Ronnie. She does things *big*, and her pops have the money to spoil her.

"Did I tell you . . . her and her girls doing the dance routine from Aaliyah's 'Are You that Somebody?' video?"

"For real? That's . . . yo wait, ain't there guys in that video?"

Silence.

Jarrell cocks his head to the side, his grin growing wider. "Hold up? Is Ronnie making you . . . dance with her?"

"Man," I grumble. "She even got us doing costume changes."

Jarrell eyes spark before he bust out laughing. "BAHAHA-HAHA! Son, I'm dying! Why didn't you just tell her no?"

"You kidding? Her pops would kill me! I got no choice."

"Maybe we can borrow some of my auntie's curl activator and you can get your Ginuwine body-roll on," he snickers. "Man, the whole hood gonna find out you can't dance for shit."

"Whatever. I don't care what people think."

Aight, I care. That dance is mad complicated, and Ronnie keeps snapping at me when I mess up. Swear I've watched it about ten thousand times and still can't get it right. Might turn gray the way she stressing me.

"Yo! Is La'Tasha dancing too?" Jarrell asks, eyebrows wiggling. "You know I'm feeling her. You need to hook it up."

"She ain't checking for you. But Ronnie's cousin is. You know she's had a crush on you since the fifth grade?"

"You mean Dragon Breath Brenda? Nah, I'm good on that, thanks."

We hop on the bus, heading back to Brevoort. I grab my new *Vibe* magazine out my book bag and flip to the page I left off.

"Yo, who's that on the cover? Will Smith?" Rell ask.

"Yeah. It's the fifth-anniversary issue."

"Man, not for nothing, but *Vibe* be having the illest covers," he says, putting on his headphones. "I still got my Biggie and Faith cover posted on my wall."

This month's issue is thick with new music reviews and an exclusive interview with none other than Pierce Williams, an A&R rep at Red Starr Entertainment, one of the hottest record labels in the industry. He's known for discovering and developing new talent. The interview is a big deal since he don't mess with the press like that. In his words, "I like to be seen, not heard, ya heard!" He's definitely seen, alright. Duke is everywhere! In pictures at the most poppin' clubs with celebrities like Janet Jackson, Naomi Campbell, even Elton John.

He recently signed Fast Pace, this cat from Sumner Houses in Bed-Stuy. Everybody was bumping his tracks last summer, after he was featured on a DJ Clue mixtape. I always wondered how rappers got their start in music. But when it happens, it happens fast. One day they on the corner, the next day they got a video on MTV.

The bus jerks and moves through traffic, hitting every stop up Fulton Street. Jarrell's head bobbing hard to some beat.

"Hey," I say, tapping his leg. "Yo, what you messing with?"

He frees up one ear and sighs. "Steph. Been listening to his stuff all week."

He said it like he didn't want to admit it.

"Yo, at E. Rocque's party, you see how everybody started wildin' out when his song came on? DJ had to run it back twice!"

"Yeah. Cash was fronting like he didn't wanna give me back my damn CD. Chump."

"Now that's the kind of parties I fucks with. No stress, no stiff suits, no damn dance numbers like we a Broadway musical. Just folks vibing to good music."

"That's 'cause Steph had the type of flow that anyone could get with."

"I'm telling you, if Steph was still alive, he'd be killing them."

Jarrell reaches up to press the signal strip before our stop.

"Ha! He's killing them while he's dead."

The bus stops short, and I damn near hit my head on the seat in front of me. Jarrell skips out the back exit and I follow. The bus roars off, exhaust swirling around us as his words echo over and over.

Killing them . . . while he's dead.

"Yo, let's stop at the bodega. I'm thirstier than a mother-fucker."

As we head down our block, I stare at the gray pavement, the cracks in the ground as the world goes silent, and an idea so crazy pops into my head that my legs stop working.

Jarrell glances back at me.

"What? What's up?"

I blink. "You're right."

"Huh? Right about what?"

"You're right. He *is* killing them . . . while he's *dead*."

Jarrell face screws up into a frown. "Quady, you been smoking or something? What are you talking about?"

"Steph. He could drop an album!"

Jarrell crosses his arms. "Steph? Our boy Steph? You want him to drop an album from six feet under?"

A rush zips through my veins as I picture it all. This could work. It's gotta work!

"Mad rappers come out with albums after they died. Biggie did it. Tupac did it."

Jarrell snorts. "Yeah, a couple of times."

"Bob Marley still making money and he's been dead for a minute."

Jarrell nods. "Rastas do love dem some Marley."

"So I'm saying, if they all did it . . . why can't Steph?"

Jarrell cocks his head to the side. "You wanna know why?"

I roll my eyes. "Yeah, why?"

"'Cause all those people you talking about already had a deal!" Jarrell shouts, throwing his hands up. "They had the clout, the juice, the je ne sais quoi. And they all had deals with labels to drop their album for them!"

That's true. They were all established before they passed. People never heard any of Steph's music before that party.

But if Fast Pace could get signed just off a freestyle . . .

I snatch Jarrell's Discman out of his hand, pop out the CD,

and hold it up to his face like a mirror.

"So. Why don't we get Steph a deal?"

Jarrell stares at the CD until my idea hits him in the gut. He steps back, eyes almost popping out his head before the craziest grin grows across his face.

9
Jasmine

When they finish spitting out their plan, all I can do is stare up at the two goofy faces standing in front of me.

"You . . . you serious?"

Quadir nods. "As a heart attack."

Jarrell sucks his teeth. "Yo, son, why you gotta be so corny?"

"What? What I do?"

"'As a heart attack?'" He shakes his head. "This dummy."

"Man, if you don't stop breathing down my neck . . ."

"You really thought that shit was cool, didn't you?"

"Aight! Enough," I yell over them.

The living room falls silent as I lean back into the sofa.

"So . . . you want to get my brother signed? To a label, like for real?"

"That's the plan," Quadir says, eyeing Jarrell, twiddling his fingers.

"Even though he's . . . gone."

Quadir takes a deep breath and sits next to me.

"It's like this Jazz: Steph recorded mad music before he died, right? All we're gonna do is take some of his tracks and make a demo. Once people start hearing him, he'll blow up, and labels will be begging for more."

"But . . . he's gone."

"See, that's the thing . . . he's not dead."

"Not to us," Jarrell adds with a grin.

"Um, am I missing something?"

"We're gonna pretend he's still alive."

I can't find the words to accurately describe how I feel. I can only spit out, "Y'all are wildin'! How you gonna do that?"

"Okay, so, boom. Steph kept a mad low profile, right?" Jarrell says. "I mean, cats just knew him as a hot freestyler, but no one's ever heard his real music before, besides us."

"What if people find out it's him and find out he's dead?"

"Trust, they won't. We gonna keep all of this on the low low."

"Think about it, Jazz," Quadir says. "If we don't do this, no one will ever know just how nice with it he really was!"

"And for real, yo, you see how many wack emcees there are out there! He would've been the hottest rapper to come out of Bed-Stuy since Biggie."

"And Jay-Z," I mumble.

"Huh?"

"Jay-Z."

"Psst, I mean, I guess," Jarrell chuckles.

"You guess? Boy, did you actually *listen* to *Reasonable Doubt*? The way he spits over the horns on 'Can I Live'? 'Recruited lieutenants with ludicrous dreams of gettin' cream. "Let's do this," it gets tedious. So I keep one eye open like CBS!' That shit was sick! Your ears broken or something?"

Quadir smirks. "Yup. You Steph's sister alright."

I gulp, thinking of what Steph would say. *"Easy, Jazz, you don't have to bite duke's head off."*

Quadir touches my shoulder. I thought his hands would be all rough from playing ball, but nah, they soft like butter leather.

"Listen, I know this sounds mad crazy. I mean, who knows how far we'll get. But we gotta at least try. All we need . . . is his music."

Ohhh, so that's why they're here. That's why they made sure to come right after school when Mom's not home. They want to run up in Steph's room and cop all his stuff, and they need my permission to do it.

I look across the room at the picture of Steph they used for his funeral. It was taken at last summer's block party, Steph making all the kids dance in front of the DJ booth, grabbing the mic, playing emcee, with the biggest smile on his face.

Who can kill a kid with that smile?

The question has been stewing in my head for so long that I

can't even concentrate at school. I want to know all the whos, whats, wheres, whens, hows, and most importantly, the why. Why did they take my brother, my best friend, from me?

"Y'all know where Steph worked at?"

Quadir blinked. "Huh?"

"Steph said he had a part-time job at this shipping company. I went by there to pick up his last check, but they never heard of him. But that don't make sense because Steph was giving Mom money, and some nights he'd even come home late."

Jarrell and Quadir share a quick look.

"Nah, I don't know nothing about no job," Jarrell says, rubbing the back of his head.

They know something. Something that may help me find out what really happened to Steph. But I can't go searching for answers alone.

"Alright. I'm in."

The boys grin. "Aight! Yo, thanks, Jazz!"

"But under one condition. Y'all have to help me find out who killed Steph."

Jarrell waves his arms. "What? Aw, hell nah."

Quadir tries a softer touch. "Jazz, I don't think that's such a good idea. We don't want to go barking up the wrong tree or nothing."

"But we have to try, right? Somebody gotta know something. I can't just move on like Steph didn't exist. He would do it for me. He would do it for you!"

Quadir swallows, rubbing his hands together. It's something I picked up on when he's thinking hard. Jarrell clears his throat with a sharp nod.

"Uh, Quady, can I see you in my office?"

"Be right back," Quadir says with an uneasy smile, and follows Jarrell into the kitchen, where their whispers echo off the hanging pots and pans.

"Son, no way," Jarrell starts.

"Yo, just chill, b. How else you expect to get Steph's stuff?"

"Psst! I don't know, but not like this!"

"We can't just try?"

"What you gonna do, Inspector Gadget? You and Pink Panther in there gonna run around the hood playing *Law and Order*?"

"So who you plan on being? Scooby-Doo?"

"Son, this shit ain't funny. We cruising for a bruising even considering this shit. Mess around, and we gonna end up just like Steph! Nah. Nope. Negative. Not happening."

Quadir took a deep breath. "Jazz is right, though. He'd do it for us."

Jarrell grumbles. "Aight. But we got to keep this on the low low for real, though."

"No doubt."

The boys walk back into the living room.

"Aight, Jazz. You got a deal, but with limits. We'll ask around if anyone knows . . . anything."

"Cool." It's a start.

"Okay, so if you could just hand over Steph's music, we'll bounce and get to work."

Before I even realize, I'm up on my feet, blood surging.

"Hand what over? Whoa . . . y'all really thought you were gonna do this without me? Nah. We in this together."

"We good, Jazz, we got it covered."

I shake my head. "I know my brother's music better than anyone. You need me."

"Yo, this ain't no game," Jarrell grumbles. "Shit could get real out here, and we can't have some girl slowing us . . ."

"Oh, so you don't think chicks can hold it down?"

Jarrell rolls his eyes. "Here. We. Go. Not chicks . . . girls! You just turned fifteen."

"And! What my age got to do with pushing music?"

Quadir, always the peacemaker, tries it. "Jazz . . . I don't think you . . ."

"That's right, you DON'T think. 'Cause if y'all even think you doing this without me, you tripping. I ain't no little kid, and you ain't messing with MY brother's music without me. So stop with the bullshit, and let's get to work."

I storm down the hall to Steph's room, before hearing Jarrell chuckle.

"What you laughing at?"

"Hmph. She tooollldddd you!"

"Man, shut up and come on."

No one has stepped foot in Steph's bedroom since the funeral. Untouched, the door creaks like a crypt when I open it, light blazing through the small window. Someone built some type of invisible glass force field that won't let me pass the threshold. My muscles ache to take a step, but my bones froze to the floor.

The boys join me a few moments later, smart-ass tongues locked to the roof of their mouths, taking in the neatly made bed, the book bag hanging on the back of the chair, and the dust floating in the air, all from the safety of the hallway.

A roach the size of a tic-tac crawls up Snoop Dog's face. Jarrell takes two quick strides, brushes it onto the floor, and gives it one stomp with his massive foot.

"Nah, can't let homie disrespect Snoop like that!"

And just like that, the force field is broken, and we tiptoe inside. The room feels smaller. Steph surrounded us with his scent, mixed in with the stale air, clogging up our noses and my eyes water.

Don't cry. Don't let them see you cry.

I pinch my arm and clear him out of my throat.

Quadir takes one look at me, then opens a window, letting a breeze run in.

"Close it," I snap, my voice scratchy. If we leave it open, his scent will vanish, and I can't take losing my brother again.

Quadir and Jarrell glance at each other. They're having second thoughts. I sure am.

"Um, he keeps . . . kept . . . all his music under his bed in shoeboxes."

They turn to the bed, the comforter dangling off the side kissing the floor, and gulp.

"Aight," Jarrell says. "Let's see what we got." Jarrell lifts the edge of the comforter, then throws it back, gasping at the assortment of shoeboxes packed underneath, nearly lifting the bed off its legs.

"Damnnnn!" the boys shout.

I'll admit, I only expected to see a few boxes, not a whole shoe store.

"Three stacked up, six across, at least three deep," Jarrell says, doing the math in his head. "Son, that's fifty-four shoe-boxes!"

"And this is all music?" Quadir asks me.

"No, I think some of it is his journals and rhyme books. Maybe magazines and comics."

Jarrell kneels to the floor and quickly pulls out boxes one by one. Quadir helps, scattering them around the room. I sit cross-legged by the window and grab one, lifting off the lid. A box of black-and-white composition notebooks, the edges colored, some folded, others with sheets ripped and sticking out sideways.

"Yo, this kid was a beast," Jarrell chuckles, sitting next to the bed, a box on his lap. He lifts a tape and shakes his head. "Some of these date back to the sixth grade!"

Quadir laughs from the opposite side of the room with a box of *Vibe* magazines, Steph's favorite pages folded.

"He's been collecting these for almost six years. Like, when we were in elementary school!"

We spent almost an hour opening boxes, shouting out the inventory: tapes, CDs, journals, *Spider-Man* comic books, all tucked away and surprisingly organized.

"Son, we got enough for like . . . ten tapes at least," Jarrell laughs.

"We gotta go through them, pick the best ones," Quadir says, his nose in a journal. "Yo, listen to this. . . ."

Words from the Blind Soldier

The soldier I knew well,

He wouldn't talk but he always answered.

I would read his blind eyes.

He would nod. . . . I asked him in abundance,

How could a Blind Soldier enter a war?

How would he know what he was fighting for?

How would he know if he was fighting for wrong or right?

How could he understand the struggle between Evil &

    Righteous?

Would he still be a soldier?

When his eyes read nothing he asked me . . .

"Would you?"

"Damn. That's deep," Jarrell says, pensive. "I didn't know Steph could write like that."

"Neither did I," Quadir mumbles, glancing across the room at me, searching my face before reaching for another box.

"Oh snap, check it," he laughs, dangling a porn magazine like a carrot in front of an ass. "I found his sticky pages."

"Aye. Give me that!" Jarrell says, ripping the magazine out

of his hands and grabbing the box. "I'll take those. Youngins like you don't need to be seeing all this."

I let out a chuckle lifting the lid off an Adidas box before my heart hiccups out my mouth and splats on the floor. Quadir turns to me, still laughing.

"Hey, Jazz, what's that? Condoms?"

With a mouth full of cotton, I don't know what to say. My shaky hands can't hold the box steady.

Quadir crawls across the floor, still laughing.

"What's up? Let's see what we got," he says, leaning to peer over the half-open lid before his head pops up to look at me. Jarrell's too busy checking out girls' titties to notice our dead silence.

Inside a large ziplock bag, the kind of bag that Mom marinates chicken in, is at least a hundred mini vials of crack with red caps. Lying on top of the bag like a paperweight is a black gun and a red Motorola beeper.

Quadir's shock matches mine, which means he had no idea either. I open my mouth, eager to defend Steph against whatever Quady could be thinking about my brother. But the words are stuck and tangled up in fast-growing questions. Steph? A hustler? He wouldn't.

"Yo, what's in that one?" Jarrell asks behind us.

Quadir and I lock eyes. Panicking, I shake my head slightly. *Please. Please don't tell. I don't want anyone to know.*

Quadir takes a breath, grabs the beeper, and closes the lid.

"Nothing man. Just some old sneakers."

Jarrell shrugs, continuing to flip through his magazine.

He gives me a once-over and crawls back to his side of the room.

I push the box back under the bed, wondering how I can unsee what I've seen.

"Hey. Look what I found in this box," Quadir says, holding up the beeper.

"Yo, when did he get one of these?" Jarrell asks, grabbing it out of Quadir's hand. "Your mom bought him one?"

"Nah. He must have found it or something," I say, playing along with Quadir's story.

"This shit is like new. Looks like he missed a bunch of calls and codes. 343. 044. 943. 943. Again, 943."

"What'd all those mean?"

"Well, 343 means call back. 044 means Thursday. 943 means where you at? Last one says 911," Jarrell says.

"Emergency," Quadir mumbles, shooting me a look. "Someone was definitely looking for him."

I swallow, trying to keep a brave face.

"Well, we should keep this," Jarrell says. "Use it, in case anyone wants to contact us about Steph's music."

"Can I hold it? Just in case anyone tries to call him. They might not know he's . . . gone and I want to be the one to tell them."

"Who else besides us would hit him?"

Quadir's jaw tightens, ignoring Jarrell. "What if someone hits him thinking he's still alive. May owe them money or something."

"Why would he owe anybody money?" Jarrell barks, outraged.

Quadir glances my way again and it hits me: if Steph really was hustling, he wasn't working alone. He would've had to answer to somebody to get that product. Maybe he owed that somebody money and that's why they killed him. But it doesn't make sense. Steph had no reason to sell drugs, ever.

"I'll be careful," I promise, grabbing it from Jarrell.

Jarrell left with some of the tapes to transfer to CD, leaving Quadir and me alone to make the track list. I brought him out into the living room just in case Mom came home early. I don't know what she would've been mad at more: the fact that we was in Steph's room, messing with his stuff, or that I was in a room alone with a boy. Even if it's just Quady.

"Aight, so I think we should decide what kind of rapper we want Steph to be."

Quadir sits on the floor, leaning against the sofa, sorting through Steph's CDs while I use my science notebook to take inventory.

"What you mean 'kind of rapper'?"

"Steph got a large catalog. And if we gonna put him on the map, we gotta decide if he's gonna be an underground rapper like Mos Def, a conscious rapper like Nas, a gangsta rapper like Dr. Dre, or a crossover, like Puff Daddy. That way we know who we aiming for. And that's how record labels will find him."

"Why can't he be all of them? I mean, Biggie did it! On *Life After Death*, he had tracks that touched everything.

'Hypnotize' was for the club, 'Ten Crack Commandments' was for the goons, and 'Going Back to Cali' was for the West Side."

"Yeah, but you talking about his second album. What really put Big on the map was 'Juicy' from *Ready to Die*. But . . . you onto something, though!" He hops to his feet and starts pacing. "We need to attract the shorties. That's what Big did with 'One More Chance.' And chicks be loving rappers who gonna bark at them like DMX or lick they lips like LL Cool J. If we get the chicks, the fellas will follow."

Dag, I'm kind of disappointed Quadir thinks so little of women. We don't all want those type of guys. Some of us want someone we can keep it real with.

"Steph would've wanted to show everyone all his skills," I say.

Quadir stops pacing and crawls back on the floor.

"Well, how about we do a 'A side, B side' type thang. A side will be all his bangers, B side, the hood shit. Good?"

"Yeah. That'll work."

I tear out a sheet of paper and divide it into two, labeling each side A and B as Quadir sorts through the CDs.

"Aight, so this pile over here is the party hits, this pile over here is that real hip-hop shit, and this pile . . . I don't even know."

"Definitely this one for side B," I grabbed a CD from unknown pile. "He sampled that Black Moon 'I Got Cha Opin' beat. Then you got to add this one too. Steph murdered that Smif-N-Wessun's 'Bucktown.' Oh, and this one, he has that Gang Starr flow."

He smirks. "What you know about Gang Starr?"

"Why can't I know about Gang Starr?"

He laughs, leaning back on his elbows. "I don't know. 'Cause you a girl!"

Steph must not have told him how we practiced together, how we spent nights studying tracks on HOT 97, how Steph been grooming me for the ring.

So I close my eyes and spit a few bars of "Above the Clouds," letting the words slice out and fill the room. Haven't rapped anything since Steph died. It feels . . . good, but my heart aches when I open my eyes and Steph isn't there.

Only Quadir, with his mouth hanging open. "Damn! You got flow, Ma!"

First time anyone called me "Ma" like a real compliment.

"Thanks," I mumble, shying away from his stare. "You really think this is gonna work?"

"I don't know. Music is kinda funny."

"How so?"

"Seems like everybody's trying to get on nowadays, there's so much of it. Music from the East, the West, even the South with Master P and Silkk the Shocker."

"You right. It's a whole bunch of different instruments in the band room making noise. Hard to hear the clarinet over the trumpet."

"Yeah like that!" He laughs. "Yo, it's mad cool you doing this, Jazz."

"Well, yeah. He's my brother. I mean . . . was . . . my brother."

My mouth feels stiff. I have a hard time talking about him in the past.

Quady smiles. "Nah, Jazz, he'll always be your brother. Always."

I swallow. "Well, he was . . . good. He ain't did nothing to nobody for them to kill him! He ain't never stole or hustle or . . ."

Quadir shoots me a look, and a lump lodges in my throat. Neither of us is ready to talk about *that* box under his bed.

He jumps to his feet again, heading to the stereo.

"Hey . . . it's uh . . . it's mad quiet in here. How about some music?"

"Um, yeah. Sure."

"Let's see what y'all got."

Lauryn Hill was still on heavy rotation. The next track that played: "Every Ghetto, Every City."

Quadir laughs. "Ha! Figured you rocked with L-Boogie. Chicks at school love the album!"

I ain't feeling him trying to throw me in the category with all them other girls that be sweating him.

"What, you not feeling it too?" I ask, meeting him at the stereo.

"Nah, this joint is tight! I like that she can sing and spit bars. When she was still with the Fugees, she was killing them." He smiles. "Softly."

"Rell's right, you do have some corny jokes," I laugh. "But nah, for real though, girls got bars. Not just L-Boogie."

"I know! Lil' Kim's *Hard Core* was fire!"

I roll my eyes. "I mean, I guess. If you like those sort of chicks."

"What you mean by 'those sort of chicks'?"

"You know, the ones who gotta be extra sexy for you to listen to them, and they ain't saying nothing of . . . substance."

"Oh, they saying a lot. You just not listening close enough."

"Nah, I mean ladies who are really saying *something*. Like Lady of Rage, MC Lyte, or Queen Pen. You ever listen to Queen Latifah? She talks about woman equality. Kim ain't saying nothing, just talking about sex."

He shrugs. "So. What's wrong with sex?"

And just at that moment, the next song plays: "Nothing Even Matters" featuring D'Angelo. The most romantic song on the entire album. It starts with this real pretty piano before the drums kick in that remind me of hearts fluttering, and Lauryn sings . . .

Now the skies could fall
Not even if my boss should call
The world it seems so very small
'Cause nothin' even matters, at all . . .

Quadir's ears perk up as he stares at the speakers.

"Damn," he mumbles. "I ain't hear this one yet. This is . . . nice. I mean, like, beautiful."

The room shrinks, heat cranking up to a million.

"Um, yeah. It's nice."

We listen in silence, just the two of us, and the whole world fades away. Like nothing really matters . . . except us. Quadir looks at me, his eyes softening, and I swear I could melt right into them.

We inch closer, too close I guess, 'cause our feet drag against the carpet, and sparks fly.

"Shit," he gasps, eyes widening as he takes three steps back and clears his throat. "Oh damn, um, what time is it? Yo, I have to go . . . I promised my mom that I . . . uh . . ."

I wipe the sweat off the back of my neck. "Yeah, and I gotta go pick up Carl, but I um . . ."

"Yeah. So I'll holla at you later." He grabs his book bag and rushes out the door.

"Cool. Yeah. Later!"

I said that mad casual because if I keep pretending like it's no big deal, then maybe I won't feel like my face is on fire, and that my armpits aren't soaked, and that I definitely wasn't imagining us kissing on the sofa.

10
OcTobeR 3. 1997

Steph steadied himself on the narrow windowsill, feet propped up on the radiator melting the bottom of his Timbs. Project heat is the type of heat that makes walls sweat, pipes hot enough to burn the skin off knuckles, and windows fog with condensation.

It was tricky, balancing the hot and cold while keeping from falling out the window and cracking your head open on the pavement, eight stories down. But Jarrell's room had one of the best views in Brevoort. From high up he could see old cats chilling on benches sharing stories, women helping each other push carts of laundry, babies playing in the courtyard, teen lovebirds kissing by the stairs. Salsa, reggae, and jazz battling between Biggie lyrics. The sounds of basketballs bouncing on the court, dice hitting the wall during a game of cee-lo, grandpas slamming down chess pieces on fold-up tables against the young hustlers taking a break from making a dollar. There was beauty and joy hidden in the struggle.

"Jarrell! Jarrell!"

Jarrell, squeezed to his computer desk, never took his eyes off the screen.

"Ugh. Yes, Mummy?"

"We need a pack of chicken! And rice. We out of rice!"

Jarrell sucked his teeth and turned to Steph. "Yo, I swear she always sending me to the store. I don't think she ever been up in there herself."

Steph snickered, digging into a plastic bag of what remained of his red and peach gummy rings. They were his favorite sweets to stock up on from the candy shop on Coney Island. With only a few pieces left, it would soon be time to officially say goodbye to summer and everything he loved—endless basketball games, open fire hydrants, barbeques, and ice-cream trucks. Everything he used to do with his dad that he made his friends and family uphold.

Jarrell's room was the size of a hallway closet. One bunk, one twin bed, and a tall dresser were all that could fit. He could barely squeeze in the lopsided mini desk leaned against the wall for his computer.

"Son, you done yet?" Steph asked, impatient.

"Slow down, kid, I'm working on it." Jarrell hunched over his keyboard and tapped his mouse, opening up a new window. Ten more minutes left on the CD transfer. "What's this for anyways?"

Steph shrugged, rubbing the sugary crystals between his fingers. "Just a little something I'm working on."

"Aight, well, while you here, let me copy that Firm album for you. The cover is mad fly, they made it look like that movie *Casino* with Robert De Niro."

Steph hopped off the windowsill. "You got music . . . like, on your computer?"

"Yeah. Music ain't nothing but files you can save on the hard drive."

"Oh, word?"

"Watch, the whole world is gonna start using this thing called email where it, like, sends letters over the phone wires. Like a fax machine but with no paper, all electronic."

"Like beepers?"

"Exactly. Haven't tried it yet 'cause Mummy is always on the phone, and I need a free line to hook it up."

Steph watched his friend, intense and focused, typing wildly, as if he'd been using computers since fresh out the womb. Knowing someone who even owned one in the hood was like an alien sighting.

"Yo, this must've cost you a grip," Steph noted, keeping his voice light.

Jarrell swallowed, not meeting Steph's eye. "Um . . . yeah. Got a guy who hooked me up."

Steph shook his head. "'A guy,' huh? Rell, you ain't getting in no shit with Mack, are you?"

"I told you, I know a guy! Damn, why you clocking me? It got nothing to do with him."

Jarrell sucked his teeth, refocusing, with five minutes left to burn.

"Aight," Steph said, shrugging, dusting the sugar off his hands. "I'm just saying, you pretty nice with this computer stuff, that's all."

Jarrell's shoulders tightened. He hated lying to his friends. Yes, he "paid" for it, but not nearly the amount it was worth when it mysteriously fell off the back of a delivery truck. Not everyone was as lucky as Steph to have had a father to steer him down the right road. Jarrell had bread crumbs to follow rather than a real map. That's where Mack stepped in. Steph's father may have taught Steph how to be a man, but Mack had taught Jarrell about the streets and how to survive.

And when you're in the thick of it, it's hard to tell which lesson should be above the other.

"Keep it up and you gonna blow up," Steph added. "Probably be working for Microsoft, Wall Street, or for like the FBI or something."

"Nah, chill. I ain't trying to be no pig! What I look like?"

"Man, there's some good cops out there . . . my pops knew some."

They both fall silent. Anytime Steph brings up his father, all the air sucks out the room. Talking about his legacy poked at the throbbing pain bubbling skin deep.

"But I'm serious, though. You should, like, go to college

and get your degree in computers. You'll be making some serious bread."

"I don't know nothing about that college life," Jarrell laughed. "Plus, nobody in my family went."

Steph rolled his eyes. "Why you gotta be like everyone else? Just 'cause they didn't, don't mean you gotta do like they do."

"Well, my pops always say school ain't for everyone. Somebody gotta take out the trash at night, y'knowwhatumsayin?"

"That somebody don't gotta be you, though. My pops used to say, 'Dreams don't settle, so why should you?'"

Jarrell rubbed the back of his neck. "Man, ain't college expensive? Like thousands of g's?"

"So?" Steph barked. "You get scholarships, grants, and financial aid or whatever."

"What's that?"

"It's when they give you free money to go to school."

"Aight, what's the catch?" Jarrell chuckled. "'Cause nothing in this world is free."

"The catch is . . . you work legit, stay out of trouble, and help the next kid get into college. Kinda like when you get put on and bring your homies with you."

Jarrell sits up straight. "Like Big did with Lil' Cease?"

Lil' Cease was Biggie Smalls's main right-hand man that he met on the block hustling. Took him on tour, and hooked him up with Junior M.A.F.I.A., with Lil' Kim, Capone, and Nino Brown.

"Exactly! Who knows where Cease would've ended up? My pops used to call it 'reach back, pull forward.'"

"Yo, I like that," Jarrell laughed. "And there's probably all the cute honies up in college too. So, you thinking about going?"

Steph grabbed the basketball by his feet and tossed it in the air. "Maybe."

"Maybe?" Jarrell scoffed. "After you finished beating me in the head about this college shit, you don't even know if you want to go?"

Steph looked back out the window at the world below, full of the people he loved.

"I don't know. I may have a deal before then." Steph smirked. "You never know."

The CD drive popped open.

"Ohhhh . . . so that's what's on here," Jarrell said, holding the CD on his pinkie. "You ain't gonna let me hear it?"

Steph quickly snatched it off his finger. "Nah. It's just beats and bullshit anyways. But thanks, son. I'll check you later."

"What's the rush? You got a date or something?"

He unzipped his book bag and slipped the CD into his Discman, heading for Jarrell's bedroom door.

"Nah . . . business. But aye yo . . . I'm serious about that college shit. Think about it. Aight?"

Jarrell nodded. He had never seen Steph so pushy about anything except music.

"Aight, son."

"Oh snap, while I'm here," he said, jumping over to Rell's bed and pulling out a shoebox. "Can I borrow your kicks for . . . hey, what the fuck is this?"

Jarrell froze. "Nothing. Put that back."

Steph did what he was told. "This shit ain't NOTHING!"

"It ain't mine," he mumbled. "I'm just holding it for Mack."

"Well, Mack's dead wrong."

Jarrell sniffed, squaring his shoulders. "He ain't been wrong about nothing yet."

Steph had never been a fan of Mack and the way he seemed to steer Jarrell into thinking it's his way or no way.

"And quit going through my shit," Jarrell laughed, trying to lighten the mood. "How you this nosey and you don't ever let us in your room?"

Steph knew he couldn't talk Jarrell into giving it back, not even if he tried. "Ha, yeah, you right," Steph laughed uneasily. "Aight, I'll holla at you later."

Steph said his goodbyes to Jarrell's mom and ran out the door, down the stairs since he hated taking elevators.

Damn, Pops, you saw that, he thought with a smirk around the fifth floor. He had talked one of his best friends into considering college. Something his father actively did around the neighborhood. Maybe he could do the same, take up where his pops left off. Problem was not everyone in the hood was feeling his pops talking foot soldiers out of business. But what was under Jarrell's bed just solidified that before Steph could make that move, he had a lot more work to do to keep everyone he loved safe first.

And the key to that was on the fresh CD in his book bag.

11
JaRRELL

Optimus Prime swoops down and lands on my keyboard.

"Yo, I swear to God . . . I'mma throw this shit out the window!"

DayShawn grins from the top bunk and flips down to the bottom bunk with DaQuan, playing with their Transformer action figures.

"Jarrell!" Mummy screams from somewhere. "Jarrell! We need sugar! And milk! And a loaf of bread. Jarrell!"

"I'm busy, Mummy. I'll go later!"

"Huh? Meh can't hear yuh!"

"Mummy, meh said meh go lata!"

There's too many of us in this apartment. Mummy,

Grandma, the twins, my cousin Teddy sleeping on the sofa, Uncle Clinton on the love seat, and Auntie Mita always dropping by to gossip. That's why I spent all my time up in Steph's spot. At least it was quiet, and I didn't have to worry about stepping on Hot Wheels left in the middle of the floor. Can't stand sharing a room with these two Tasmanian devils.

"Arghhh! Yo! Would y'all be quiet already? Y'all act like you never play that game before. And pick up your toys, yo. Y'all act like we live in Toys"R"Us and y'all can leave shit wherever."

The twins flop on my bed, giggling, as the doorbell rings.

"Jarrell! Jarrell! Yuh friends are here!"

"Finally!" I asked them to stop by and see my progress.

"Aye yo, y'all go play in the living room!"

The twins act like they hard of hearing.

"What up, kid?" Quady says, walking in with Jasmine trailing behind him.

"Son, I can't work under these conditions," I grumble, pinching my temples. "These kids are driving me dumb crazy."

"What? They just kids," Quady laughs, playfully hemming them both up. "Are y'all gonna be good?"

"No," the twins answer in unison.

"Well, if y'all be good, we'll take you to the store to get some candy. How about that?"

The boys glance at each other with a smirk and run into the living room.

"See, all you gotta do is bribe them."

Jasmine sits on the bottom bunk behind me, shaking her

head. "That trick works on Carl for about five minutes."

"Yo, Steph better blow up," I say. "I gotta get my own crib! I'mma have mad rules like, take your shoes off at the door and no running. Matter fact, no one under ten gonna be allowed in my spot."

"Chill with that, son," Quady says, all serious. "We ain't doing this for money."

I roll my eyes, waving him off.

"Yeah, yeah, yeah. We doing this for 'the love of the game' or whatever. Save that shit for the movies."

"I'm serious. If we go in this trying to get rich—"

"Then we get rich! Now quit stalling, and let me show you what I've been working on."

Quady sighs. "Aight, what you got?"

I turn my focus to the screen as Jasmine and Quady surround me. "Here it is. After I digitized everything, I took that list Jazz made and broke it up. Party hits, volume one. Conscious hits, volume two. There's about twelve tracks on each. Here, I burned a copy."

Jasmine holds the CD, grinning as Quady pats my shoulder. "Good look, Rell! Way to hold it down."

"That ain't nothing. Check this out." I open another program. "I took a couple of old photos, scanned them, then . . ."

"Photos! Nah, hold up! You can't use pics of Steph!" Quady says. "People gonna recognize him! How we gonna explain that?"

"Would you relax? I got this! Check it out."

There was a photo of Steph after a basketball tournament I

I found in our yearbook. He was in a black hoodie, sort of turned to the side, his head tilted down.

"See? Little shadow, some fake facial hair, and boom! A *new* Steph."

Jasmine leans in closer to the screen.

"Damn."

"Anybody ask, Jazz, just say it's your cousin or something. Now, we take this picture, put it on a background"—I open another window to show them the progress—"and boom! Got us an album cover."

Quady punches me in the shoulder.

"Yoooo, son! Where'd you learn how to do all this?"

"Summer school, last year. I'm nice with it, right?"

"Shit. You've been holding out on us!"

"I can't believe you did this in two days," Jasmine adds.

I lean back in my chair, hands behind my head with a smirk.

"What can I say? I'm the man."

She rolls her eyes. "Uhhhh . . . I didn't say all that, now."

Quady laughs. "Aight, so now what?"

"Well, we gotta come up with a rap name. He can't go by anything he used before, or people are gonna know it's him."

"But don't we . . . want them to know it's him?" Jasmine asks, like she's offended.

"Nah, 'cause if labels know he's dead from jump, they ain't gonna wanna mess with him."

"Rell's right, Jazz," Quady adds. "We gotta fake them out first, for as long as possible. Get Steph in the club and on the radio until they come begging to sign him."

Jasmine shrugs. "I mean . . . I guess. But maybe it's a good thing that people might recognize him. Maybe someone will come forward with some info."

Quady winces. "Um. Yeah, right. But let's keep the name different."

Jazz squirms, looking uneasy.

"This is gonna work, Jazz," he says softly. "Trust me."

I peep something unsaid pass between them and roll my eyes.

"Aight, so let's think of some names."

"How about Fresh to Death? Get it?"

I rub my temple. "Yo, Quady, can you for once not be so damn corny? How about Killa—"

"Killa nothing!" Jasmine snaps. "Steph ain't no thug. Never even held a gun."

Quady and I share a quick look. It's like Steph was a whole other person to her. Like she didn't know the real Steph.

Or maybe we didn't know.

Quady starts pacing around the room, thinking, stepping over toys, sneakers, and socks.

"What about Professor S?" she offers. "Ghost Writer? Ghost—"

"Taken. Taken. And we can't name him Ghost nothing and try to compete with Ghostface Killah. Wu-Tang Clan ain't nothing to fuck with." I shake my head. "Damn, who knew this would be so hard?"

Quady suddenly stops, staring up at the wall above my bed.

"Architect," he mumbles.

"Huh?" Jasmine says. "What was that?"

Quady spins around, a goofy grin on his face.

"The Architect!"

I look behind him at the wall he was staring at, where Mummy hung an old wooden cross over my bed and one of Steph's old lines come back to me.

"Respect for the most high architect in full effect . . ."

"Yoooo . . . kid, that's it! Architect!" I look at Jasmine. "That is . . . if it's aight with you?"

Jasmine stares at the cross and smiles, nodding.

"Yeah, Architect."

"Aight, bet. We got a name and a demo. All we need now is to get some copies made."

"Can't you burn them on your computer?" Quady asks.

"Not to sell to the whole hood! You trying to start a grease fire on my baby? Nah, we need one of them professional CD burners."

"Well, where we gonna get one of those? And with what money?"

Jasmine grins. "I got an idea."

12
Quadir

"Yo, where we going?" Jarrell asks as we cross Malcolm X Boulevard, heading down Fulton Street.

"Just relax," Jasmine says with a smile.

He groans, twisting his lips up, and we slow down, letting her walk ahead. That's when I peep it, a little booty sticking out under her crop jean jacket. Jazzy Jazz isn't all legs and arms no more.

The other day at her spot, it just felt mad . . . regular. Like, kicking it with the homies on the corner, drinking quarter waters and talking about music. Maybe that's why when that song came on, the one with L-Boogie and D'Angelo . . . I lost my head. I found it, but it ain't been working right since. I almost kissed her. Jazz! Jazzy Jazz!

Man, I'm bugging.

"I don't like not knowing where I'm going," Jarrell whispers to me. "Your girl is wildin'."

"Chill! She ain't my girl!"

He sucks his teeth. "Man, not like that and you know it! You ain't stupid enough to do some dumb shit like that. Unless you want Steph to 'Thriller' dance his way out of the grave and snap you in half."

I punch his arm. "Yo, shut up, man! That ain't funny!"

"I'm just joking! Damn! What got your panties all in a bunch today?"

I take a deep breath, thinking about that scene in *Scarface*, when Tony went bananas on his friend for checking out his sister, and my stomach starts knotting up.

"I'm . . . just saying, she says she got an idea, let's see what it is. Unless you got a better one."

Jarrell grumbles, "Aight, fine. Just don't want her thinking she running the show, that's all."

We walk through Fulton Park, near Boys and Girls High and up two blocks to the corner. Jazz opens up a foggy glass door between a storefront and a bodega, and we climb up a narrow flight of stairs with smelly carpet. She tests the knob and pushes the door open a crack.

"You gonna have to squeeze in here," she says, her voice low as she slips inside first.

"This some bullshit," Jarrell says, approaching the door real casual before shoving himself through the crack. He stops midway. "Yo, I'm stuck."

I take a deep breath and push at his shoulder. "Suck it in, man!"

"Ow! I am!"

"No, you not," I laugh. I can't help it. He looks ridiculous, wedged in like a doorstopper.

"Yo, this shit ain't funny."

"Aight. Ready?" I take a few steps, giving enough distance for a running start.

"Bet!"

I sprint up with both hands extended and shove him inside, collapsing on the floor on top of him. Jasmine stands over us, shaking her head.

Inside reminds me of my neighbor's apartment. She got so much junk that you can't even see the floor or open the door fully. Mom calls her a hoarder and keeps threatening to call the landlord. This place is like some kind of electronic repair shop filled with computers, camcorders, cassette decks, stereos, and boxes filled with rolls and rolls of blank CDs. The far wall looked like a shelf in Blockbuster. Six TVs, each playing a different movie, connected to a stack of VCRs by the window.

"What the . . . ," Jarrell mumbles, stepping over extension cords taped to the floor. "Where are we? Half this shit looks stolen."

"We at a friend's," she whispers. "Now be quiet, and let me do the talking."

We check out the next room and Jarrell stops short,

pointing to a machine in the corner.

"Look! See that? That's a CD duplicator. Son, it's exactly what we need."

"Hi, Kenny," Jasmine says from down the hall. But she doesn't say it regular, though. She says it all smooth like. We follow her voice, running up behind her.

Kenny's head pops up from behind the back of a TV. He's mad scrawny, rocking a bright-green knit sweater with thick glasses that slip down his nose.

"Jasmine? Oh . . . wow. What's up? What are you doing . . . here? How'd you get in?"

"I came to see you, silly," she giggles. "You need to learn how to lock that door."

She's never giggled like that around us. I try to swallow back my rising . . . overprotectiveness. Yeah, that's it. Or at least that's what I think it is. It can't be jealousy 'cause I'm not checking for Jazz like that.

"My dad must've left it open. He's making some deliveries."

"Your pops a bootlegger, right?" Jarrell asks with a smile. "He's one of those people in the movie theater with a camcorder that tapes whole movies that got folk walking in front of the screen and shit."

Kenny worms his neck around her, adjusts his glasses, and frowns. "Who are they?"

She waves us off. "Don't worry about them. They ain't important."

"Oh. Wow. Well, it's good to see you. Why haven't you been to any meetings? People been asking about you."

Jasmine's face drops, eyes quickly glancing at us.

Meeting? What meetings?

She clears her throat. "Um, yeah. I've been busy with school and stuff. But, yo, remember how you said you'd help me with anything?"

Kenny gulps. "Yeah . . ."

"Were you lying?"

"No, no. Of course not. Whatever you need."

I know this is all business, but I ain't feeling how duke is staring at her all hard.

"Yo, should we be doing this?" I whisper to Jarrell.

He looks at me like I got two heads. "You bugging. Shorty's about to hook us up."

"I just don't feel right about using Steph's sister like this."

"*We* ain't. This was her idea. Remember? You the one that wanted to play along."

"Cool, 'cause I need a favor." Jazz holds her hand out behind her back and Jarrell slips her the CDs. "I need you to make copies of these."

"How many?"

"About a hundred."

"Of *each*? That's a lot. My father . . . he may notice."

Jasmine smiles. "Or he may not. You guys seem so busy up in here. But if something happens, you can let him know it was me."

"No, no, I can't let you get in trouble. That . . . wouldn't be right. Um, when do you need it by?"

Jasmine smiles. "Yesterday."

He blows out some air, gripping the back of his kufi.

"Okay. But, if I do this . . . you gonna come back, right? You know you can't just . . . leave."

Jasmine tenses up, her lips in a straight line, and she mumbles. "Yeah, I know."

"So that's it?"

We stand outside the Utica Ave station stop, a few blocks from home, for a quick team huddle.

"Yup," Jasmine sighs. "I'll pick up the copies on Wednesday after school."

"Yo, good looking, Jazz," Jarrell says.

"Yeah . . . uh, thanks," I say drily.

"Aye yo," Jarrell says. "Shit. I forgot. Supposed to pick up some bread for Mummy before dinner. She's gonna kill me! I'll holla at y'all later."

Jarrell don't even say bye before he takes off running into the supermarket.

"Well, I better get home," Jasmine says. "I still got homework."

"I'll walk you."

She shrugs. "You don't have to."

I roll my eyes. "You live across the street. It ain't nothing."

"Oh. Yeah, right."

"Aye yo, how you know homeboy? From school?"

Jasmine squirms, focusing on the ground. "Um, kind of."

"Oh. And what was he talking about in there? Something about a meeting?"

We cross Malcolm X Boulevard and head up Chauncey, passing the courts, a late game going down.

"It's nothing. Hey, did you know that Malcolm X was born in Nebraska?"

She switching up and dodging the subject. Ain't like I'm trying to be in her business or nothing. But, what we asked of homie . . . was kind of huge. Don't do that type of stuff for your biology classmate.

"Nebraska? I thought he was from Harlem. You know they all think I'm Muslim too, 'cause of my name."

She smiles. "Nah . . . really?"

It feels good to make her smile.

Wait! Son, what are you doing?

It hits me that we walking mad slow, strolling like we on a date or something. And just the thought of this image getting back to Ronnie somehow . . .

"Damn, Quady, what's the rush?"

I look back and Jazz is a solid twenty feet behind me.

"It's uh, getting late," I say, widening the space between us.

"Late? The sun ain't even set all the way," she laughs, gazing up at the pink sky. She sighs, her smile fading. "Um, Quady . . . about the other day . . ."

"Don't worry about it, aight. The music just . . . carried us away."

She frowns. "Nah, not about that. I mean, what we found under Steph's bed . . ."

"Oh. Oh! Yeah."

She crosses her arms. "Did you know . . . he was hustling?"

My heart picks up the pace. "Um. Nah."

"I . . . don't think he was. And I don't think how he died had anything to do with all that."

When we hit Patchen Ave, I open my mouth and say something real stupid.

"How . . . do you know for sure . . . though?"

She shoots me a look. "'Cause he was my brother. And yours too, I thought."

I nod. "You right. My bad."

"But I think that's what the police are gonna assume. Just cast this off as some drug deal gone bad or something. Police ain't never been here for black folks. We have to do for ourselves always. That's why . . . I need to know what really happened."

"So that's why you didn't want Rell to see the box?"

She bites her lip. "I just don't want the people he loved, looking at him . . . different."

We stop in front of her building door. I nod at a few cats I recognize from the courts chilling on the benches and can see the light on in my apartment across the street.

"Jazz, I hear you. But what if you find out something . . . something bad. How you gonna take it?"

Jasmine takes a deep breath and chuckles before heading inside.

"Anything's better than not knowing."

I walk in just after seven and find Mom sitting on the sofa in front of the TV, hair already wrapped up for bed.

"Hey, baby," Mom says. "Dinner is on the stove and . . . what is China? HA! Yes, knew it! I knew it!"

It's Mom's favorite hour of the day: *Jeopardy* at seven and *Wheel of Fortune* at seven thirty. Mom shouts answers and curses contestants out for not being as smart as her, but dead-ass, my mom is like a genius. She's waiting for the New York tryouts to be on one of the shows. Either one, don't matter. She kills it in geography, US history, science, and eats word-search magazines for breakfast. If there's ever a hip-hop category, she'd smash that too. Mom swears she was at the party in the Bronx where DJ Kool Herc first started scratching records for the break.

"What is carbon?" she yells at Alex Trebek while the contestant gets it wrong. "Tuh. Stupid white girl. How was practice?"

I load up my plate with instant mashed potatoes, corn, roasted chicken, and pour myself a cup of iced tea. Mom used to work at Chase as a bank teller until they let her go. She picks up retail jobs here and there during the holiday seasons, but they don't always last long.

"Ma, practice don't start until next week."

"Well, where you been all afternoon then?"

"Chilling at Rell's."

"Oh yeah. And how's my favorite troublemaker doing?" she says with a grin, setting up a tray table for me.

"About to punt the twins out the nearest window if they keep acting up."

I squeeze on to the sofa. Steph and Rell always snapping

on me, saying I'm rich because I don't live in the projects like them. Truth is, our spot is much smaller. We live on the top floor of a walk-up, railroad-style apartment. That means the whole place is the length of the house and the rooms are all connected. So my parents gotta walk through my room to get to their room and I have to walk through my parents' room to get to the bathroom. The TV sits right next to the stove, and all the closets are in the hallway by the stairs so if Ms. Proyer downstairs makes fried fish for dinner, all our clothes smell like grease. It was worse when my sister lived with us; we looked like a can of sardines up in here. But now she's shacked up with her boyfriend in Queens. Such a traitor, leaving Brooklyn for Jamaica Ave.

"I saw Ms. Davis on the train this morning heading to work. She looks . . . good. Considering."

I play with a piece of chicken, slowly losing my appetite.

"How is she?"

"Said she's doing okay. Keep on keeping on. Jasmine found a little job after school."

Jasmine must be lying about helping us. Good. Her mom would dead our project the moment she found out.

"Oh word, that's cool."

Mom smiles real big. "When I got home today, that coach from Bishop called."

My head snaps up. "What he want?"

She shrugs like it's no big deal. "Just to see how you're doing. Practice already starting over there."

I stuff my mouth so I don't have to talk.

"Baby . . . Bishop is a really good school."

"Yeah, that cost almost six g's to go to."

"So? I said we'd find the money."

"How?" I snap. Mom's been out of work for over a year now.

"Quadir. College recruiters are gonna come looking. I don't know how all this works, but wouldn't it be better if you were on a winning team? A, what's it called, division one or something?"

I shake my head. "Mom, we gonna need to go over the sports category again before you hit them *Jeopardy* tryouts."

She laughs. "I'm serious, Quady. That coach said if you're ready, he can find scholarship money. If you go to this school, you could get into a really good college, then med school, and become a doctor!"

Me being a doctor was always her dream. Since I was a kid she's been pushing for it. I guess all moms hope their sons make an honest living and move them out the hood.

But that's never been my dream.

"So you want me to just leave my friends? My teammates? Ronnie?"

Mom rolls her eyes. "If Ronnie really loved you like you swear she does, she'd understand you doing this for your future."

"What if she's my future?"

Mom purses her lips. "And what is her future? Aside from buying expensive stuff her little grown-ass behind don't need to be wearing."

I wasn't in the mood to debate about Ronnie again. Plus, I can't leave now. Not with our plans for Steph in full effect. I need to be close and in the mix.

"It's just too much money, Mom. We barely keeping the lights on."

Mom sighs and shakes her head, tuning into Alex Trebek again.

"What are invertebrates?" she shouts and looks at me, hard. "Animals without a backbone."

13
JARRELL

"Yo, what's this? A crackheads anonymous meeting?"

Mack don't even look up before letting his dice fly and hit the brick wall behind my building, landing on a four, five, and six.

"HAAAA! Yo, pay up, playboys!"

The fellas, all huddled up, drop they dollars on the ground. There's DJ Mo-Breeze, D-Block, Reck 'Em . . . ahhh, forget it, too many of them to name. They all meeting up for the daily cee-lo cypher. Cee-lo ain't like no regular dice game. I tried to teach my cousin who lives in North Carolina and he looked at me like I had three heads, guess 'cause we play with three dice rather than just two. Cats be serious about this game.

The rest of the homies are chilling on benches, people-watching, smoking lah, playing music. Just a typical day in Brevoort.

"Well, look who it is," Mack says, dapping me up. "J-Money in the building!"

Mack's wearing a fresh Fila velour sweatsuit and the butter Timbs, looking like he copped them from Foot Locker that morning. He always got the fly gear, the crisp haircuts, and the baddest shorties.

"You want in?" he asks, chewing on a toothpick.

"Nah, I'm good," I say. I had business to take care of first. "What up, Cash?"

DJ Cash gives me a head nod from the bench, taking a few puffs from a blunt.

"What y'all getting to?"

"Ain't shit," Mack says. "Just kicking it, enjoying the weather before the cold comes in, you know what I'm saying."

"Word, word. Well, I got something for y'all."

I reach into my book bag and grab the stack of CDs Jasmine dropped off that morning.

"Here y'all go," I say, passing them out.

Mack looks at the cover and chuckles. "Son, what's this?"

"It's a friend of mine's. He's nice with it."

Mack flips the CD around and I hold my breath, hoping he don't look too close and recognize Steph.

"Yo, man, is this a joke? You a promoter now?"

The only way we were gonna get the word out about Steph . . . I mean, Architect . . . is by starting with the streets.

And all these cats were either DJs, knew DJs, threw parties, or bumped music from the banging sound systems in their cars around the block.

"Yeah . . . something like that," I laugh, trying to act cool even though my heart is pounding something serious. "Son, all you got to do is play some of these tracks at your next party. I'm telling you, gonna have people rocking. And when they start asking about it, send them my way."

"This kid, always scheming," Mack laughs. "Ever since I met him. Only six-year-old I knew hustling five-cent bags of chips for a dollar."

Cash takes the CD and snaps his fingers. "Oh, is this that joint you gave me at E. Roque's party couple of weeks ago?"

I grin. "Yup! Track number seven, 'Go Ma.'"

Cash looks at the fellas. "Yo. Shorties were wildin' over this tune. I ran it back twice."

All the homies nod. "Oh, word? Like that?"

"Yeah! That shit is butter!"

Cash's words sealed the deal. Any tunes that get the shorties dancing is the tunes fellas want at their next party.

Mack nods his head, rubbing his chin. "Aight, kid. We got you. But, before you bounce, let me holla at you for second."

He throws his arm over my neck, yoking me up. Mack is like three times my size, so it don't take nothing for him to pull me away from the others.

"Aye, I can't breathe," I cough out.

"Man, stop bitching," he laughs, loosening his hold. "So,

yo, you think about what we talked about the other day?"

"Um, yeah. Yeah."

Mack squeezes harder. "Don't bullshit me. I'm serious."

"I'm . . . thinking."

"All I'm saying is, you got real potential and—"

"I know! Damn. I'm . . . just not sure if I'm ready. . . ."

"You ready, you just shook. But it's aight, playboy." He releases me and pats my shoulder, leaning in a little closer. "Yo, you still got that deuce deuce?"

I gulp. "Yeah."

"You didn't use it for something stupid, did you?"

"Nah!"

Mack stares me down, and then pokes me in the chest. "I only gave you that shit for your protection. You see what happened to—"

"Yo! What the dilly, Mack! Rell!"

Dante comes speeding in our direction.

Mack sighs. "What up, Dante."

"Mack, I was looking for you. Yo . . . ," he says, lowering his voice. "Word is, some kids off Bainbridge been trying to creep on your turf and make a name for themselves."

I try stepping away. Less I know about Mack's business, the better. But Mack keeps me locked close.

"Oh, word," he says, rubbing his chin, his face unreadable. "Aight. Good looking."

Dante brightens, as if he did right. "Aight, check y'all later!"

Dante rushes off quick as he came. Mack shakes his head with a smirk.

"I swear, that kid be telling me everything. Even shit I ain't worried about."

Giving the fellas the demos should handle most of Bed-Stuy. We had the rest of Brooklyn to take care of. And the street vendors on Fulton was gonna be the fastest way to do it.

Fulton Street starts from all the way in Cypress Hill, running through Bed-Stuy, Clinton Hill, and stopping way downtown close to Borough Hall. Folks from Crown Heights, Fort Greene, even Brownsville hit Fulton for one reason or another. Clothes, shoes, sheets, towels, jewelry, TVs, music, weed, crack, groceries . . . you name it, Fulton Street got it or knows how to get it.

You hit Fulton Street on a Saturday, you gonna see everybody shopping, from grandmas to teen moms. Saturday had the most foot traffic. Especially around the A&S on Fulton Street Mall.

"Let's start with him," I say, pointing to the young cat, setting up two brown folding tables with the newest bootleg movies and CDs.

"Why him?" Quady asks.

"'Cause he's playing that Nasty Nas."

Quady taps my arm. "Nah, bump that. Let's start with duke over there."

To our far right, homie with the fresh Caesar cut, thick gold cable chain, and blue Starter jacket has his tables set up with the black crushed-velvet tablecloth and red boom box bumping DMX.

"Homie got style. He gonna recognize good music."

"Aight, let me do the talking."

"Why you?"

"'Cause I'm nice with it! And ain't nobody wanna hear no cornball jokes from some light-skin Eddie Murphy wannabe."

Quady rolls his eyes. "Whatever."

Homie sees us approach and starts rearranging the table, looking wild busy.

"Sup, sup, sup! How y'all doing? Got that new Jay-Z, Big Pun, Cam'ron. What you need, I got it!"

"Like your style, son," I say. "But what we need is a pusher."

He chuckles. "A what?"

"I got this new joint here . . . everybody's gonna wanna get with."

Homie rolls his eyes. "You a rapper?"

Damn, why people keep asking me that?

"Nah nah, my main mans is though. He's the truth, for real."

"Yo, kid, I got like five of you coming to me every day looking for a hookup."

"But you ain't heard nothing like this!"

He blows out air and laughs. "Please, I've heard it *all* before."

"Just listen. And if you don't like it, we'll move on."

He rolls his eyes. "Aight. But only cause it's mad early, and I don't got no customers yet. Let me hear what you got."

I give him volume one and skip to track seven. Steph's voice bumps through the speakers and . . . I can't really explain it . . . but every time I hear him, it makes me miss him more.

"Aight, homie, ya man got flow," he finally says, glancing me over. "I'll take three."

"Just three? Nah, you gonna need more than that. Probably gonna sell out of these by the end of the week. Make it six."

"Aight. But need to be on consignment. Split the profits seventy/twenty."

"Man, are you smoking something? Your math all messed up. Seventy plus twenty don't even make a hundred!"

"Listen, I'm out here doing all the work, and taking the risk, so I name the price!"

Quady looks nervous. Glad I ain't.

"Yo, let me break it down for you—we giving you that good shit. Sound quality straight, no scratches or nothing. Not that bootleg crap you be getting from Chinatown. Think about how many people come back trying to return CDs. We give you this, they gonna want more. Now I know you taking all the risk, but we providing the product. How about this? Take five, we do a sixty/forty split. And if you sell out by the weekend, we bring you back two dozen and we split fifty-five, forty-five. Twenty-four times ten, hell, let's say nine if you trying to be nice, is two sixteen, minus ninety-seven for our share plus another five for delivery is roughly, a buck-o-two. So we straight?"

Homie nods his head real slow. "Aight, that sound good."

"Quady, give this good man the goods."

Quady blinks out of a trance and hands him five CDs,

and I offer homie a handshake.

"Pleasure doing business with you. And if you need more, I put my pager number inside on the bottom left-hand corner."

Homie still seems lost. "Uh, yeah. Likewise, young man," he says, as he reaches for the Stop button on his boom box.

"Nah nah nah, man. Let it play. Let people hear. I'm telling you. They coming. This is just volume one. We got volume two if you interested next time."

Homie rolls his eyes. "Yeah, yeah. We'll see."

I give Quady the look and we walk off quick.

"Son! How you do all that math in your head like that?" he whispers.

"Easy," I chuckle. "And duke so lost he don't even know I hustled him into giving us fifty percent of his profits."

Quady daps me up. "Good lookin', kid."

We make the corner and head down the block, where Jasmine is leaned up on a mailbox.

"Well?" she says.

"Aight, you up!"

"Hope he don't peep game," Quady sighs.

"Son, the man can't add to a hundred!"

"I know, I'm just saying."

"I got this, Quady," Jazz says all soft. "Don't worry."

Quady looks at her and nods. "Aight."

Why it feel like she was asking his permission or something?

Jazz passes us and heads down Fulton Street. We follow, staying hidden by the corner, watching her walk all casually down the street before stopping in front of Homie. Once again, duke makes himself mad busy as she approaches.

"Sup sup sup, how you doing, young lady. Got that new L-Boogie, Mary J., Eve, 112. What you need, I got you."

"Ooo . . . what's this you playing now?" she asks, bobbing her head. "This is tight. I think I heard this last night at a party." She sings the hook. "Yeah! That's it! Yo, me and my girls were just rocking to this."

Homie's eyes light up. He quickly grabs the CD case and reads off the cover. "Oh yeah, that's that new . . . new, uh, Architect. Yeah. Kid's about to blow up!"

"Architect? Never heard of him, but I like his style."

"You hear that flow?" he says, bopping his head too. "That rumble. Yo, he's coming for cats' necks! You heard it here first, ma!"

Jazz smiles and picks up the CD. "How much?"

"Ten, but for you, sweetheart, I'll do nine."

Jazz pulls crinkled up dollars out her pocket. "Thanks."

"Thank YOU! And that's just volume one. I got volume two coming . . . uh . . . end of this weekend."

"Oh word? He got two? Oh, I'm definitely coming back! You the only person I've seen sell these."

Homie smiles real big as Jazz walks off and we meet up with her two blocks down.

"Well, it worked," she says with a grin.

"Aye yo, good idea, Quady," I laugh.

"Told y'all," he smirks. "It's all about the ladies."

"Aight. That's one down," Jasmine says, staring up the street with a sigh. "Twenty-five blocks to go."

14
Jasmine

Mom is mad obsessed with cleaning now.

Since she went back to work, she's been taking extra hours to save up. But when she's not working, she's cleaning. That means I'm cleaning, and we ain't doing no regular cleaning. We do that deep, deep, deep clean. That wash all windows, scrub the bottom of the stove, dust the tops of shelves type cleaning. But it's all good—as long as my music is playing, I'm cool.

"What I tell you about them baggy pants, Jasmine?"

I glance down at my Guess jeans; the wide black belt and silver buckle have them sitting right on my hips.

"You want to dress like a boy or a girl?"

"Girls wear their jeans like this, Mom. It's the style!"

"Hmph, some style. Why can't you dress like Ms. Stewart's daughter, Tania? She has nice taste."

Ain't no way I'm dressing like Chicken-Head Tania in her crop shirts and tight booty shorts that's been on the floor of every brotha's nasty bedroom in Brevoort.

"That just ain't me, Mom."

She shakes her head, lifting the left side of the sofa so I can vacuum underneath.

"How's school?" she asks.

Lauryn Hill is on repeat again. It's crazy how much I love this album. It like . . . speaks to my soul for real. Mom likes it too. I peep her bobbing her head to "Lost Ones."

"School's okay." Honestly, I wouldn't know. Been distracted and mad busy selling Steph's demos and making some serious cash. I can't believe people really feeling my brother like this. I wish I could tell Mom about it. She'd be so proud.

"You ain't giving the teachers problems this year, are you?"

"I told you, that wasn't my fault. Ms. Grant was trying to teach out of a textbook that had one paragraph about slavery. ONE! It didn't even talk about the Nat Turner rebellion or Harriet Tubman leading slaves to freedom through the Underground Railroad, or the freedom papers or . . ."

"Lawd, you have so much of your father in you. He used to flip desks back in high school when they refused to celebrate Black History Month. He went around trying to organize a Black Panther Party right in school. Your grandmother came down and knocked some sense into him."

I laugh. "And you loved him even then?"

"Of course! First man I ever knew who called me 'Queen' and really went out of his way to make me feel like one. We never had much money, but I never felt so . . . royal."

Daddy *had* to have serious game to kick it to a hard rock like Mom.

"How's that job going?" she asks.

"It's . . . uh . . . it's okay. Busy. How's the investigation going?"

Mom blinks twice. "Oh. It's . . . well, these things take time, Jasmine. Steph ain't even been gone a month yet."

"It's been eight weeks, Mom," I mumble to the floor.

Mom shakes her head, like I said something crazy. "What? No it hasn't."

"It's October, Mom. Halloween is next week. Steph died . . . in August."

Mom huffs, waving her arms around. "Well . . . whatever. The police are handling this, Jasmine! Let them do their job. Stop worrying about that and help me in this kitchen."

You can't tell, but my room has been cotton-candy pink since I was a baby. I've been begging Mom to let me repaint it. Dark blue, green, purple . . . anything, but she always says no. So I do the next best thing: I cover it up with posters, just like Steph did. Tupac, TLC, MC Lyte, Queen Latifah, Roxanne Shanté, Missy Elliot, Yo-Yo . . . every poster that came in a *Word Up!* magazine or a cover of *Vibe*, I added to my wall until all that's left is the ceiling.

Maybe I'll put Steph up there, when he's on the cover of *The Source* magazine. Like he's watching me from heaven.

I left my Lauryn CD in the living room with Mom, and I wasn't trying to go back out there so she could find something else for me to clean. It's aight, though. Funkmaster Flex is on HOT 97. Plus, I'm rereading Assata Shakur's autobiography. Daddy bought it for Mom, but she was never really interested. Me, though, I couldn't get enough. A militant revolutionary so committed to black liberation she even took on an African name. This should be required reading for all women.

Gotta stop by Kenny's and cop some more CDs before I meet up with Rell and Quady tomorrow. But then that means . . . he may ask me to go to a meeting. And I don't know how long I have until they come looking for me.

Bzzzz Bzzzz

Oh shoot, that's Steph's pager! This is the first time it's ever rung. Someone must be looking for him.

Bzzzz Bzzzz

I jump up and grab the pager from the hiding spot under my desk. If it keeps buzzing, Mom may hear it.

917-224-4747

I hit *67 to block my number and call back. A man's voice answers on the first ring.

"Steph? Steph, you there? Where are you?"

There's some static and his voice is real low, so he must be on a cell phone or something. I hold a blanket over the phone so he can't hear me breathing (I peeped this in a movie once). There's some clicking, a window rolls up, and I hear Biggie in the background. That "Kick in the Door" beat is unmistakable.

"Hello? You there? Hello? Hellooooo?"

He don't sound like some kid. He sounds older . . . and white. What he want with Steph?

Just as I was about to speak up, I hear it. It's faint with the window closed, but outside, someone's car is bumpin' the same song. It drives by and it's silent again. Both on the phone and outside.

He knows where Steph lives. Where I live.

"Hey, kid. You don't want to play games with me. Call me back."

Click.

15

QUADIR

"This is it," Ronnie whispers in my ear. "Don't fuck it up."

Damn. No pressure.

Ronnie has on this long black velvet dress with sheer sleeves and two slits that stop way up her thigh. I'm trying hard not to stare, but she looks so damn sexy, I can't keep my hands off her. She won't let me kiss her 'cause I'll mess up her makeup, which already got her looking like a whole other person.

I'm also trying to distract myself from thinking about all them people in the hall waiting for our big entrance.

Ronnie adjusts my pink satin tie and vest that matches one of the dresses she's changing into tonight. The rest of the friends in her royal court are laughing and dancing behind us. All the fellas have on fly black shirts and slacks, the ladies sleeveless black dresses. They look mad relaxed, probably 'cause they all cheerlead together and dance at parties. I'm the only nondancer in the crew.

"You okay?" she asks, patting down her swoop bang. She put in these long extensions that stop around her mid-back, even though her hair was long already. She really don't need all this extra stuff; I already thought she was pretty before.

"Yeah, I'm cool."

She looks me over like she don't believe me and starts to say something, but then the party planner gives us our cue, and everyone rushes into formation. The double doors swing open, bright spotlights falling down on us.

I don't have much time to scope out the room, but I swear all of Brevoort is up in here to witness me make a fool out of myself. Neighbors, classmates, cats from the courts, even some ladies from church surround the dance floor. Rell is in front of the mini stage, already laughing. Man, I hate him sometimes.

There's pink everywhere. Pink tablecloths, pink balloons, pink twinkling Christmas lights, pink flowers, and a giant pink cake with *Happy Sweet Sixteen Veronica* written on each layer in gold glitter. I ain't never seen anything like it. It's like a wedding, and the thought of that makes me want to run into traffic.

We file onto the dance floor and take our positions, Ronnie and I the last to enter. Everyone's cheering and taking pictures before a hush falls over the crowd. The DJ turns on Aaliyah's

"Are You That Somebody?" and we break out into the first steps of the dance number. I swear we watched that video a billion times and practiced the routine all summer, but I'm still shook. I also wasn't expecting Ronnie dancing in some sexy dress with splits and heels, showing the whole hood her goods, so I keep counting out all the steps to the Timbaland beat.

DUM dum. Dum dum dum dum DUM.

During one of the turns, I spot her pops standing by her moms taking pictures with a disposable camera. He straight up looks like Deebo from that movie *Friday*, all swole in the chest and arms. That man never smiles, but he takes one look at Ronnie and all that hardness melts off him. But when he looks at me, his eyes go dark, and I know I better not mess this up or he'll kill me.

We're midway through the dance. Ronnie is smiling, looking all happy while I'm sweating bullets. Her heel slips and she almost falls, but I catch her and smooth it out, pretending I tripped instead. I rather take the L for us both. Her eyes go wide and she laughs.

At the end of the song, it turns into this type of flamenco dancing, the fellas tap dancing while the girls wave lacy fans. When we finish, I have to dip Ronnie, but I'm nervous 'cause her dress is mad low cut and I don't want her titties falling out, so I dip her a little and pull her back up. She cuts her eyes at me while the crowd goes wild, cheering and clapping. They bum rush us on the dance floor, giving us hugs and daps.

"Yoo . . . you looked good out there, kid," Jarrell cackles. "Only fucked up once."

"Twice," Ronnie corrects him, shooting daggers at me.

I can't believe it—even after everything, she still ain't happy.

DJ starts spinning some music. Ronnie runs off with her friends to change into her next dress, and it's the first time all day I take a real breath. The party is bumping after that. People laughing, drinking, eating. Jarrell's up in the middle of the dance floor. Rell's pretty light on his feet for a big guy. My man got all the moves.

Ronnie returns in this long, poufy, pink dress and one of those gold tiaras like she's a princess. She holds on to my arm and we walk around the dining tables, greeting her subjects. Everyone is telling her how beautiful she is, how wonderful her party is, how lucky I am to be her boyfriend. I'm fake smiling the whole time 'cause deadass, I'm not really in the mood to party no more.

The DJ throws on a slow song, K-Ci & JoJo's "All My Life," and couples start floating to the dance floor. Even Rell grabs a shorty. I know I have to dance with Ronnie now, but I'm not really feeling how she played me after I saved her. But her pops got that look in his eye, so I take her hand and lead her to the floor. She wraps her arms around my neck and I hold her waist as we sway.

That's when I finally notice Jasmine in the corner, sipping out of a black cup. She don't have her regular two puffs. Her hair is slicked up into one bun and she's wearing this short black dress that must've been her mom's but still got her leather African medallion necklace. She looks mad uncomfortable, like she don't know what to do with her arms.

Ronnie follows my stare and rolls her eyes.

"Grandma made me invite her. She feels bad for her mom."

Jasmine seems as miserable as I feel.

"That's nice of you, though."

Ronnie shrugs. "Yeah. I just wish she didn't come so busted looking. Like, don't she own a hot comb?"

"Damn, Ronnie, that's mad foul."

"What? You see how laced everyone showed up. She couldn't leave that Africa shit home for one night?"

I don't feel like arguing with her, so I don't say nothing. A group of girls standing by Jasmine keep whispering and giggling at her. Either she doesn't notice, or she does and is pretending like she don't. I don't know which is worse but all I wanna do is grab her, clock out this wack-ass party with all these fake people, and just chill.

Ronnie sucks her teeth. "I'm saying, after I bought that dress for her, didn't think I'd have to teach her how to rock it too."

"Hold up, *you* bought her that dress?"

She shrugs. "Well . . . yeah. She's was your best friend's sister, right? Everyone know they don't got money like that. Anyways, Grandma dropped it off this morning."

Damn. I'm surprised. And that dress don't look like it came from a thrift store either. Looks like it cost a grip.

Jasmine catches me staring and smiles.

Ronnie taps my chin with her finger. "My parents are still going out of town this weekend."

That was our signal. We finally, *finally*, supposed to "do

it," and even though she had me waiting long enough, and she laced Jasmine up, I still wasn't in the mood.

The song changes to Monica's "Angel of Mine." That's when her pops taps me on shoulder.

"Mind if I cut in."

He didn't say it like he was really asking, so I slide to the left. With Ronnie distracted, I don't even try to be smooth about it—I walk right toward Jasmine.

"Hey."

"Hey," she says real quiet, and it's the happiest I've seen her.

"What's up, y'all," Rell says behind me. I didn't peep him following me, and for a split second, I'm kind of disappointed.

"Nice party," she says.

"Quady, while you were getting your Usher on, I was talking to Jazz. Said the pager's been blowing up—everyone's looking for Steph!"

Jasmine nods, grinning.

"For real! Son, we gotta get busy and make volume three!"

"Word?" Rell laughs. "You think we got enough for a volume three?"

"Man, we got enough for a three, four, five, and six if we really wanted to."

"There's a bunch of songs we left off the first two volumes," Jasmine adds.

"Jazz, you remember that one where he was talking about stickup kids?"

She smiles. "Yeah yeah! That's like a DMX banger. What about that one about the Brevoort courts? You know, that one you said sounds like Jay-Z's 'Can I Live?' What we call it?"

"'B-City Blues'?"

"Ha, that's it! That's it!"

We laugh, and Rell raises an eyebrow. "Aight, I see you two got the catalog down."

"Um, yeah. But for real, we gotta get to . . ."

Steph clears his voice on the mic before the song starts playing, and there's an "Ohhhhh" from the crowd as they rush the dance floor. The three of us look at each other in shock.

"Oh shit!" Rell laughs. "Yoooo! What y'all waiting for? Come on!"

We head to the dance floor, and just as I reach for Jasmine's hand, Ronnie snakes between us.

"Oh snaps, I love this song!" Ronnie laughs, dancing up on me.

Jasmine don't say nothing. She just gives me a small smile and bobs her head on the edge of the dance floor. Ain't nothing I could do. Ain't like I could push Ronnie away.

They run Steph's song back twice, just like at E. Roque's party. The spot is popping. I swear they loving him as much as they love Big. Before the DJ can run the song again, another DJ takes over.

"Yo yo yo yo . . . can I have your attention please. Can I have your attention please!"

His voice sounds familiar, but I couldn't place him. Ronnie's pops jumps onstage with another mic.

"Hey, y'all! I wanna thank y'all for coming to celebrate my

baby girl's sweet sixteen." Everybody cheers and claps.

"Now. I got a special surprise for my baby. A friend of mine came to show some love, so show him some love. Y'all give it up for my boy Fast Pace!"

Fast Pace strolls up from backstage, giving Ronnie's pops a dab while the room wilds out.

"Oh my God!" Ronnie screams and rushes to the stage.

It's really Fast Pace, hitting that tiny stage with his squad. I ain't never seen, you know, a real celebrity in person before. He's much shorter than he looks on TV, his voice raspy like Rakim.

"Aye yo, what's up, everybody! Happy birthday, Ronnie! Man, you grew up fast! When your pops told me it was your birthday, you know I had to come through! Yo, B-Voort, where you at? Brooklynnnn!!!!"

Fast Pace performs his hit single "Dirty Dozen." It's been all over the radio. I mean, it's aight. Steph shit is better, though, and I ain't just saying that 'cause he's my boy. Even Moms says she don't see the big deal.

After he wraps up, Ronnie runs onstage and gives him a big hug. This party is going to be legendary. Everyone is gonna be talking about it for years. Exactly what she wanted. He takes a few pictures, signs autographs, and heads for the exit. The DJ scratches into a reggae set, and everyone starts dancing again. I thought I'd see Rell on the floor with his peoples, but instead he comes running up to me.

"Yo, kid, now's our chance!"

"Huh?"

"Son, come on!"

We rush out the doors, where Fast Pace and his crew are climbing into a caravan of Escalades parked out front. Rell pulls a CD out his blazer pocket.

"Son, what you about to do?" I ask.

"What d'you think? I'm about to give it to Fast Pace!"

"Nah, he ain't gonna take that seriously."

"Son, he's from Brooklyn. Steph's from Brooklyn! Why not put him on?"

Why put on his competition? I don't know if I would. Especially as weak as he is. I check out all the people Fast Pace rolled with and spot the DJ loading up his stuff in the first truck.

"Yo, you got another one of those?"

"Of course!" He slips out another copy, volume one.

"Aight, you give one to Fast Pace and I'll give one to the DJ."

"What? How come?"

"Trust me!"

Rell shook his head. "Aight, let's go."

We split, and I rush over to the DJ as he slams the trunk closed.

"Uh . . . excuse me . . . um, sir?"

He turns, surprised to see me. "What's up?"

"Hey, uh, nice job in there. Um, don't I know you from somewhere? You sound . . . familiar."

"Ha, maybe. I be around, nah mean?"

Suddenly it hits me. "Yo, you're DJ Rex! You on HOT 97!

I recognize your voice, you be on the late-late-night show during the weekdays. You be spinning that ill West Coast set."

He smiles. "Yo, what you doing up so late, young king?"

I shrug. "Thinking. Man, I listen to you all the time!"

He laughs. "Aight, well, my bad, yo, we gotta dip. Fast Pace is performing tonight at the Moxey. This was just supposed to be a quick stop 'cause he owes shorty's father a favor, and we already running late."

I glance over at Rell, trying to talk up Fast Pace's bodyguard. He don't look too interested.

"Word, well, I know you probably get this a lot, but my mans . . . he got this demo. I was hoping you'd check it out. He . . . uh . . . couldn't be here tonight, but he's the truth! Everybody in the hood be rocking to his shit. He's from Brooklyn, just like Pace."

Rex raises an eyebrow. "Hmm."

"I'm not asking no favors or nothing, but maybe you can take a listen, and if you like it, I don't know, maybe you can share it with some of your peoples."

He laughs. "Aight. Only 'cause you rock with me. But I can't make any promises."

I smile and give him the CD. "Either way, appreciate you."

"But you said you'd come over after school," Ronnie says, real hard. If we weren't on the phone I'm sure I'd see her neck rolling. "How you gonna be a man if you can't keep your word?"

"What you want me to say?" I groan at my desk. "Coach added another hour of practice."

Aight, that's a lie. Rell and I were collecting money from vendors on Fulton Street. I've been so caught up running around selling Steph's demo, going to school, practice, and homework, I haven't had much time to be the boyfriend Ronnie wants me to be.

"So why didn't you page me?"

"I didn't have change for the pay phone. I didn't know you were looking for me like that. Damn."

"Well, if you had a cell phone, you'd know."

This again. She always starting. If my bedroom had a bigger window, I swear I would jump out it.

"You know," she adds. "Even Derrick down the hall got a cell phone, and his parents ain't making no money."

"Yeah, so how he get it?"

"You know how! He got that work in."

"I ain't with that, Ronnie. I keep telling you, I'm not down with your pop's business."

"Ain't like you'll be selling. I told you, my dad can hook you up with something else."

"We shouldn't be talking about this over the phone," I warn.

She sucks her teeth. "You sure you were at practice? 'Cause Naomi said she saw you and Steph's sister walking and talking like you go together or something."

Busted. I knew someone was gonna spot us eventually.

"Go together?" I say, trying to act real surprised. "It ain't even like that. She just lost her brother. I'm just trying to be there for her, that's all. You trippin' for real."

"Am I? You don't think I've peeped you been acting mad distant lately?"

"Maybe because I just lost my best friend," I mumble.

"That ain't it," she snaps. "Quady, we been going together for a year. I know you. Something else is up." She sucks her teeth. "You skipped coming over when you knew my parents weren't gonna be home, and now you acting brand-new. I just don't know why you won't tell me what's going on. We used to talk about everything."

It's funny how girls be peeping the small stuff. I mean, I didn't think I was acting different. It's like she got some type of superpower and can see inside my head. And if she could, I wouldn't know how to explain my weird feelings about Jasmine.

The front door opens.

"Quady!" Mom shouts. "I'm home! Got some KFC!"

"My moms home. I gotta get ready for dinner."

"Baby," Ronnie says, real soft. "I miss you. I know practicing for that dance was mad . . . stressful. But I miss hanging out with you. Kicking it, just me and you."

I don't even know what to say. I mean, Ronnie don't ever show this type of emotion. Damn, maybe she's right. I haven't been paying her a lot of attention, and it's been hard living a double life, trying to keep Steph's music under wraps.

"I miss you too, baby. I promise, we'll go to the movies next weekend. Just me and you. Okay?"

"Aight. That's what's up."

I hang up and head into the living room. Mom's already

made my plate and setting up the TV trays.

"Hey, baby, how was your day?"

"It was cool. How was work?"

"Fine, already busy and it's not even November! Sad I missed my shows, but I'm right on time for *Living Single*. You know I love me some Regine! That girl can wear some wigs." She giggles to herself and plops on the sofa next to me. "Oh! Picked up a magazine for you."

"Bet! Thanks, Mom!" She tosses me the November issue of *Vibe*. Magazines were the only things I looked forward to every month.

"Mm-hmm. Now you got that, you gonna hand over last month's? That one with my other fine-ass husband, DMX, on the cover."

"Ew, Mom!"

"Listen, we all got our one. And he's mine. Oh . . . but let me tell you what happened today!"

I kinda want to chill in my room alone and read, but I can tell Mom wants to talk to someone. With my dad gone all day and night sometimes, she can get lonely. So I let her tell me about all the crazy customers in the shoe department while I flip through a couple of pages, knowing I'll do a more thorough review later. I'm just at the Mariah Carey feature when I flip past a picture I recognize. There, in the bottom right-hand corner, is Steph, under the Who's Got Next? column. I jump to my feet.

"OH SHIT!"

"What! What!" Mom screams, frantic, pulling her feet up.

"What? A mouse? What! What!"

I calm down, biting my fist to keep from exploding.

"Oh nah, Mom . . . it's, I mean, uh, nothing. They just, talking about . . . this new Nas album I've been waiting for!"

Mom slaps my arm. "Jesus, Quady! You scared the hell out of me. Anyways, what was I saying?"

16
Jasmine

I still can't believe it. Even when Quady ran over with the magazine yesterday, I couldn't believe it.

My brother . . . in *Vibe*. Like, for real!

Some journalist reviewed his demo. Quady thinks he got it from that DJ that was rolling with Fast Pace. I don't care how it happened, I'm just happy it did! If Steph was alive right now, man, I don't know what he would've done. We probably would still be celebrating. I like to think he's celebrating in heaven, with Daddy. Wish I could show Mom, but I don't know how she'd react. She still thinks I'm working at the shipping company.

After school today I bought two issues. One to keep, and

one to put in Steph's room on the wall, where it belongs.

Bzzzz Bzzzz

The pager goes off. It's been going off nonstop since Ronnie's party.

212-558-2838

Hmm. A Manhattan number?

I walk into the kitchen to use the phone. As soon as I pick it up, I notice there's no dial tone.

"Hello?"

"Hello? Jasmine?"

Someone must've been calling at the same time. "Who's this?"

"It's Kenny."

"Kenny! How'd you get this number?"

"They . . . um . . . gave it to me."

"'They?' They who . . . ?"

Oh . . . *them*. I plop down on the kitchen stool, twirling the phone cord between my fingers.

"Right. Uhhh . . . what's up?"

"Um, yeah. They wanted me to call to see when you plan on returning to continue your . . . initiation."

I gulp hard. "I . . . um, I've been . . . kinda busy, helping my mom and stuff."

Kenny sighs. It's quiet. Doesn't sound like he's at his dad's place. He must be with *them* . . . and I bet they listening in on this convo.

"Well, they just wanted me to remind you that you made a commitment that you need to . . . fulfill."

My neck tightens. "I understand."

"So see you at the next meeting, right?"

"Uh, yeah. Sure."

There's a long pause until he says, "Peace, Jasmine. My black is beautiful."

"And so is mine," I recite back the practiced line and hang up, putting my head between my knees, breathing in hard. I look up at the picture of Daddy on the windowsill.

"What should I do?" I ask him, wondering what he'd think of *them*. I mean, they believe in everything Daddy ever taught me. Just their methods are . . . different.

My mind is spinning so fast I almost forgot why I came into the kitchen, until I feel the pager in my hand.

"Oh damn." I dial back the Manhattan number and squeaky voice answers on the third ring.

"Hi, um, someone paged from this number?"

"Oh! Hello, this is Gordon Fletcher. Can I speak to Architect?"

"What'd you need?"

"I'm calling on behalf of Pierce Williams at Red Starr Entertain—"

"Red Starr? Oh shit!" I clear my throat and put on my best white-girl voice. "I mean, yes. Hi. This is, uh, Q . . . JJ Entertainment. How can I help you?"

"Oh, are you with Architect's managing firm?"

"Um . . . yeah!"

"Got it. Well, Mr. Williams heard Architect's demo and saw his feature in *Vibe*. He's interested in setting up a meeting. Say, the Oct Bar? Tomorrow night, around nine thirty?

"Mm-hmm, yeah. That'll be perfect."

"Now, please remind your client not to be late. Mr. Williams is all about promptness."

"Will do. Thank you so much."

I slam down the phone and run around the room, screaming inside my sweater.

17
QuadiR

As soon as we step past security, I release the breath I've been holding since we got off the train in Times Square. I don't wanna say I'm scared 'cause that'd make me sound like some chump. I just never tried to sneak into a club before.

"Aye yo, I can't believe those IDs worked," I whisper, feeling way more relaxed with the music thumping through my chest.

Rell smirks. "I told you Mack had the hookup. You were all shook for nothing."

I wasn't shook. I just didn't want to embarrass ourselves.

Oct Bar is real classy inside. All orange, yellow, and red with black leather sofas, disco lights, and a glass staircase.

The bar has this kinda clear amber color with mirrors, like my uncle Frank's ashtray. The place looked like money with shorties walking around in high heels and skirts, carrying designer bags, glossy lips sipping on martini glasses. I shouldn't say shorties—I'm talking real women, like my sister's age. Brown skin, dark skin, light skin, Puerto Ricans, whites, all fine as hell. The fellas look fly too. Versace shades, Gucci belts, gold chains and rings, buying bottles at the bar. I'm glad Rell came over and made me change my clothes. We couldn't walk up in here in sneakers and durags. Rell scopes out the scene, a big ol' smile on his face, rubbing his hands together like he's about to be up to no good.

"How do I look?"

Rell has on his COOGI sweater, black jeans, and gators. That sweater cost him over two hundred dollars. Steph told him he was crazy for buying something so ugly.

"Cool. How about me?"

I had on my nice hard-bottoms, brown slacks, and a gold button-down shirt I borrowed from my pops.

Rell smirks. "Like you sixteen in your daddy's clothes. And I keep forgetting without a durag you look like a Chia Pet fried in corn oil."

"Man, shut up."

This tall straight-gorgeous Amazon woman passes by in a blue backless shirt held up by strings. She winks at me and I smile back.

"Damn, kid. Last time a shorty looked at me like that was never." Rell chuckles, shaking his head. "Ain't no way shorty got a bra on with that top."

"Aight, let's focus. Where Jazz tell us to meet this dude? 'Cause if we don't handle business soon, you gonna get us in trouble up in here."

Rell chuckles. "You mean before or after you told Jazz she couldn't come with us?"

"I'm saying, even with that body, we couldn't get her up in here with all these real ladies!"

Rell's head bounces back. "Ohhhh, so you checking out her body now, huh?"

Damn, busted.

"NO! I mean, nah, I . . . I didn't mean it like . . . man, whatever. She's too young!"

"Son, she's a fifteen-year-old project chick! That makes her at least twenty-one mentally. Besides fool, you sixteen. You act like you R. Kelly and she Aaliyah or something."

I ain't have nothing to say back to that. Feels weird even having a conversation about Jasmine like she's a real girl or something.

"Aight," he says with a smirk. "Just don't let Ronnie hear you talking like that or that's your ass. Come on. Jazz said see the hostess and she'll bring us to his VIP table."

"Bet."

We follow the hostess up two flights of stairs, where it's less crowded, but the vibe the same. From the landing, I spot his white blazer before I see his face, sitting on a red velvet sofa surrounded by these fly-ass ladies in the VIP section. He's laughing and joking while his homies pour champagne into glasses. A scene straight out of a music video.

As we approach, we catch the end of his conversation with this Asian girl he got his arm around.

"So, baby, like I was saying, how about you and me take a little trip? Nothing too fancy, I just got this spot up in the Hamptons I like. Me and Puff be there all the time."

The girl gushes and nods. "Really?"

"I'm telling you, baby, when you roll with me, it's nothing but high class." He laughs, that type of laugh like he's the king of the world and she's twirling her hair falling for it.

This dude is smooth.

But before we even touch the velvet rope, a skinny, brown-skin dude in a tight, shiny, gray suit swoop in on us.

"Hi! You must be Architect! I'm Fletch, and you're right on time. Thanks for coming!"

I shake his hand. "Oh, no, nah, we—"

"Mr. Williams! Mr. Williams? He's here!"

Pierce glances up at us with a big grin and throws back his drink.

"There he goes! Just the man I was looking for!" He looks around at his party. "Aight, Come on, y'all. Everybody out!"

He takes the Asian lady's drink, nudging her away.

"Sorry, baby, you gotta go. Got business to take care of. I'll call you, okay? We'll set that trip up soon. Real soon, okay?"

She rolls her eyes, mumbling something under her breath before pushing through us and storming away.

"Don't worry about her," he says, waving it off. "Come, come. Have a seat! Fletch!"

Fletch jumps. "Yes, sir," he says, his voice shaky.

"Get me another bottle for my guest. And some of them strawberries too. Make sure they fresh, I don't like no bruised berries in my champagne."

"Yes, yes. Right away, sir!"

Fletch scurries down the stairs. Over the balcony, we see DJ Clue in the booth, spinning for a crowded dance floor, the party poppin'.

"What y'all standing there for," Pierce says. "Sit down! Make yourselves comfortable!"

Rell pops down on the mini chair across from him, all hyped. I sit down slow, suspicious of anyone this friendly.

Pierce rubs his hands together and points at Jarrell.

"So let me guess. You're Architect. Man, you look nothing like your picture and you definitely gained some weight, but I can work with that! We gotta hook you up with a stylist 'cause you looking like some hood kid straight outta Brooklyn, and that's not what's hot in the streets right now. You feel me? We need you looking like money! Designer everything!"

Jarrell smirks, then all cocky says, "Who me? Oh nah, man. I'm not Architect. He ain't coming."

Pierce's smile drops to a straight line, and right then and there I knew Rell fucked up.

"Shit," I mumble.

Fletch returns with a waitress and four bottles of Cristal.

"Fletch!" Pierce barks. "I thought you told me this is Architect?"

Fletch frowns, eyes ping-ponging between Rell and me.

"They . . . I mean he told me he was!"

"No, we didn't."

"Then . . . who the fuck are you?"

"We his representatives," Rell says, trying to sound tough, but I've know him long enough to know when he's shook.

"His what?"

Fletch's eyes go wide as he holds up his hands. "I swear, sir, they told me—"

"Managers! We're his managers!" Damn, Rell just gonna continue to dig us a grave.

Pierce rolls his eyes in disgust. He's heated for real.

"Man, get the fuck out of here with that bullshit! What are you, twelve? I don't have time for games with pointless lackeys." He rips some money off a bill clip. "Here, take this five dollars." He slams it on the table and we both jump back. "Go buy yourself a metro card and take your asses back to BK and tell your 'artist' I don't deal with big-headed male groupies like yourselves, aight? I'm with Red Starr Entertainment! We ain't no little bullshit-ass label. We the real deal! I put people like Fast Pace on the map!"

I glance at Rell. He's speechless.

"Well? The fuck you still sitting there for? Get out before I have you thrown out! In fact . . ." He waves at two brolic cats standing by the VIP entrance, ready to break our arms with they pinkies. I could see the headlines now:

Two High School Juniors Found in Dumpsters Outside Times Square Nightclub

Nah, I had to jump in.

"Whoa, whoa. Yo, we meant no disrespect, Mr. Williams! Just that Architect had a family emergency—"

"Yeah, a death in the family," Jarrell adds, and I kick him under the table.

"And he didn't want to miss this meeting with you. He admires you! Ever since you started at Def Jam and all the work you did with artists like Redman, Method Man, and LL Cool J. He would never disrespect you like that! But, like I said, he had an emergency, and he didn't want to cancel . . . so he sent us instead. We sorry for the confusion. We ain't trying to waste your time."

Pierce chuckles. "Death in the family? What d'you think, I'm stupid?"

Them big dudes are standing right behind us, breathing down our necks. He could snap his fingers at any moment and have us yoked out of here.

"Word on my mother, I'm telling you, if he could be here, right now, he would. Music was everything—"

"IS everything to him, sir," Jarrell says. "We've been helping him with his career from the start. He trusts us to handle business."

Pierce eyes us down. He's suspicious, and I don't blame him. I don't know if I would've believed us. He nods and waves the bouncers away. Jarrell exhales and clutches his chest like he's a second away from a heart attack.

"Aight. I hear you. Tell ya man that Red Starr Entertainment is looking for its next big breakout artist. Need someone who got flow and originality. I listened to his demo. It's good. But I need great. Nah, fuck that, I need outstanding. Nah, fuck that, I need excellence!"

He snaps at Fletch. Fletch runs over and hands him a CD.

"The beats on this . . . certified bangers. I need your man to make a single off one of those tracks in a week."

Jarrell does a double take. "A week?"

Pierce raises an eyebrow. "Is that a problem?"

I touch Rell's arm. "Nah. We'll let him know."

Pierce looks us over again. "Aight. Now get out of my face."

We jump up, ready to dip. After dodging a bullet, no sense in overstaying our welcome.

"One more thing," he says to our backs. "Tell your man if he fucks up and pulls some shit like this again, the only place his music is gonna be heard is at his funeral."

Jarrell chuckles and I punch his side.

"Yo, would you shut the fuck up," I grumble through my teeth and nod back at Pierce.

"Deliver that song by the end of the week or I'll come looking for it. And y'all don't want me to come looking for y'all."

18
NOVEMBER 3, 1997

"So nobody knows nothing yet?"

Quadir practiced his handles in front of the bodega, the bouncing clashing with the car stereo passing by. "No witnesses, no nothing. All those people? Nah, someone saw something."

It had been eight months since Big's funeral. As "I'll Be Missing You" by Puff Daddy and the Bad Boy family stayed on top of the charts, and more and more people came with new stories about Biggie's life, none of those stories answered the most important question: Who shot Big?

Steph popped a few Dipsy Doodles into his mouth. He

wanted something salty before eating his last piece of taffy saved in his jean pocket. The last taste of summer, he thought as the leaves kick up in the late autumn breeze.

"If they haven't figured out who killed Pac, what makes you think they gonna figure out who killed Big?"

"'Cause, for real, it's connected!"

"Bet you it was someone in Pac's crew," Jarrell sniffled into a tissue. "They think Biggie had something to do with him being popped, so it was eye for an eye! You saw *Boyz n the Hood*, you know how shit be out there. It's like the wild, wild west for real."

Jarrell blew his nose, coughing into the sleeve of his Nautica jacket. Another cold, right on schedule. He always caught one around the end of fall that messed with his asthma, but he hated carrying around the bulky inhaler the doctor gave him after his last hospital visit. It clashed with sneakers, socks, belt, and whatever else he planned to wear.

"Nah, I got a cousin who lives out there. She said it's not a war zone like people think," Steph chuckled. "Probably like the way white people think it's mad crazy in Brooklyn. But look at us. Kicking it, drinking our quarter waters in peace."

"So why ain't anyone saying nothing?" Quadir asked. "Cops don't have no witnesses or nothing?"

The question kept Quadir up at night. He read every newspaper and magazine that discussed the investigation, but no other information had been released except for the basic details:

- Biggie, along with the his Bad Boy crew including Puff Daddy and Lil' Cease, left a party the day after the Soul Train Music Awards early, due to overcrowding.
- Biggie's Suburban SUV stopped at a red light on the corner of Wilshire Boulevard and South Fairfax Avenue, near the venue.
- A Chevrolet Impala SS pulled up alongside the SUV.
- The driver of the Impala, a black male dressed in a blue suit and bow tie, pulled out a 9mm and shot into Biggie's passenger-side door.
- Biggie was taken straight to the hospital where he was pronounced dead thirty minutes later.

"It just don't make no sense. They expect us to believe with the streets being mad crowded and the police and fire department shutting the club down, Big gets popped a few feet away, and no one saw nothing? No cameras. No paparazzi. *No one?*" Quadir shook his head. "Yo, deadass, I think it's a conspiracy. The government is in on it. Trying to take out hip-hop 'cause we taking over. First NWA, now Big."

For a change, the boys didn't argue with him. With so few answers, the impossible did not seem so far off.

"Son, you right," Steph said, clawing the taffy out of his pocket. "With all those people, someone . . . definitely saw something."

"So what, you expect people to snitch?" Jarrell asked, his face turned up as if the words stank.

There it was. The *s* word. The one word that hit worse than a curse.

Quadir stopped bouncing his ball to face Jarrell, his eyes wide. "Well . . . yeah . . . kinda. Not like that . . . I mean, just leave an anonymous tip or something."

Jarrell shook his head. "Son, snitches get stitches. You don't ever want be labeled a snitch, 'specially in the hood! That shit will follow you like a disease."

Steph held his breath, palming the taffy in his pocket. He knew what his father would say, but things were different now.

"But . . . that's just mad stupid," Quadir said incredulously. "You telling me, if you see someone get murked, you ain't gonna say nothing?"

Jarrell sucked his teeth. "Son, if I want to stay breathing, I ain't saying shit. And you wouldn't either. If cats out here know that you know *anything* . . . they won't hesitate to pull a trigger on you and your whole family. I don't even feel comfortable talking about this out here."

Jarrell looked over both his shoulders with a wary eye before sneezing into his jacket.

"Steph," Quadir said. "What'd you think?"

Steph gulped. "I . . . don't know.

"You don't know?" Jarrell barked. "Son, keep it real with me. Is you a snitch?"

"What? Nah, I ain't no snitch!"

"Yo, 'cause for real, though, you acting wild suspect, and I can't be associated with snitches."

Steph's eyes narrowed as he stepped to him. "Well, I told you I ain't, so back up off me!"

Quadir quickly intervened. "Y'all! Chill. It ain't even that serious."

Steph stood inches from Jarrell's face, breathing hard, not saying a word.

Jarrell sized him up with a snarl. Same height, but he had at least thirty pounds over him. Cold or no cold, he could still take him, but crazy that he'd even had to consider it. In all their years of friendship, Steph had never stepped to him. *What's going on with him?* Rell thought.

"Then what you trying to say with all that shrugging shoulders and shit?"

Steph crossed his arms. "I'm saying, what if you knew someone that knew something . . . about how my dad died, what would you do?"

Stunned to silence, Quadir and Jarrell share a quick look. They weren't expecting to talk about anyone so close to home.

"That's . . . different," Jarrell struggled to say, stepping back.

"How?" Steph snapped.

"'Cause I know you! You my brother! If I knew anything, you'd be the first one I tell!"

"So. Someone knew Biggie. Biggie was a lot of people's brother. He was a father, a husband, and a son. But that don't mean shit. Why? All 'cause of some code about snitching, and now his family can't get justice."

The boys stop talking, not knowing what else to say. Steph

returned to his spot on the corner, trying to quiet the thoughts bouncing in his head. What if someone did see something, would he blame them for not coming forward, if only to protect his or her family? He'd do anything to protect his. Wonder what Pops would say about all this, he thought. He wasn't down with the no-snitching rule. He was all about protecting the community at all costs.

Even if that meant losing his life to prove that point.

"Aye, man, sorry about calling you a snitch," Jarrell said. "But yo, word on Moms, I'd kill the mutherfucker myself who did your pops. A hit and run . . . man that's some sucker shit, for real."

19
JARRELL

Quady ain't say a word on the train ride back to Brooklyn. He ain't saying much now in front of the corner store. But he's pacing. Pacing like he's about to run a hole into the ground. No way I can sneak him back in my spot; he's too hyped up to be indoors just yet.

"Yo, kid, would you calm down? All this back and forth is giving me a headache. Pacing around like some old lady. You sixteen or sixty?"

"Calm down? Are you serious? What we gonna do?"

I take a bite of my bacon, egg, and cheese, and a quick sip of ginger ale. I always think better on a full stomach.

"Psst! I don't know."

"Rell, this ain't no joke. How the hell are we gonna give him a whole new song when Steph's dead?"

"You being mad soft right now! Just chill."

Quady cuts me with his eyes.

"Yo, Pierce ain't no pretty-boy, kid. He used to be a mad gully street dude. Everyone knows that. He's like the East Coast Suge Knight. He'll come for US!" He sighs. "Maybe we should tell him."

"Tell him? Nah, no way! Not when we *this* close."

"This close to what? Being killed? If we tell him, maybe he'll go easy on us."

"Then everybody's gonna know! Cat's out the bag and shit, and we did all this for nothing!"

"Well, what else you suggest, then?"

"Shhhh . . . I'm thinking!"

Quady throws his hands up. "Thinking. This fool is thinking!"

He starts pacing again, and I try to keep a cool head for the both of us.

"You said he has mad music, right?" I remind him. "So let's use one of his old songs."

"We can't just give him an old song. It has to be a song on one of these tracks." Quady palms the disc Pierce gave him. "What we gonna do? Say, 'Oh nah, we didn't like any of your shit. But here you go. This is the remix!'"

A light turned on above my head and I snap my fingers. "Yo! That's it!"

"Man, I was joking!"

"Nah, you onto something, though. Okay, so boom, remixes are just tracks from original songs laid on a new beat, right? I mean, they do it all the time with reggae remixes. So that's all we gotta do! Put Steph's track on one of these beats."

Quady raises an eyebrow. "Is that . . . is that something you can do on your computer?"

I sigh. "Nah. What we need is a professional . . . with a studio. Like a real producer who knows what they doing."

"How we gonna find a studio and a producer and do it in a week? And how we gonna explain why we asking him to do it? 'My main man's dead, but we want you to produce this track—just don't tell anybody.'"

I nod. "Yeah, exactly like that."

Quady throws his hands up. "Son, this shit is . . ."

"Oh snaps!" Dante strolls around the corner grinning. "What's the dilly? Look like you coming from a party or something."

Quady clears his throat as Dante leans in for a dap. "Yeah. A . . . birthday party."

"Oh, word?" He gives Quady a once-over. "What's up? Why he looking mad stressed?"

"Me? Oh nah, I ain't stressed. I'm good." Quady damn near twitching as he lies.

"Aight, so where's the party at? Why ain't nobody invite me? You know if I don't know about a party then it ain't really happening, you know what I'm saying?"

"Yo, hold up," I say, chuckling. "Dante. You *do* be

knowing everybody. You don't happen to know any . . . producers, do you?"

Quady shakes his head behind him.

"Producers? Hahahaha! Y'all trying to be rappers now? Spit some bars!"

"Nah, nah . . . my cousin . . . from Jamaica! He got this song that he did, but he wants to . . . fix it. Make it better. On the low low, nah mean?"

"Oh, no doubt. I got the brotha for you. His name is Kaven, he got a studio on Pulaski."

"Pulaski?" Quady says. "Nah. Hell no!"

"What's his problem?"

I take a deep breath. "That's where they found . . . Steph."

"I don't wanna be anywhere near that place! Ever," Quady barks, and starts pacing again.

"Yo, chill, son. It's cool. The spot is like mad blocks away from there. And the producer is the truth. My mans and them in Marcy fucks with him."

I frown. "Oh word? You fucks with people in Marcy?"

Dante laughs. "Hey man, I'm Sweden!"

"Sweden? What does that mean?"

"Means I fucks with everybody. I got peoples all over. I'm neutral."

"Hmm. Sweden?" I guess that makes sense. Dante don't have a crew that I know of. Seems like he just knows a bunch of people and all they business, but no one knows nothing about him. Mad incog-negro.

"Yeah . . . Sweden," he says, smiling. "They this country

with all these blond white people who just mad happy and don't rep no sets or nothing."

"Yo, I think that was an answer on Jeopardy," Quady says, rubbing his chin.

WOOP WOOP!

Three unmarked cars screech up on the curb surrounding us, red and blue lights spinning on the dashboard. The ginger ale slips out my hand, fizzing on the ground.

"Aye yo," Quady screams, squinting away from the headlights blinding him.

"What the fuck?" Dante yells.

"Get down on the ground!" A man shouts, but I can't tell from where.

"Hands up!" Another duke barks.

"Down on the ground now!"

"Down now!"

"On the ground. On the ground now!"

"Don't move!"

I'm so confused that when the plainclothes 5-0 jump out with they guns drawn, it don't even register to me that they about to shoot *us*.

"Oh shit," Dante says under his breath.

"Get down!"

"Don't move!"

"The wall! Now!"

Damn, what they want us to do first? And I can't get on the ground. I'll ruin my sweater.

"Hands in the air," one says, coming closer. "Hands in the motherfucking air!"

Quady's mouth hangs open as he backs up, his hands in the air, staring at the gun pointed in his face. He gulps and turns toward the wall, shaking.

"What we do? We ain't do nothing!" Dante shouts as he's shoved up against the wall by some bald-headed white guy in a gray polo and black jacket, his badge hanging like a necklace on his chest.

A man with a salt-and-pepper mustache and curly hair turns to me. "You! Turn around!"

"Huh?"

"I said turn around!" He mashes my face into the wall.

"Ah! Yo, chill!" I scream, my cheek throbbing.

"Yo, chill with all that! He didn't do nothing," Dante hollers.

That only makes him madder. He pins me up against the wall, elbow digging into my back.

"Ahhh! Shit!"

"Spread 'em," he barks in my ear. He pats down my back, sides, ass, legs, ankles, balls, and head. With the lights shining in our faces and me pinned against the wall, I couldn't get a good look at the cats hemming us up, rummaging through all our pockets. I can't breathe the way duke has my face pinned into the wall, sniffing bricks like a dog.

"What you doing this for, man?" Dante says. "You got us up against this wall like—"

"Yo, stop talking," Quady snaps, his voice cracking.

A calypso pan is ringing in my ear and it stings like hell. I know I should be scared like Quady, but I'm so confused that nothing feels real. Like it's all a dream or something. Across the street, a few people watch from their windows. I keep my head down, hoping no one recognizes us and word get back to Mummy.

This ain't no regular stop-and-frisk, and we damn sure didn't do nothing out here to have anyone call the cops on us. So many lights and cars, you'd think this was a drug bust and we the plug.

Dante sucks his teeth. "This some bullshit."

Salt-and-Pepper pulls a dime bag of weed out of Dante's pocket and shakes it in the air.

"Well, hello! Look what we got here?"

"That . . . that ain't mine! You probably put that shit there! Y'all always planting shit on brothas."

Damn, we fucked now.

"Calm down. I ain't here for this little piece of shit," the cop says. "Which one of you knows Steph? Any of you assholes know where we can find Steph?"

Steph? Nah, I must have heard him wrong. My ear is still ringing. Quady and I look at each other. There ain't no way . . .

"Steph. Anybody know him?" the other officer says. "Tall, skinny, got braids."

"Yo, that's like half of Brooklyn," Dante says with a smirk. "You gotta be more specific, b."

Salt-and-Pepper slaps Dante upside the head. "Hey, shut the fuck up! You wanna spend the night downtown? Now, Steph got a scar on his cheek and he's usually on this corner. Nobody knows who I'm talking about?"

I glance at Quady, eyes bugging out. Damn, he really *is* talking about Steph.

Dante sucks his teeth. "Man, y'all about two months too late as *usual*. That kid's dead."

The cop's whole body stiffens behind me. "What?"

"Steph's dead. Steph's been dead!"

"You better not be lying," Salt-and-Pepper growls through his teeth, shoving him harder.

"Yo, word on my momma, Steph got popped right before Labor Day."

"He ain't lying," Quady says softly, eyeing the ground.

"Don't y'all cops talk to each other or nothing?" Dante snaps. "Last time I heard, y'all were supposed to be investigating his murder."

The cops look at one another. They silent, but you can sense their confusion. No one knows what to do. Finally, Salt-and-Pepper eases his elbow from between my shoulder blades.

"Alright," one of them says. "Have a good night, gentlemen."

The army that had surrounded us seems much smaller and less like killers as they retreat back into their whips.

"Yo, that's it? Y'all fuck with us, then bounce?"

They don't say nothing as they slam their car doors and

speed off down Patchen Ave.

Dante's in the street, screaming at their taillights like he got a death wish. Quady limps over, hands on his knees like he about to faint. I wipe the blood off my ear, rubbing it between my fingers.

"Yo," he gasps, looking up at me. And I know we thinking the same thing.

Why the fuck are they looking for Steph?

20
Jasmine

Here we are, cleaning again. Except Mom's purging stuff now. Throwing away papers, broken toys, and collecting old clothes to donate to the shelter.

"Jasmine, pass me them baby coats," she says from the living room. "Not like we need them."

I step over Carl and rip the coats off the wire hangers. Life just don't seem fair. While the boys are out partying, I'm stuck up in the house, cleaning out a dusty hallway closet. Quady told me I couldn't come, probably so he wouldn't be seen with me. He rather be up in the club with girls like Ronnie, with fake nails and hair, dressed in designer clothes made by folks who don't care about black people.

I need to get the idea of "us" out of my head. Not because I don't think I'm good enough. But because I can only take so much heartache.

"And how many times I gotta tell you to put your book bag in your room?" Mom fusses. "I'm trying to keep this place clean!"

"Yesss, Mom," I sigh. I didn't notice the opened top zipper, and just as I grab my bag, a stack of the CDs slips out onto the coffee table. Within seconds, I shove them back in, but that was all the time Mom's eagle-eye vision needed before she snatches up the last runaway. I keep quiet, hoping she won't recognize him. But I should have known a mother always knows her son.

"It's . . . Steph," she says, rubbing her finger along his picture. "Wh-what is this, Jasmine?"

I'm trying to keep calm and figure out how to frame it. I wasn't expecting to tell her so soon.

"Jasmine! What. Is. This? Why his picture look so funny?"

"It's a demo," I mumble.

"A what?"

"A demo. Of Steph's music."

"He made this? How come I didn't know?"

"Nah. Um . . . me, Jarrell, and Quady did it."

"What?"

"We made a demo of some of his songs."

Mom's hands are shaking.

"So y'all made a tape . . . of my baby's music, selling it . . . so they making money off my baby? You using your own brother, Jasmine!"

"Nah, Mom, not like that!"

"Then why?" she screams, grabbing my shoulders. "Why you do this? Why you do your brother like this?"

"It's *for* him, Mom! It's all for him!" I can feel myself choking up but refuse to cry. "Mom, Steph was real good at this music thang. I know you didn't really listen, but . . . people are buying his music, playing it at parties, and I've been saving all the money I'm making."

"Them thugs are buying from you with they drug money!"

"No! It's just regular people, like me, that like good music! Mom, I wanna use this money and hire a detective. One of them private ones, to find out what really happened to Steph. They cost $250 a day, and I—"

"What did I tell you? The police are handling it. We don't need no fake gumshoe getting in their way."

I can't believe she's tripping like this. I'm doing this for Steph! Don't she want to know what really happened? Don't she want to see the person that killed Steph in jail?

"Mom, I'm saying . . ."

Mom grabs the CDs out of my bag, storms in the kitchen, and dumps them in the trash, snapping them into pieces.

"I don't want to hear NOTHING about this no more. You get those tapes back from them boys. Tell them to stop using my baby to fill they pockets. No more 'demo.' No more talk about hiring a detective. And I don't want you ANYWHERE near them two again. You get on that phone and tell them they done."

"But—"

"Go to your room, Jasmine! Don't make me say it again."

I grab my bag, head to my room, and close the door. (I could've slammed it, but I ain't *that* brave.)

21
Quadir

"This it? You sure?"

"Yeah, this is the place," Jarrell says, raising an eyebrow.

"This don't look like no studio."

The rusted gate to the basement of a beat-up brownstone looks like a door to Satan's playhouse, and I ain't about to skip inside some vampire's lair. We don't even know who could be in there. Probably won't be a body to be found after they finish eating us . . .

Headline: The Case of Two Bed-Stuy Teens Mysteriously Vanishing Remains Unsolved

Ever since them cops hemmed us up, I've been having nightmares about being locked up and dying. Elevators feel mad tight, walls in school squeeze in, even the subway cars seem smaller. I keep opening all the windows around the house, and Mom closes them behind me, calling me crazy. I couldn't tell her what had happened without ratting myself out. I couldn't tell Ronnie—she'd only be mad I went to a party without her—and I couldn't tell Jasmine 'cause . . . well . . . I don't want her assuming the worst.

A blue tarp covering a broken window flaps in the wind. The red cement stairs are crumbling into a pile of rocks.

Jarrell steps over a puddle of water pooling by a storm drain, shaking his head.

"I better not fuck up my kicks in this place," he grumbles, and presses the buzzer.

The gate unlocks automatically, and I let Jarrell step inside first. We walk down a dark hallway as I try to hold in my panic before we step into the light.

"Damnnnn," Jarrell says with a grin.

The basement looks nothing like it does outside. Polished oak floors, green leather sofas, glass audio booths, and pristine equipment surrounded by warm orange lighting. This spot is mad official.

Kaven stands by the audio board, his arms crossed. Behind him, a security monitor with four different angles around the outside of the house. He sizes us up in silence.

"So, you Dante's people?" he asks in a husky smoker's voice as he sits in a black swivel chair.

Kaven didn't look how I expected him to either. He's about Jarrell's height and weight, a bald head with rolls stacked on his neck, grays peeking out his goatee. Old like my pops but dressed like he's late for a Wu-Tang Clan concert. When Dante mentioned him, I thought it would be some young guy, not an Old G.

"Yeah. I'm Rell. That's Quady."

"What y'all need? Dante didn't give no details."

Kaven didn't seem like the type interested in small talk. He probably hasn't smiled in ten years. Jarrell gives him the scoop, leaving Steph's and Pierce's names out of it. Kaven listens, swiveling in his chair, deep in thought.

After a few moments, he asks, "How you know your man's good?"

"Trust me, fam," Jarrell says. "He's the real deal. He's serious about his music."

"It's his dream," I add. I always feel the need to put that in perspective.

"Why can't your boy come and lay some fresh tracks instead of working off his old stuff?"

"He's . . . not available."

He chuckles. "Is he dead?"

Jarrell blinks hard.

"Wh-wh . . . what makes you think that?" I choke out.

"That's the only reason homeboy wouldn't show up on his own. You said he all about his music, and only a grave can stop you from your dreams. So, is he dead?"

"Uh . . . sorta," Jarrell says.

"Dead to the world," I jump in. "He got some family stuff to take care of."

Kaven pulls a bottle of Guinness out of the mini fridge under his desk. "I don't work with zombies."

Is it just me, or this Old G a mind reader or something? Jarrell brushes his hair down, something he does when he's nervous.

"Look man, all we need you to do is listen to my boy's lyrics on these tapes, cut it up, and lay it on one of these tracks."

I hand him the CD Pierce gave us at the club. I'm surprised it survived unscratched in my pocket the way them cops were throwing us around that night.

"These beats? Where you get them from?"

"Don't worry about that."

"And here's his music," Jarrell says, passing him three tapes. "He got more than this, but this is a good start."

Kaven sighs, rubbing his temples. He pops one of the tapes in and Steph's voice whistles out the speakers. A few bars into the song, Kaven's eyes go wide, the bottle almost slipping out his hand.

"You good?" I ask.

He clears his throat, composing himself. "Yeah."

"And yeah, I know," Jarrell says, smiling. "The sound ain't all that good. Think some of these tracks he recorded in his bathroom or something, but can you fix it?"

Kaven nods a few times then says in a flat voice, "It's straight. I can work with it."

"Bet. One more thing though, you gotta keep this on the

low. Nobody can know about this, y'knowwhatumsayin?"

Kaven glances from Jarrell to me, then back. I don't know about Rell, but this duke making me mad uneasy. I bet if Steph was here he'd be feeling the same way.

He measures us with a straight face and says, "Aight. But I don't work for free."

"How much?"

"Eight hundred."

"Eight hundred! You talking American dollars?"

"Rell, chill, son."

"Nah, did this fool really say eight hundred dollars?"

"We got no choice," I groan. He already knows too much.

Jarrell sucks his teeth. "Aight, son, we got your word on this. You won't tell nobody?"

"You got my word once that money is in my hand."

Jarrell rolls his eyes and digs into his pocket, slicing out a few bills. "Here. That's four hundred. I'll give you the rest when we get our shit."

He smirks. "Smart kid. Y'all can show yourselves out."

Heading to the bus, I tap Jarrell's arm. "Yo, you peep that?"

"Peep what?"

"The way duke got all . . . weird or something when he played Steph's music."

"Nah. I didn't see him do nothing but take our four hundred dollars."

I look back at the house, wondering how far them cameras could go. Could he see us walking, hear us talking about him?

"I'm saying, it almost like—"

"Yo, would you stop tripping? I mean, you know Steph taking over Brooklyn! He probably heard a track somewhere and was surprised we the ones doing it. So let the man do his thang. Come on, I wanna hit up Fulton before we head back to the crib."

I want to argue but maybe he's right. Maybe it's nothing.

Still, my gut is saying something different.

22
NOVEMBER 6, 1997

Beatboxing is an art form.

Steph combed through stacks of cassettes tapes and CDs on the windowsill, his lips making the music he couldn't lay down on a track yet. He still needed a couple of stacks before he could walk into the studio. But he was ready. Felt like he'd been ready his entire life.

"Son, I thought you said you wanted to study," Quadir said with a laugh from his desk, tossing a paper ball at his head.

Quadir's room was small, kept neat and tidy, with dark slate-blue walls, bad lighting, and a tiny window with a direct view into Brevoort's front courtyard.

Steph held up a CD from the edge of Quadir's twin bed.

"You ain't really studying. And what you doing with a Mint Condition single?"

"What? That 'Pretty Brown Eyes' song is on point! Now come on, man! I told Ronnie I would call her at eight."

"Damn, you barely been together and she already got you on a schedule."

"Whatever."

Steph smirked. "You like her?"

"What? Yeah. What kind of question is that?"

"I don't know, I just never thought she was your . . . type."

Quadir's back tightened. "How you figure?"

Steph shook his head. "Nah, never mind. It's nothing."

Quadir didn't take his eyes off his friend, who had hit the very nerve he had pretended wasn't pinching the top of his spine. But . . . who cared if Ronnie wasn't "his type." She was the baddest chick in school, and she wanted him. When someone hands you a bag of money, you don't leave it at the front door, do you?

"Hey, uh, sorry my mom didn't cook nothing," Quadir muttered, hoping Steph couldn't hear his stomach growling. "Just . . . things been tight around here lately."

He shrugged, indifferent. "It's cool man. Don't sweat it."

Steph had watched Quadir ravenously devour school lunches, even picking at his friend's leftovers, for over a month. There's being hungry and hunger, and he was smart enough to recognize the difference and not draw attention to it.

"Anyways, you got that new *Vibe*?"

"Yeah, right on top."

As Steph moved from the CDs to Quadir's meticulously organized stack of magazines, he noticed a purple pamphlet sticking out the side. Bishop Loughlin Memorial High School.

"Hey, what's this?" he asked.

Quadir jumped to block him. "Hey! Give me that!"

He dodged out of his reach, laughing. "Whoa! Where you get this from?"

"Some coach stopped by last week's game," Quadir relented.

"A coach?" Steph flipped through the book. "Yo . . . that's what's up! You gonna go?"

"To Bishop? And leave my peoples? Why'd I wanna do that? Plus, cost mad bread to go there."

"It's a good school, though. It got everything you want . . . you could have it all here!"

Quadir blew him off. "I ain't going to some wack-ass prep school. You tripping."

Steph sighed. "You know what, man? I'm mad proud of you."

"What?" he chuckled. "Why you sounding like my pops now?"

"Nah, man, I'm serious. You got a fly-ass chick, honor roll, captain . . . and now schools are checking for you."

"So?"

"I'm saying, wouldn't hurt to step out the box and see what they talking about."

Quadir fidgeted in his seat, the proposition making him antsy. Especially if stepping out his comfort zone meant leaving his friends behind.

Steph glanced at the clock and jumped up, sliding on his jacket. "Aight, yo. I'm out."

Quadir checked the time. "Where you going?"

"Gotta hit the block and make some bread. You know how it be."

Quadir measured his tone, his words only half in jest.

"Son, I'm playing," Steph laughed.

Quadir raised an eyebrow. "Yo . . . you good, man?"

Steph nodded as he slipped out the bedroom door with a smirk. "Always."

23
Quadir

You know when a song really makes you feel something? Nah, not no horny stuff. More like, a song got your head in the clouds, dreaming.

I had "Nothing Really Matters" playing on repeat, and all I could think about was Jasmine. Been avoiding her calls just to keep from lying to her. I wasn't ready to tell her about the cops looking for Steph. She would go bananas playing detective behind them, and it's just not safe. But I kind of miss politicking with her about music. Yeah, believe me, I know it ain't right, me thinking about another girl like this. I'm saying, sometimes music have you looking at the world through a different set of eyes.

Sitting at my desk, I drum a pencil against my open history textbook. Daydreaming about Jasmine ain't gonna help me pass my midterm on Monday. Maybe I should head down to the courts, play some hoops to clear my head. Some extra practice would be good for next week's game. That coach from Bishop said he wanted to stop by and say hello. Mom's going to come too. I hate how hyped she is about all this. It's just a school. A school with a championship-winning team and alumni that play in the pros, but still . . . it's just a school.

I slip the Bishop High School brochure from its hiding place between my magazines. Mom keeps dropping new ones on my desk, and I keep throwing them away. But this one, I keep, and flip through it, always stopping on the exact same page— a basketball player in his uniform, posing for a picture with the school newspaper club. Imagine that, playing ball AND writing for the newspaper? Maybe that's what Steph meant, going here and having it all.

KNOCK KNOCK KNOCK

"Uhh . . . come in?"

Jasmine opens the door, smiling. "Hey."

I jump to my feet, my headphones yanking me back down.

"Jazz! What you . . . how you get in here?"

"The front door, duh. Your mom let me in. Guess you couldn't hear us talking."

"Nothing Really Matters" plays loud out of my headphones and I scramble to turn it off.

"Uh, yeah. Guess I was in the zone. Studying."

She smiles and shifts the box from under her arm into her

hands. "Got some more CDs."

I grab the box from her and set it on my bed. "You went there by yourself?"

"Yes," she chuckles. "I'm a big girl, you know. Plus . . . I, uh, got no room at my house to keep them, and you and Rell ain't been returning my calls. Something's up?"

"Nah! Nothing."

I crack my knuckles against my hip bone. I don't like her rolling there alone with all those grown men who could take advantage of her. If I was there, I could protect her. Funny, I don't feel the same way about Ronnie. She always seems like she could handle herself.

Jasmine sits on my bed, gazing around the room. I ain't never had no girl on my bed before. I mean, yeah, my sister and Mom, but not no real girl.

Still, she got me sweating. I'm so nervous I don't even know what to do with my hands. I rip out my headphones and switch CDs. If she was a regular girl, I'd put on some R&B like Next, SWV, or Faith Evans. Set the mood or something. But with Jazz, I have to put on some Gang Starr or Heltah Skeltah to impress her.

Wait . . . why the hell am I trying to impress her?

"Steph used to talk all the time about how nice your room was. He said you were very . . . organized."

"Oh, word?"

She tilts her head toward my desk. "You going to Bishop?"

I follow her eyes to the brochure sticking out of my textbook.

"I, uh, well . . . maybe."

"Cool. That's what's up!"

"Really?"

"I mean, yeah. It's a good school, right? Good basketball team. It'll get you into college and everything. Ain't that what you want to do?"

"I'm still thinking about it."

She nods, giving me a closed-mouth smile.

"So, you heard about Mos Def and Talib Kweli dropping an album together? They calling their group Black Star."

I shrug. "That's . . . cool."

She cocks her head to the side. "You *do* know what Black Star is, right?"

"Their group name?"

She laughs. "The Black Star Line was created by Marcus Garvey, one of the leaders of the Black Nationalist movement. It was a shipping company that took black people back to Africa, when black people were free from slavery, but not really free because of segregation. He wanted black people to be proud of their heritage and stop assimilating with our capturers. Why continue to live in a country where they treat us like animals?"

"Whoa. I never thought about it like that. So what happened?"

"The government sabotaged the ships then arrested Garvey, and deported him back to Jamaica."

"Why they do that?"

"Because if black people really woke up and realized how

fucked up we've all been treated, we would've burned this country down to the ground. It'd be LA riots times a thousand." Jasmine gazes out the window, across the street into B-Voort.

"Jazz . . . you okay?"

She takes a deep breath, tears slowly trickling down her cheeks. "Our crib feels . . . mad empty," she says, her voice cracking. "I miss him."

"Yeah. I miss him too."

"I know I shouldn't be crying—he wouldn't want that—but it's been so hard . . . being without him." She sniffs and wipes her face. "Making these demos, it's like he's still with us . . . but not the way we want. Not in the way we need . . . you know? All this, and we still don't know what happened to him."

Her eyes water up bad. I don't know what to say or do to stop her from crying. I thought the demos would be like a Band-Aid and help kill time while we heal. But for Jasmine, it's like being cut over and over again. Because she still doesn't have answers, she still doesn't know who killed her brother, she still doesn't have closure.

"Time's been going mad slow. Summer just flew by and then . . . it happened. I mean, we didn't even get to Coney Island or nothing," she chuckles through tears.

Coney Island?

The idea lands mad hard on my forehead.

"Yo, that's a good idea." I jump out my chair and grab my jacket. "Let's go!"

169

Jasmine looks up at me. "Go? Go where?"

"Coney Island!"

"What? Right now? You buggin'. It's late and too damn cold to go to the beach. They probably closed anyways."

"Nah, I bet this is the last weekend before they close for the winter. I'm saying, we can at least get a hot dog from Nathan's or something. We got to let loose, have some fun for a change. We've been all business since . . ." I can't say it. Not to her. "Come on Jazz, we *both* need this."

She stares up at me with those big, bright eyes, and it's hard for me not to wrap her up and tell her she'll be okay.

"Aight," she says softly. "Let's go."

A chilly breeze kicks up from the beach as we exit the Ocean Avenue station. We stand on the corner, gazing across the street at all the twinkling lights as the dizzy carnival music drowns screams coming from riders on the Cyclone roller coaster.

Crossing the street with face-splitting smiles, we enter Astroland Park, walking past the kiddie swings, the Haunted House, and the Scrambler, toward the boardwalk ramp.

"Damn, not a lot of rides still open," I say, glancing around the near-empty park.

"The Wonder Wheel is," she says, pointing up at the massive Ferris wheel ahead of us. "Want to?"

I think of the scene in that movie *He Got Game*, with Rosario Dawson riding on top of Ray Allen in the passenger car . . . of them getting it on . . . and try to shake the image out my head.

"Um . . . how about something to eat instead?"

We head to Nathan's on the boardwalk, ordering two hot dogs, fries, and lemonades. Some speakers down by one of the bars is blasting HOT 97. Funkmaster Flex is on for his live Saturday night mix. We sit on a bench facing the ocean.

"Steph used to love Nathan's french fries," Jasmine says, popping one in her mouth with a red toothpick that looks like a devil's pitchfork. "They so bomb!"

"Word. It's like, how they know the right amount of salt to put on each piece of potato?"

Jasmine looks out at the beach, shaded by darkness. "Did you know this was one of the first beaches in New York that African Americans were allowed to come to, but they weren't allowed on any rides?"

"Word?"

"Yeah. My dad said that his great-grandfather used to come here and bring his dad. He had never been to the beach before."

I dip a fry in our shared ketchup cup and nod toward her head.

"So what else you got stored up in there?"

She laughs. "What you mean?"

"I mean, you stay dropping black history gems everywhere we go. So what's up? What else you got?"

Her lips turn down, eyes losing some of their happiness. "You ain't got to make fun of me, Quady."

"Nah, deadass, Jazz, I think it's cool. They don't teach you this stuff in school."

Jasmine stares at me, as if she's staring through me. That's when I notice she doesn't really wear makeup. A little lip gloss, but her face is always smooth and glowing.

"Okay, you know how you always say Biggie's the biggest to come out of Bed-Stuy."

"Yeah."

"Well, you want to know someone bigger than Big? Lena Horne."

I laugh. "Jazz, for real?"

"I'm serious. Lena Horne was born and raised in Bed-Stuy, went to Boys and Girls High when it was still called Girls High. Same school Shirley Chisholm, the first black woman to run for president, went to. Gwendolyn Bennett, the renowned poet and figure of the Harlem Renaissance . . . shall I go on?"

"Aight, so what you trying to say?"

"Guess I'm saying . . . there's a lot of ways to put Brooklyn on the map. Not just rapping."

I hold on to the cold fact that she slid into my hand, gripping it tight.

"I knew you had something else stored up there," I joke.

Jasmine sips her lemonade, puckering her lips at the straw. "Steph used to call me a nerd."

I shrug. "Maybe you that a little bit."

"Shut up," she laughs, pushing my arm, and it feels good to laugh with her. My laughs been cut short lately. Like I haven't taken a real breath since Steph died.

"He would've loved this," I say into the wind, letting it carry my voice away. I inhale deep, waves crashing against my eardrums. Feels like we're in our own universe, listening to the Fugees "Killing Me Softly" on the radio, eating hot dogs, being still, staring out into the void together. I'm cool just being this way. Why didn't we ever hang out like this before?

Jasmine is humming along with the music. Nah, more than humming, she's actually carrying a note, her eyes closed, her lips moving over the straw.

"Hold up, Jasmine. You can SING? Like for real?"

24
Jasmine

My eyes pop open and glance up at his with a gasp. Quickly, I swallow the words boiling up in my throat. I thought I had my urges under control. But I lost myself in the moment. The waves, the wind, and Lauryn Hill pulled me out of my seashell and into the spotlight.

"What?"

"You can sing," Quadir says, his eyes wide and in awe.

"Nah. I mean . . . not really."

He grins like I let him in on a secret, and it was too late to turn back.

"You lying. I just heard you. If you're humming that good, I know you can blow."

Shit, how did I let the ocean carry me so far away?

"It's just . . ."

"Come on, show me what you got! Take the stage."

"Out here? With all these people? You buggin'!"

"People?" He waves his arms around. "What people? Few drunks on a bench and the hot dog guys? Just sing! For real, when's the last time you really *sang*?"

"I—I don't remember." But I do remember. It was with Steph. Chilling in his room while Mom was at work. I sang this exact song, pretending to be Lauryn while Steph pretended to be Wyclef. The memory haunts me.

Quadir nods toward the boardwalk extension that reaches farther out into the water.

"Sounds like you need to."

At the end of the extension, with no one around, I walk up to the ocean, grab hold of the wooden railing and close my eyes. You could still hear the faint beat of the song through the crashing waves. The song bridge was coming. I tighten my grip on the rail, stare out into the sea and sing.

"Whooooooooaaaaaaaaa. Whoaaaaaaaaaaaa . . . La La La La La La. . . .Whoaaaa . . ."

I belt it out. All my pain. All my frustration. I let the ocean have it all. The notes held deep in my belly, rip through my lungs, weakening me.

When I turn around, Quadir is standing a few feet away, his face blank, the streetlight shining above making him glow orange.

"Well," I say, my chest heaving.

Quadir shakes his head slightly. "Wow."

I snort. "Wow? That's all you got to say?"

"Nah, I mean. I don't really want to say no more. Not if it's gonna stop you from singing."

My face is on fire. I smooth down my edges and try to hold back a smirk, quickly walking by him.

"Um, you ready for the bumper cars now?"

"That's it? That's all you gonna sing?"

"That's enough."

Quadir follows me off the extension. "Enough for who? Yo, we need to get you into the studio or something!"

I wave him off. "Nah, I'm good."

"Why not?"

"I just don't want to."

He jumps in front of me by the ramp leading back to the park. "That don't even make sense. Like for real, you see us working to make Steph's dreams come true, what's stopping you from going for yours?"

"Cause Steph's dream . . . it's just a dream! I'm not like Steph. I don't got it like that."

Quadir frowns, crossing his arms. "You're afraid."

"Afraid?" I scoff, before counting out the facts. "Steph's dead. Dad's dead. Mom's barely holding on, and Carl is just a baby. Only one out of hundreds really make it. I can't risk spending years and money chasing some dream and not be able to take care of my family. They *need* me. So no, I need to keep my head down, go to school, get good grades, become a teacher . . ."

"But why can't you can do both? Chase both dreams."

I shake my head. "We don't even know if this plan of yours is going to work."

"It will," he says, holding both my arms and pulling me a few inches closer to his chest. "Aight? You just got to trust me."

I want to trust him. I want to lean in and kiss him too. But my mind is too foggy to do either.

"But what if it doesn't? What if . . ."

The beat echoes faintly over the crashing waves, and I crane my neck toward the street.

"Hold up. You hear that?"

Quadir frowns. "Hear what?"

The wind and waves threw me off for a moment but I could recognize his voice anywhere.

"Steph! That's Steph."

I take off running down the ramp, heading back to Ocean Ave.

"Jazz, wait!" Quadir shouts, following me.

The song is coming from a car parked on the corner, near the train station. Its sound system thumping through my chest could be heard from two states away. I still feel a tingle whenever I hear his music out in public.

Yup, that's my big brother you're rocking to.

The song suddenly scratches out. I'm confused until I hear Funkmaster Flex drop his famous bomb sound effect and run the song back.

"Oh my God! Oh my God!" I scream, turning back to

Quadir. "Quady! Steph's on the radio! He's on the radio! Right now!"

Quadir slows to a stop, blinking at me. "Stop playing. You serious? You sure?"

"Yes! Listen!"

Flex runs it back again. Another bomb, and says, "Yo, this track got the city on lock. Watch out for this kid!"

"Ohhhhhh!" Quadir screams. "Yooooo! Steph's on the radio! He's on the radio!"

Quadir picks me up, jumping up and down on the corner, wildin' out.

"Oh shit," he says suddenly. "We got to get to a phone and call Rell before he misses it!"

Holding hands, we rush across the street, weaving through traffic, Steph our sound track. We pass a group of brothas hanging out on the corner chilling by the car, and just as we're about to slip into the train station, one deep, heavy voice stands out in the crowd.

"Aye yo, don't this duke sound like that kid done a few weeks ago?"

Wait, what did he just say?

I rip my hand out of Quadir's and double back.

"Jazz, what—"

"Shhh," I whisper. "Don't look at them. Just listen."

Quadir nods, eyes scanning around me. I kneel down, pretending to tie my sneaker so I can sneak a better look.

A tall, light-skin brotha in a red bomber jacket leans up against the car, smiling. His face swollen with acne, light-brown hair braided back.

"Oh yeah," he says. "That kid from the studio? Yeah, but that ain't him."

The brown-skin brotha in a black leather and Timbs laughs. "How'd you know?"

Red Jacket sucks his teeth. "Son, you *know* why, stop playing yourself."

There's a hiss in his voice, something unsaid. They gotta be talking about Steph. They knew his voice. I glance up at Quadir, his eyes flinching as he listens.

"Aight, son, I'mma holla at you later," Red Coat says before they dap. "Gotta check on my girl."

"Aight, later kid."

Red Coat starts walking in the opposite direction, down toward the apartment buildings behind the train station.

I jump up, my feet moving in his direction before Quadir yokes me back.

"What you doing?"

"We gotta talk to him. Find out what he knows about Steph."

"Girl, you bugging," Quadir says, yanking my hand.

I dig my heels into the ground. "Why not?"

"Son, do you wanna be fish food? We can't just roll up on some cats, saying 'what happened to my brother' and think we gonna walk away alive. That's like asking them to turn themselves in to the cops."

"But they know something! We can't just let our one lead walk away."

Quadir grips my wrist, holding me steady. "Jazz, *think*. If one of them really did murk Steph, what makes you think they won't do the same to us? You talking about taking care of your moms and Carl—think about what happens if you don't come home."

My eyes swell with tears, but I hold them back.

"Okay. But, we gotta tell someone."

"We will," he nods. "We will. I promise."

He pulls me toward the subway, and we hop on the next train out.

I replay Red Coat's words over and over on the ride home.

"He mentioned something about a studio. What studio was Steph recording in?"

Quadir dug his fist into his palm. "I thought you knew. He didn't tell us. But it had to be the Funky Slice down on Fulton. That's where everybody record they demos."

"Thought he talked to you guys about everything."

Quadir shakes his head and mumbles, "Not everything."

25
JARRELL

Pierce throws a chair across the room, nearly crashing it through the glass door of his massive penthouse office.

"What the fuck you mean, he ain't here? Who the fuck this mutherfucker think he is?"

"Sir, please!" Fletch is at it again, trying to calm duke down. But that's like trying to tame a lion in a slaughterhouse. Hope Fletch is getting paid mad bread to deal with this grown-ass baby-man.

"Tell me again, Fletch." Pierce says, leaning forward, cupping his ear. "Come on. Tell me, what's they excuse this time? I want to hear it."

Fletch gulps. "Um . . . that he's . . . on tour."

"Tour? On TOUR?" Pierce screams, knocking a pile of CDs off a side table. "You expect me to believe that shit?"

I glance at Quady, sitting next to me in front of Pierce's giant glass desk. He gives me a look and shakes his head, checking over his shoulder at the goons chilling on the plush white sofa. Okay, so I guess I didn't expect homie would get this mad. I thought if we gave him the new single and tell him Steph was on tour, he'd be impressed! Booking shows already, it would've proved Steph could make mad bread. I mean, what's wrong with that?

"There ain't no goddamn tour, Fletch! They playing us!"

"Sir, I think you should calm down," Fletch begs. "You remember what happened the last time you wrecked your office. They almost escorted you out the building! They won't replace these windows again for free!"

I look out the window, down at Times Square, sixty-seven floors below, and wonder how many cats he's sent flying.

"No Fletch, I ain't gonna calm down. You know why? Because I'm dealing with fucking children. A bunch of knuckleheads who think they hot shit! You know how much audacity you have to have to say 'I'm on tour' and can't make it to a Red Starr meeting? I got folks with Grammys and hit records on the charts cancel appearances just to make it to a meeting with me! Red Starr don't wait for you. You wait for Red Starr!"

Pras's "Ghetto Supastar" video (with Mya's gorgeous self) is playing on a huge TV behind Pierce. His whole office is mad official. Music plaques, crystal lamps, statues, awards, and framed photos of Pierce with celebrities hung everywhere. Everyone from Snoop Dogg to Jesse Jackson to Arnold Schwarzenegger.

Pierce grabs a CD off the floor, shaking it in my face.

"You see all this? I got hundreds of artists *begging* for me to sign them, and ain't one of them ever send me their bullshit-ass 'managers' to a meeting. Ain't one of them talking big shit about being on tour. So tell me, Fletch, why the fuck shouldn't I drop this clown right now?"

Fletch takes a deep breath, flipping through notes on his clipboard. "Because, so far, he's sold approximately six thousand albums across the city. Sir."

Pierce's neck snaps in his direction. "Hold up, did you say six thousand?"

"You asked me to take an unofficial tally. I called his management, who was able to count the amount of cases and copies made and checked with a few references. His single has also been receiving heavy airtime on the underground radio scene and premiered on HOT 97 last weekend."

"Whoa . . . ," Quadir mumbles, sitting up straight.

Damn, I didn't even know we were hustling like that. And big ups to Jasmine for coming through with the statistics.

Pierce tosses the CD back on the floor, rubbing his chin.

"Hmm. Let's . . . uh . . . think on this some more," he says, plopping in the grand gold throne behind his desk.

Quadir clears his throat, clasping his hands over his knees.

"Yo, we ain't trying to waste your time. Arch had another emergency."

"Yeah. One of *grave* importance," I add.

Quady kicks me under the chair, and I hold in a moan.

"I swear I'mma fuck you up when we get out of here," he grumbles through his teeth.

Aight, I know, I know. That was foul, but I couldn't help it. It's like they just throwing these setups at me.

Pierce's eyes ping-pong between us, then he smiles. And it ain't one of those nice smiles, it's one of them sly joints, like he's up to something. Never trust a dude who smiles like that.

"You know what the problem is with y'all," he says, folding his hands over his stomach. "Y'all just don't seem hungry enough. There's cats out here that are HUNGRY for this shit, and y'all out here looking full."

He smirks at the goons behind us.

"And you know what, I'm actually kinda hungry myself. Think I'm in the mood for a chopped cheese and a slice of red velvet cake." He leans back, with his hands behind his head. "Go visit my man Knowledge on 135th and Frederick Douglass."

Quadir and I look at the goons, who don't move, and turn back slow to Pierce staring at us.

"Wait, are you talking to . . . us?" Quady asks.

He chuckles. "There ain't no one in here but you."

"Hold up, you want us . . . to go get you . . . a sandwich?"

"Not just any sandwich. I want a chopped cheese with lettuce, tomatoes, mayo, extra onions, and peppers. Tell Knowledge I sent you."

"135th Street?" I ask. "Son, that's Harlem!"

"Yeah. And? Oh, and I want that shit in . . ." He glances at his Rolex. "Thirty minutes. Want to enjoy it before my meeting with the executives. In there is where the *big* decisions are made. And depending how hungry I still am will decide if I bring up your boy's name or not."

Quadir looks at me, his eyes wide.

Pierce shrugs. "So . . . if you want to put your boy on, you better hop to it and get my mutherfucking sandwich! You now have . . . twenty-nine minutes."

Quadir jumps up and races out the office. I follow, wondering why he's walking so fast, pushing the elevator button like the killer was on our heels.

"Well, guess that's it then, huh?" I sigh, rubbing out a scuff on my sneaker.

Quady's face screws up like he smells a fart. "What'd you mean?"

It hits me, he ain't rushing to dip out the office. He's rushing on a clock.

"Nah, Quady, bump that! I ain't taking my ass all the way to Harlem to get duke a sandwich. Who he think he is? Trying to play us like some chumps!"

Quady steps to my face. "Son, did you hear them numbers Fletch was talking about? We so close! Let's just give him what he wants."

"You tripping. I ain't gonna be no gofer for that power-tripping pretty boy. Let them overgrown Mutant Ninja Turtles surf uptown and cop him that bubble-gut sandwich."

"We got to do this . . . for Steph."

I groan so hard it scares the receptionist as the doors of the elevator open.

"Let's take the A train. It'll be faster."

We come up from underground at 125th Street, Harlem's mecca. Reminds me of Fulton Street, with all the street vendors and people shopping. The Apollo Theater sign is a few blocks away, looking just like it does on *Showtime at the Apollo* my auntie likes to watch. I ain't gonna lie: I've never been up here. Everything I know about Harlem I learned from my peoples and TV. What I look like, coming up here? For what? Brooklyn got what you need. No sense going exploring.

We jog up Frederick Douglass, Quady checking his watch every five seconds. I'm panting and out of breath. Feels like we've been playing ball for ten hours.

"There it is," Quady says, pointing ahead at the only bodega on the corner.

A bell rings as we bust through the door. The place looks mad empty. I mean, not empty of people, but the shelves look like they haven't been stocked in a minute. Plus the joint is smoky. I spot some old grandpa in the corner with a Newport between his lips, reading the paper.

"Yes," he says, not looking up at us.

"Um, we trying to get a chopped cheese."

He turns the page. "Then why you asking me? Does it look like I work here?"

Quady rolls his eyes. "Aye yo, back here."

We rush through the short aisle to the deli. Behind the

counter, a tall black man with long graying dreads wrapped up in a crown, slowly slices some onions with a butcher knife the size of a machete.

"Peace, Gods," he says.

"Are you . . . Knowledge?" Quady asks, staring at his knife.

He stops to glare at us. "Who wants to know?"

I've had enough of all the back and forth. "Aye yo, my man. Can we get a chopped cheese? Asapually."

"It's for Pierce," Quady adds.

"Pierce sent you? Really?" He smirks, wiping his knife clean and firing up the griddle. "He must be realllly hungry to send y'all up here to talk to me."

Quady bounces on the balls of his feet. "Yeah, and we only have . . . fifteen minutes. So could you . . . hurry up?"

He sighs. "Everyone is such a rush to do this and that. If you slow down, perhaps you may learn something."

This duke is talking slower than a slug.

"Mister, I don't mean no disrespect, but we on a time crunch here."

"Okay. I'll make your sandwich. But first, you got to pass the test."

"Test?" I bark. "He ain't say anything about no damn test!"

"Got five simple questions. Get them right, I'll make y'all sandwich the way he likes. And if you know anything about Pierce, you know he's very particular."

"Yo, my man, we just came to get a sandwich," I snap, hand clapping as I talk. "I already failed my midterms. What's the deal?"

Quady waves me off. "What kind of questions you talking?"

Knowledge begins pulling out bread, cheese, and meats from the deli fridge.

"Question one: Where was hip-hop first founded?"

"What the hell is this, hip-hop 101?"

"Uh, New York," Quady says, scratching at his durag.

Knowledge smiles. "That is incorrect."

"What? You crazy? Everyone knows hip-hop was BORN in New York."

"Hip-hop was founded at a party hosted by DJ Kool Herc at 1520 Sedgwick Avenue. The Bronx."

I suck my teeth. "Yeah, but Brooklyn made it hot!"

Quady pushes me back. "Would. You. Shut. Up! You trying to do this or nah?"

"Come on, son! He's playing us on some tech foul bullshit!"

"Ready for your next question?" Knowledge offers, a laugh in his voice.

"Man," I groan. "Why it feel like we in school right now?"

"Life is a school called the school of life, young God," he says with a shrug. "And one should never stop learning their lessons."

Quady blinks real hard and grins. "You're a Five Percenter?"

Knowledge only smirks back.

"Aw hell, no wonder."

Steph's pops taught us all about Five Percenters. It's like this religion founded back in the '60s, an offspring of the Nation of Islam but with a twist. Let me break it down: ten percent of the people in the world, the elites, know the truth of existence, so they keep eighty-five percent of the world ignorant and under their control. That leaves the five percent, the enlightened ones, whose mission is to enlighten the rest through teaching their lessons in supreme mathematics and alphabets. The problem is, their rules aren't always cut-and-dried. Today the sky can be blue, but tomorrow it's purple. Still, it's kind of cool they consider black men Gods. And a bunch of cats in hip-hop practice it heavy. Like Wu-Tang, Busta Rhymes, and the God MC Rakim.

"It's a wrap, son. We out," I say, pulling Quady toward the door. "Let's go before we start talking in circles."

Quady grabs my shoulder. "Chill, I got this."

Knowledge is wiping his counter clean, watching us. Duke look like he could sell water to a well.

"You sure?"

"Yeah, trust me." He nods at the ol' head. "Aight, next question."

"Question two: Name the original members of the Wu-Tang Clan."

"Son, that's crazy," I say. "Everybody and they momma is in Wu-Tang! How are we supposed to know?"

Quady pushes me out the way, listing them on his fingers. "RZA, GZA, Method Man, Raekwon, Ghostface Killah, Inspectah Deck, U-God, Masta Killa, and Ol' Dirty Bastard."

"Correct. Question three: Who was the famous mastermind behind the Juice Crew, and name three of its members?"

"That's TWO questions. The man's cheating!"

Quady talks over me. "Marley Marl. He helped put people like Biz Markie and Roxanne Shanté on." He looks at me. "He produced Big's 'Juicy.'"

"Correct," Knowledge says, throwing some red beef on the griddle.

"Aight, son," I laugh, dapping Quady up. "I see that *Vibe* subscription is paying off."

"Question four: Who was the other queen featured on Queen Latifah's black feminist anthem, 'Ladies First'?"

Quady struggles. "Um. Uhh . . . ummm . . . damn. Jazz would know this one."

"Oh snap, I know! Monie Love."

Knowledge turns to me, impressed. "Correct."

"What?" I shrug at Quady. "Shorty has a cute-ass smile."

"Question number five: What famous shipping line that transported our brothas and sistas back to Africa did Mos Def and Talib Kweli name their newly formed group after?"

Quadir smiles big. "Marcus Garvey's the Black Star Line."

"Correct. Now if you really want to impress Pierce, pass me some salt-and-vinegar chips."

"A ship to take you to Africa? Why would you want to do that?"

Knowledge gives me a look that could cut through bullet-proof glass. "Because Africa is home. Why wouldn't you want to go home?"

"Why would I want to go back to some country to live in a hut with no clothes and shit?"

"That's what the media wants you to believe Africa is like.

There are fifty-four countries on the CONTINENT of Africa, with some of the finest clothes, buildings, and most intelligent people in the world that you never see on American television. It's all a mind game, to make you believe your home is dangerous to keep you under the government's thumb and ensure that you will continue to slave for them."

"But I ain't from Africa. I'm from Brooklyn."

Knowledge leans over the counter. "Okay, think of it this way—you can move, be moved, go your whole life living other places, but you will always be from Brooklyn. Brooklyn will always be your home. It's in your blood. So is Africa."

I laugh. "Word up!"

Knowledge gets busy, creating some masterpiece on a toasted hero and wraps it up in tinfoil with ten minutes to spare.

"One last thing . . ."

"Damn, son, what now?"

Knowledge tosses in some napkins in the bag and ties it closed, chuckling to himself.

"Tell my son, next time he wants a chopped cheese . . . he should just call."

Pierce bites into his sloppy sandwich with his eyes closed, ketchup hanging out his mouth.

"Mmmmmm," he moans, with a happy grin. "That's that shit right there. Perfect!" He takes a sip of his Evian water and looks up at us. "So how many questions you get wrong?"

Quady smiles. "Just one."

"Heh! One? That's it? Damn, old man must be getting soft."

I wipe the sweat off the back of my neck. "Aight, we brought you your sandwich, so what's up?" I try to keep my voice light, but I'm done jumping through all these hoops like we in a circus. My deodorant been burned out, so I know I'm stinking. Plus, my feet are killing me. Timbs weren't made for track and field.

Pierce raises an eyebrow. "Brave, ain't ya? Brave and stupid. Fletch!"

Fletch comes running in. "Yes, sir!"

"Pop that new track in. Let's see what they got."

Both Quady and I sigh in relief. Finally, now we getting somewhere.

Fletch pops the CD in a glass-face stereo, and Steph's voice comes out the speakers from all four corners of his office. Heads start bobbing. The track is tight! Kaven was worth the money.

Pierce cuts his throat with his hand and Fletch quickly shuts it off.

"Better. Much better. Now, let's see if you can do it again."

"What?"

"You told us to make a new hit and we did that," Quady says, outraged. "You can't tell me this ain't a club banger."

"Yeah, but I need another one." He chuckles, taking bite of his sandwich. "What, you think all you gotta to do is make one hit, then you good? Nah kid, you got to come with hit after hit after hit if you want to win in this game! Come with it like it's your first day on the job every single time."

I'm so blown I don't even know what to say.

"We need that real club banger! Something that even the ladies can rock to. You feel me?"

Quady looks down at his Timbs and sighs. "Yeah, we feel you."

"Good. You got forty-eight hours. Bring me something hot!"

"Forty-eight hours! But . . ."

"Is there a problem?" he barks, an eyebrow raising.

Quady looks out the window, as if considering something. Maybe he's thinking of telling him. Just come out with the truth. I ain't gonna front; I considered it myself. But the way he has us running around the whole damn city, playing us like some chump, I don't want to give him the satisfaction.

Quady sniffs and offers his hand. "Nah. We good. Forty-eight hours."

Pierce gives him a once-over, then fist-bumps. "Y'all can show yourselves out."

Outside, we glance up at the building, at all the clouds surrounding the floor we came from. We were really floating in the clouds, face-to-face with real music executives, surrounded by Billboard awards, platinum plaques, and Grammys. Who would've thought two kids from Brooklyn would've made it so far?

I know that look on Quady's face. That closed-mouth dead silence. He seems real calm, but inside, he's freaking out.

Not me, though.

Being that close to the top just put a new battery in my back.

26
Quadir

Cab to the movies at Linden Boulevard Multiplex (because she can't stand the train) = $13. One way.

Two adult tickets to the seven-thirty show = $11.

One large popcorn, a large Coke, nachos with cheese, and Twizzlers for her plus one large Coke for myself = $18.

In total, $42, just to take Ronnie to the damn movies.

"Oh my God! That was bananas!" Ronnie says, as we head out the doors of the theater, holding hands. "The way they rolled into that club, them black lights, homegirl singing 'However do you want it!' So sick!"

We'd been planning for months to see Hype Williams's first feature film, *Belly*, starring Nas and DMX. The whole hood been talking about going on opening day, and Ronnie couldn't miss out on being the first. She had a rep to keep or whatever. So regardless of the deadline Pierce threw at us, I couldn't cancel my date with Ronnie. I would've never heard the end of it.

"Oh, and my girl Kisha? She was mad fly. Did you see that house Tommy had her up in?"

The movie had everybody in it. Method Man, T-Boz, that fine chick from *A Bronx Tale*, Taral Hicks, and a bunch of Jamaicans. Jarrell is gonna be real happy about that. Hopefully he's not still pissed about me ghosting on him at the studio to, as he puts it, "see some chick."

Ronnie's looking real cute, though. Crop powder-blue sweater, tight Guess jeans, and purple Reeboks. She went to the nail salon after school yesterday and I paid extra for the ladies to spray-paint little dragon designs on her nails.

"That Tommy, he's, like, a *real* man, you know?" Ronnie smirks, snuggling up on my arm. "Taking care of his shorty like that. Buying her anything she wants. That's the type of man I could love for the rest of my life."

I don't say nothing. The whole time I'm trying to pretend I don't hear them thoughts creeping in the back of my head, how I had more fun just chilling on the boardwalk with Jasmine. Even thinking about Jasmine right now seems foul.

"Hey," she says, all sweet, tilting my chin down toward her. "What's up with you? You real quiet. You didn't like the movie or something?"

"Um, nothing. It's just . . . cold." I zip up my jacket, trying to tune back in, but my mind keeps spinning between Jasmine,

Pierce, Steph, and the movie. The whole time, all Nas's character wanted to do was bounce to Africa and start a new life. Maybe it ain't such a bad move, leaving home, starting over fresh.

"Well, anyway, I wanted to talk to you about something."

Uh-oh.

"Soooo, I saw this jacket at Kings Plaza. And I'm *really* feeling it. I mean, no other girl is gonna have it. I swear, I had them put it on layaway for me. All you gotta do . . . is pick it up."

"Pick it up?"

"Yeah. I was hoping . . . you would cop it for me."

I groan loud enough for the concession stand to hear as we walk outside.

"What kind of jacket?"

She combs back her bangs that flip in the wind. "It's just this little butter leather—"

"Leather! You want me to cop you a leather jacket?"

Ronnie frowns. "What you tripping for? It's just four stacks—"

"Four hundred dollars! Are you crazy?"

She rolls her neck. "Well, it ain't like you don't got the money. I heard you been moving weight. Tisha saw you and Rell last Saturday on Fulton."

"Weight? You know I'm not into that shit."

"So what you saying, Tisha seeing things now?"

"I don't know what Tisha seeing, but it ain't that!"

"Quadir," she says, hard. "You *really* trying to tell me that you and Rell ain't up to something?"

"For the last time, I'm—"

Shit! The demos. I completely forgot about them.

Ronnie taps her foot, waiting for an answer. And I don't want to lie to her. But she can't know. If she knows, the whole hood is gonna find out, and then it'll be wrap for Steph getting signed. We too close to give up now.

"I'm not . . . it's not what you think."

"Oh, so now you gonna lie to my face?"

She tries walking off, but I grab her arm.

"It's not! That money . . . it ain't for buying leathers and shit." I take a deep breath. "I'mma use it . . . to go to Bishop."

She squints. "What?"

It's true. After we get Steph signed and set his moms up, I'm going to use my cut of the money to go to Bishop. It's what Steph would've wanted me to do.

She huffs and crosses her arms. "So you gonna leave me? I thought we talked about this last year. That we gonna go to school *together*."

I take a deep breath. "I talked to the coach. He's gonna let me walk on the team. Baby, it's a good school. It'll help me get into a good college."

"College? That's like . . . two years away. Why you thinking about all that now?"

"You gotta start applying, like, next fall."

"You don't think I know that? You don't think I want to go to college too?"

"Huh? You do?"

"Yeah, nigga," she barks. "You ain't the only one out here with dreams!"

"But . . . you said you never wanna leave B-Voort."

"So! That don't mean I can't go to college." She counts off her fingers. "NYU, Columbia, Hunter, Brooklyn College, St. John's, City College, Fordham, not to mention all the CUNY schools. Son, I don't need to leave the city if I don't feel like it. But you would've known if you would've *asked* me."

I don't even know what to do except stand there with my mouth open.

"Look at you, just assuming I was like every other chick out here instead of trusting me. You could've *talked* to me first before you go jumping to conclusions and keeping all these secrets." She points in my face, hissing. "You know what? You just like my daddy said. You a scrub who think he better than everybody else, trying to be something he not, perpetrating a fraud. Can't keep it real with nobody. Not even with yourself! I can do better. And believe me, I will!"

She storms down the stairs, waiting at the curb as the dollar cabs pull up one by one. I slowly drag myself after her, stuffing my hands in my pockets

"So that's it?" I mumble to the ground. "It's over?"

She waves a hand over her shoulder, ignoring me.

"I'm sorry, Ronnie. I . . . can't tell you. I wanna tell you, I just . . . can't right now. Not yet. But soon."

"After everything I've done for you?" She shoots glare over her shoulder. "Man, whatever."

"You want me to take you home?"

"Nah. I'm good. I don't need nothing from you."

' ' '

Solo dolo cab ride home = $13.

"Well, look who decided to show up!"

When Jasmine left a message with my mom to come over, I was low-key hyped. Gave me something to look forward to after crashing and burning with Ronnie. The last person I expected to see sitting on Steph's floor was Jarrell.

"Aye yo, what you doing here?"

"Pssh! What you think," he says, tossing another box aside. "Looking for Steph's new track. One of us gotta keep the lights on around here."

Jasmine shakes her head, smiling. "Rell filled me in on y'all's meeting. My mom's working a double shift and Carl's sleeping over a friend's house, so we got until around four a.m."

She's dressed in some baggy sweats like she's ready for bed and smells like Jergens cherry-almond lotion that has my head foggy.

"If Pierce signs Steph, I bet he gonna want to find his killer too," she says. "Maybe even front award money for any info."

Jarrell nods. "Um, maybe. So, Quady. How was the movie?"

I clear my throat, plopping on Steph's bed. "It was . . . aight. Sound track is sick."

"Yeah, DJ Clue been spinning it all night," Jasmine says, crawling on the floor near my feet, pulling some boxes from under the bed.

"What y'all looking for? We already went through all his music."

Jarrell flips through some CD's on the desk. "Yeah, well, we checking again. Kaven ain't hearing nothing that pops. He says if we find some more, to bring him what we got."

"But we've listened to everything." I glance down at Jasmine. "Right?"

"Yeah. But . . . Rell's right. We already used most of Steph's best club bangers. The rest is all partial or unfinished tracks. None of them are, what you call it . . . for the ladies."

"We can make something work," Jarrell says, digging through some CDs on his desk. "But ya man Pierce . . . I don't know if he's gonna feel it. And Kaven charging us double for putting the studio on hold. So we gotta get this done. Tonight!"

Damn, can this night can't get any worse? Ronnie and I break up, now we about to get our necks broke for wasting Pierce's time and lose Steph's deal. I won't even have money for one semester at Bishop.

"Aight," I say, jumping to my feet, shaking the sleep out my head. "Let's just . . . start from the top and look again."

Jasmine and Jarrell groan, flopping dead on the floor.

"Come on, y'all, there's gotta be something. Maybe one of these tapes or CDs we overlooked."

I snatch a few CDs off the table and bang at the stereo. "Damn, how you work this thing?" The disc changer opens, then swivels to the right. A blank CD stares back up at me.

"Hey, did one of y'all leave this in here?"

Jarrell tilts his head up to look. "Nah."

Jasmine frowns. "What's that?"

Felt like the doors of heaven just opened. Steph always said the three-CD changer on his stereo was broke, so he could only listen to one CD at a time. No one would have ever thought to check the other slots.

Jasmine presses Play, and the first song rumbles, unlike anything we've heard Steph record before.

"Son," Jarrell laughs in shock.

I grin up at the ceiling. "Good looking out, Steph."

This is it.

Kaven looks as if his brain is off somewhere in space the way he's staring at the floor, listening to Steph. We wait, eager for him to do . . . something. Say a word, a grunt, anything. He cuts the CD off, leans back in his chair, and shrugs.

"It's not enough."

"What you mean?" Jarrell pops off. "Is your hearing aid working? This is off the hook!"

"I ain't say it wasn't. But what you got here, it's not enough for a whole song. It's just two verses. You need at least three and a hook if you want something solid."

Behind us, Jasmine gazes around the studio in awe, scoping out the equipment like a nosy kitten.

"Can't you pull from another song?" I ask.

"It won't have the same flow. That's like mixing oil and water. Just won't taste right."

"Son, I only eat ranch and blue cheese, so I don't know what you talking about, but we making music here, not salad dressing!"

Kaven rolls his eyes. "You got anything else?"

"Man, don't you know any singers that are trying to get put on? I mean, damn, you supposed to be a producer!"

He chuckles. "Not for the pennies you giving me, I don't."

There's something about Kaven I don't like. Yeah, he's a man of few words, and when he does talk, he's mad blunt but never has anything helpful to say. It always feels like he's holding in something important. Something necessary that I can't put my finger on.

I palm the movie ticket stubs in my coat pocket and check the time. One o'clock in the morning. I bet Ronnie already got some brotha on the phone, making all kinds of promises. She'll have that coat by the end of the week.

"Hey," Jasmine whispers, touching my shoulder. "You okay? You look . . . stressed."

Stress don't even cover it. It's not that I didn't think Ronnie and I were already headed to the exit, but . . . man, I don't know. I feel grimy for jumping to conclusions about her. Despite all her flaws, Ronnie always kept it real. You gotta respect people like that.

"Yeah, I'm aight," I mumble, rubbing my face. "Just tired."

Jasmine smiles. "It's gonna be aight. We'll figure something out. I mean, we didn't come this far to come this far."

I chuckle. "That's something Steph would say."

"Yeah . . . something our dad used to say."

Jasmine looks not only exhausted, but real sad, and I suddenly remember how hard all of this has been on her. Here I am, stressing over a breakup, and she missing her brother and her pops. I wish we were alone. Not that I want to do nothing nasty, just kinda looking for that peace and calm I always feel with her. Maybe I could convince her to sing for me again . . .

"YOOOO!"

Jasmine jumps back and the room turns to me.

"Jasmine! Jasmine can do it!"

"What?" Jarrell and Jasmine snap.

"Jasmine can do the hook and the missing verse."

Jarrell shakes the wax out his ears.

"Son, you talking about Jasmine?" he asks, pointing at her. "Like 'Jazzy Jazz' Jasmine or another Jasmine?"

"Quady . . . no," Jasmine whispers, backing into the security monitor.

"Jasmine can spit, just like Steph. And she can blow!"

"Man, how you know?"

"'Cause . . . I've heard her. She's . . . amazing."

"Nah, he's playing," Jasmine says with a nervous laugh. "I can't sing like that."

Jarrell eyes widen, and he brings a fist up to his mouth. "Whoa . . . you ain't never been this shook before. You really *can* sing."

"What d'you think?" I ask Kaven.

He rubs his hands together with a nonchalant shrug. "It can work."

"But . . ." Jarrell says, scratching his head. "What she gonna sing, though?"

I grab Jasmine's hand and run toward the door. "Give us an hour."

27
Jasmine

Mad. Scared. Excited. Stunned. I don't know what to be first.

"I can't believe you just did that," I snap as we rush into Steph's room. I've said this about ten times so far.

Quady dives under the bed and pulls out a shoebox full of notebooks.

"Jazz, I know you hate me now, but once you do this, you gonna love me!"

My breath hiccups on the word "love."

Get a hold of yourself, Jasmine. He has a girlfriend.

"All you gotta do is spit one of Steph's poems. Some of his stuff could easily be verses on a song. Just put your own swag on it."

He flips through the pages, landing on one he bookmarked toward the end.

"I can't just spit Steph's stuff's like it's my own!"

"Why not? Rappers write songs for other rappers all the time. Big wrote rhymes for Lil' Kim!"

"I am *not* no Lil' Kim, and I ain't about to be," I snap.

"You ain't got to. Just gotta come as hard as her."

I hold my breath and count to ten. "I'm. Not. Ready!"

"Yes. You. Are!" He shoves the book in my hand. "You have to be. For Steph. For all the other ladies out there. 'Cause it's *your* dream too."

I grip Steph's book, trying to hold in tears. "I can't believe you got me out here about to play myself."

"Imagine it's just us, Jazz. No one else. That's all you have to do."

The poem sitting in my hand weighs a ton.

"We still need a hook. I'mma need a while."

Quadir looks at the clock on the wall and winces. "You got thirty minutes."

I grab a pencil off his desk and plop on the bed.

"That's all I need."

As soon as I step in the booth, I know I'm never going to be the same. The energy baked into the walls could power a whole city. I soak it in, the voice inside me ready to roar.

Most of the narrow space is painted indigo except for the dark-gray sound-absorbing foams glued to the panels. It's humid, there's a sweet hint of weed in the air, the floors slightly sticky, but within moments, I already feel at home.

"Have a seat," Kaven says behind me, handing me black headphones as big as my head. I place them like a tiara in front of my puffs and hop on the leather stool.

"What's all this?" I ask, pointing to the wall on the right, tagged up with different names and designs.

"Every emcee that comes and blesses the mic . . ." He gives the mic three taps. "Leaves their name on the wall."

"Reminds me of 5Pointz. You know, out in Queens? With all the graffiti?"

Kaven smirks and adjusts the mic to my height. "What you know about that, young queen?"

Out the glass panel window in the engineering room, Quadir and Rell watch over the audio board.

"My dad took us there."

"Aight, you ready?"

I place Steph's notebook on the music stand with all my notes and take a deep breath.

"Ready."

But I wasn't ready. When Steph's voice invades my earphones, spitting the first verse, I forget how to talk. By take number eleven, a tadpole has grown into a full-grown frog in my throat.

"Okay, queen," Kaven says over the intercom, his voice flat. "Take five."

I nod back in response, my neck sweating, clothes sticking. Kaven, Quadir, and Rell are arguing in the other room. I can't hear them, but Rell's arms are flying around, and Kaven only shrugs. Quadir catches me staring and we lock eyes.

My hands shake as I sip on my third bottle of water when he closes the door behind him.

"What's up?"

"Hey," I say, my voice almost gone.

"You good, Jazz? You need something?"

"I'm straight. Why?"

He rubs his head, glancing back at the audience watching us.

"You sure? 'Cause you not sounding like . . . you."

I blow out some nervous air pent up in my lungs. They've either sent him in here to talk some sense into me or dead the whole idea.

"What am I supposed to sound like? You only heard me sing once, and now you got me—"

"If you scared, then just say it."

"I ain't scared!"

"Ain't no shame in admitting it. You scared. You don't want to mess this up. The stress and pressure . . . it's mad crazy. But, deadass, you got this on lock, Jazz. You got the pipes. You know it. I know it. Steph knew it, too."

I rub my temples and check the time. We've been at it for almost two hours.

"It's just that, every time I hear his voice . . . maybe this was a mistake."

Quadir stuffs his hands in his pockets, pacing around.

"That day on Coney Island, when you were singing . . . you remember what set you off?"

I shrug. "Nah."

"I do. You were missing Steph bad that day."

"Oh. Yeah. Right." I try forgetting my tears as much as possible.

Quadir pulls up a stool, his back to the window. "A couple of months after Big died, I was reading this interview in *Vibe* with Puff Daddy. He said after Big's funeral, he was mad depressed. Hanging around his home, moping. Couldn't eat, sleep, nothing. Then, he heard that Police song on the radio, 'Every Breath You Take,' and a lightbulb went off. He jumped in the studio and produced that monster hit, dedicated to Big. And he kept at it. Now look at him. Bad Boy on top of all the charts!"

"So what you saying?"

He looks me square in the eye. "Pain . . . it can either *make* you or *break* you. And we trying to get made out here. You gotta keep going and remember who you doing this for. 'Cause you ain't just doing this for Steph; you doing this for you."

We let some silence hang between us as I wipe a tear away. Can't believe I'm crying in front of him again. But he's right.

"Aight," I say. "I'm ready. Will you . . . stay with me?"

Quadir eyes widen.

"Um, yeah. No doubt," he says, and closes the door, standing in front of it.

I shake the tremors out my hands and close my eyes, searching for that note, deep in the pit of my stomach. But in order to find it, I have to think of Steph. I have to focus on our memories. I have to fully feel the pain I've been wishing away. I think of the last time I saw him, and my stomach tightens.

"Queen, you ready?" Kaven says over the intercom.

I nod, digging my nails into my knees.

Steph, I hope you watching this.

The beat comes in slow. Steph's voice starts the song off first. Every time I hear him, it unhinges me. It's like he's still alive until I remember he's not. He's gone. He shouldn't be. He should be with us . . .

I see some ladies tonight

At the house party DJ savin' my life

My jeans say "ice" on 'em and my Avi is white

Ni-kes got Mike on 'em and they say he in flight

I ain't saying the price

'Cause this is Brooklyn, son

Where the crooks is from

And I ain't lookin' dumb

This the season

Where rings come

Off the hand

Like a rerun

We seen "What's Happening!!"

That's on Patchen and

Bainbridge, same kids

You know them play-the-last-car-on-the-train kids

Them make-your-mama-shake-her-head

"It's a shame" kids

Can't snitch where we from

No-name kids

Anyway, getting back to this bashment
Honies walking 'round like a fashion pageant
For real, it's like I'm steel and her ass a magnet
Guess that's how it feel when opposites attracting
I failed chemistry, but biology passed and
If you feel chemistry, let anatomy happen

Before I know what I'm doing, I humming with him, like I used to do when we'd practice in his room. And when it's time for the hook, I sing.

Nah, I don't just sing. I light the mic on fire!

Tell the DJ keep on playin' that sound
And when it hit replay, we keep on blazing it down
So Brooklyn, where you at? Brooklyn, where you at?

This one's for Brooklyn
This one's for Brooklyn
This one's for Brooklyn

I open one eye, just to check. Rell is going ballistic, cheering behind the glass, bopping his shoulders. Quadir just stands there, a grin across his face, looking mad proud. Even emotionless Kaven slowly rises to his feet, and I jump into my verse . . .

Hold up!
I brought Queens to a Brooklyn party

That's an oxymoron

Here's some more on who I be

"Mona Lisa . . ."

Mona Lisa smiling

Mona Lisa with an Afro or braids Fulani

Find me

Reading books in a Brooklyn lobby

So intrigued you took up a new hobby

Other chicks get you hooked on body

I got you Hooked on Phonics

"Every Little Step"

Now you hooked like Bobby. . . .

Hehe . . . Damn, did I say that?

New Bob Marley

DJ, can you play that?

Cause I be thirteen

I don't mean Iverson's sneaker

I mean I'm the keynote speaker

Step to the podium, break on linoleum

Stepping all over that boys' club sign with "men only"
    written

On the banner. . . .

Cause this gon' be the anthem

I'll show ya you can wear a skirt and still wear the pants,
    son!

Everybody put your hands up!

Fulton Ave, Ralph Ave . . . gotta stand up

By the second hook, I become the song. Every note, every inflection, every beat, I own. Steph comes in for his last verse, and when it's time, I blow out the final melody. The walls vibrate and my ears pop as I carry out the last note. I'm exhausted but overjoyed.

Kaven turns on the intercom and I can hear Rell cheering. "Damn, where this girl been all night?"

"Yo, you did it!" Quady says, pulling me into a tight squeeze, and I find myself softening in his arms, the safest place I've been in months. Standing there in the soundproof booth, the world is gone, and the seconds feel like days. His hands grip my back, nose inhaling my neck, then quickly, he steps aside, clearing his throat as the door swings open.

Rell rushes inside the booth and tackle-hugs me.

"Jazzy Jazz! That was hot! I can't believe it. Son, you murdered that shit!"

"I told you," Quadir says, lightly punching his shoulder.

"Whatever, you stay wrong all the time."

"Again?" I say to Kaven, leaning in the doorway

"For safety, yes. But I think we got it. You got one more in you?"

"Yeah. Let's do it."

We record the song two more times. Each time better than the last.

"Yo! That's a wrap, Jazz," Rell says over the intercom.

Quadir opens the door. "Come on out, Jazz. We done."

"Cool," I say with a satisfied sigh, when I notice a familiar scribble on the lower right corner of the wall.

"Hey, Quady, come here for a sec," Rell calls.

While the boys talk to Kaven, I jump off the stool and bend low to examine the doodle. I trace the Roman numeral three with a snake up the middle. I've seen him draw this a zillion times in his notebooks.

"Steph," I whimper, taking in the room once more. It doesn't make sense. What would he be doing here, and how would the boys not know about it? Wouldn't Kaven recognize Steph's voice?

When I walk out the booth, Kaven is playing back the song, grinning.

"Gonna sweeten it a bit, but it'll be ready by tomorrow," he says to Rell.

"Bet. I'mma cop it after school."

"I'll roll with you to bring it to . . . you know who," Quadir says. "Ready to go, Jazz?"

"Huh? I mean, yeah. Ready."

I slip on my jacket in a daze. That's not him. That can't be him. That can't . . .

"Has a kid named Steph ever been up in here?"

The words blurt out before I can stop them, and the room freezes. Jarrell and Quadir heads snaps up.

Kaven's mouth sits in a straight line for a moment too long. "Who?"

That "who" felt heavy.

"His name . . . is Steph. Brown skin, tall, braids. Scar on his cheek. You ever see him?"

Kaven folds his arms. "Doesn't ring a bell."

He's lying, a voice inside my head screams.

"Jasmine! Jazzy Jazz," Jarrell says with a fake laugh. "You bugging. You know that kid ain't from around here. It's been a long night. Why don't we *all* head home, okay?"

"Jazz, what you doing?" Quady says under his breath behind me. "You trying to blow up our spot?"

"No, it's just that—"

Kaven staring at my mouth shuts me up. It's too hard to try to explain in front of him, and like Big says, "Never let them know your next move." Kaven is lying about something. The question is, what?

Over Kaven's shoulders, the mini security monitor has four views of the house. Four cameras.

Four possible ways of finding Steph.

28
JARRELL

After school on Friday, Jasmine left a message to give Pierce a call. It hadn't even been twenty-four hours since I dropped the song off at his office. I don't know if that's a good sign or not. With Mom still out shopping, I tell Quady to come through ASAP.

"So where's your boy at now?" Pierce says over the phone, his voice short. Sounds like he's at the studio, beats playing mad loud behind him.

"He's . . . at the cemetery. You know how funerals be."

"Oh. Well, send him my condolences and shit. Anyway, this song . . . this song is hot, y'all. We definitely got something here. And who's this chick you got singing the hook?"

From my desk, I look into the living room at Quady on the sofa, holding the other receiver to his ear.

"Uh, just a . . . homegirl, from around the way," Quady says with a smile.

"Shorty got pipes. We need to get her in here too. Anyway, I played the track at a meeting with the president this morning. He loved it! His words were, 'Get that mutherfucker in the studio tomorrow!'"

Quady and I throwing each other silent cheers from across the room. I even throw the twins some love, even though I have them tied to a chair, mouths duct-taped, and they fighting for freedom.

"Aight. But first, we gonna celebrate! So I'll see y'all Sunday night at the Tunnel."

"The Tunnel! Oh shit, kid," I yell, slapping a hand over my mouth.

The Tunnel. The mecca of all hip-hop clubs. The most popping, most exclusive spot in the city. I mean, it's been in mad rap videos.

"Yeah, I already put y'all on the Red Starr list, so tell your boy no funny shit. He better show his ass Sunday night or I'll throw this CD straight in the trash like it never happened 'cause he ain't ever gonna happen. You feel me?"

"Uh, yeah," Quady starts off real hesitant. "It's just that um, he . . ."

"Yo, we'll be in the *building*, son! No doubt!"

"Rell, you bugging," Quady shouts under his breath and I wave him off.

"Good. See y'all Sunday."

I slam down my receiver and slide into the living room with a spin.

"Son! We going to the Tunnel. We gonna be up in there with all the fly honies! Forget an E. Roque party! People can't tell me shit once they see me up in the Tunnel! Yo, I gotta get my hair cut, pick up my shirt from the cleaners . . . damn, maybe I should cop some new kicks . . . you know they got a dress code. And . . . what? Why you looking at me like that?"

Quady stares up at me, leaning his face in the crook of the L his fingers made.

"Really, Rell? 'WE' going to the Tunnel?"

I'm still sitting dumb when it hits me.

"Oh shit."

29
JuLy 10, 1998

There's nothing like Brooklyn summers, filled with the type of heat that brings the crazy out of the sane and ruthlessness out of the mundane.

The boys had a regular routine during the summer: cereal and morning cartoons at Steph's house, then hoops at the courts, post up by the bodega for lunch, chill on the bench to watch all the shorties in the courtyard before dinner, then maybe a late-night game.

It would be the last summer they spent as a whole.

Steph sat on the stone bleachers of the courts, freestyling, waiting for the chance to jump in a game. A true wordsmith, he could make up a rhyme for just about anyone that passed by. The cute girl in the powder-blue dress, the grandpa with his old dachshund, the mailman hitting his route . . . they all become subjects in his impromptu poems.

Quadir laced up his sneakers, egging him on, always impressed with Steph's natural abilities that made him seem superhuman.

Jarrell strolled onto the courts, feet dragging, hands stuffed in his pockets. He had missed breakfast and didn't seem particularly interested in being outside at all.

Steph noticed Jarrell's demeanor and cut his last rhyme short. "Yo man, what's up with you?"

"Yeah, man, you ain't your usual jolly self," Quadir chuckled.

Jarrell plopped down and took a long sigh. "This kid from my science class got murk yesterday."

The boys instantly straightened. Murder deserved their full attention.

"Damn, son, I'm sorry."

Jarrell isn't afraid to show his emotions. He's not above expressing his sadness in the way most boys are taught not to. A quality Steph always admired about him.

"Yeah. It's just so fucked up. He was cool, mad smart. He even let me copy his homework sometimes."

"R.I.P. What was duke's name?"

"Rashad. Lived in Brownsville but he stayed over here on the weekends with his pops."

"Yooo . . . Rashad?" Steph exclaimed. "I knew that kid! I used to play ball with him. My pops used to coach us both.

Damn, he was nice with it!"

"Yeah, scouts were already clocking him. Heard he got caught up in . . . something. He could've . . . you know, been somebody. Ain't saying, like, we nobodies, but I wanted to see him on TV, playing for the Knicks so I could say I went to school with duke."

Quadir shakes his head. "This summer ain't no joke. I heard about this emcee out of Marcy that got murked by the cops on the Fourth of July over some dumb shit. His bars were hot! Now . . . he's gone too."

"Man, I just don't get it sometimes," Steph fumed. "We see all these cornballs dropping wack-ass albums or making it pro. Yet cats from the hood who can really spit or play ball end up dead."

"Cats be famous in the hood but not mainstream."

"Shit like this makes me think like they're trying to keep black folk in the hood forever," Jarrell barked. "Don't want none of us to make it! They either throw us in the pen or they kill us."

"Who's they?"

Jarrell sucked his teeth. "The man!"

Quadir and Steph glance at one another before busting out laughing. Jarrell jumped off the bench, his fist balled up tight.

"I ain't playin'! You know they always trying to keep a brotha down!"

Steph held a hand up. "Yo, relax, kid! Besides, you already know someone that's gonna make it."

"Who?"

"*Me*, fool, that's who. And if I make it, then we all make it. Aye yo, Rell! You owe me a bag of chips if I can make you laugh before I finish."

Yo, check it,
As I sit on this bench with bad news, tryna escape it
Hoping one day to say, "Look, Pops, we made it!"
Head Facing North
Like the jacket I sport
It's either rap's takin' off or be mad up in court
But F that,
'Cause they expect that
Plus I seen ya/senior
Two times,
Like I ain't graduate and got left back!
So picture me going to bookings,
A tree grows in Brooklyn
I hold the spot like bookmarks, but hold it down like
    bookends
Till they all know the hood like *Dawson's Creek*
I'll get us all out the hood, I know talk is cheap
But my thoughts worth g's. . . .
Twenty-carat mind of his
You might wanna sign the kid
I'm Midas with . . .
The golden touch, better yet, plat-i-num,

Rocking bigger ice than that ship in *Titanic*!
Get my man Q dipped in leather, the butter's vintage
Get Rell his own room with no little brothers in it!
Now that's something, isn't it?

30
Quadir

Weather ain't so bad, chilly but warm enough that cats are still on the courts trying to squeeze in a few games before that New York winter hits and makes you want to hibernate until May. Rell and I sit on the sidelines, watching a late-night three-on-three game.

"Son, I don't know how the hell we're gonna pull this off tomorrow," I say, clutching my ball. "You saw how heated Pierce got the last time we came without Steph."

Jarrell sucks his teeth. "My bad again, son. I just heard 'the Tunnel' and got mad excited! You know everybody be talking about that spot."

"You think we can just tell him Steph's busy or something?"

"Psst. And have them two goons Hulk-smash our faces into the ground? Nah, b," he chuckles, biting into a ham-and-cheese on a roll he picked up from the corner store. I don't know how he has the stomach to eat anything right now. "I mean, you can't blame Pierce for wanting to meet the artist he's trying to put on. It's the whole 'Red Starr don't wait for you. You wait for Red Starr' threat that got me shook."

"We need a plan. And a good one," I say, hopping off the bench to pace.

"And figure out what to tell Jazz."

Damn, just the mention of her name got me daydreaming. That was the first time I ever hugged Jasmine, like really hugged her, and I can't get it out of my head. But I gotta chill. I can't get with Jazz and fuck it up the way I did with Ronnie. I don't ever want to hurt her. And I know the truth I'm keeping is going to hurt her most of all.

A ball rolls off the court and hits my ankle. I throw it back in the game, wishing I could jump in. I low-key miss the days when all I had to do was worry about playing ball and Ronnie. Ronnie ain't even talking to me no more, and I doubt homies will let me sub in . . .

"YO! That's it! We need a sub!"

"A what?" Rell asks, glancing down at his sandwich.

"A sub! You know, like when Jordan's tired of whooping asses, he calls a sub in the game for him. So that's what we need. A sub! Like an . . . actor to take Steph's place."

"Son . . . that ain't a bad idea! Problem is we'd have to find someone who looks kinda like Steph. Pierce already saw his picture on the cover."

"Damn, how we find someone that fast, though? We talking about *tomorrow* night, and . . ."

I do a double take before staring at a figure moving through the shadows on the opposite side of the court. Something or . . . someone.

Jarrell follows my gaze, mumbling "Oh shit" to himself.

There he is: Steph. Hoodie, sweatpants sagging, cornrow-wearing Steph! In the flesh, heading straight for us. I blink a few times as Jarrell inches up to his feet. Cats are so deep in their game they don't even notice the ghost walking pass them.

"What the . . . ?"

"Yo, you see it too?"

A single streetlight by the gate flickers, straight out of some horror movie. It flashes until it steady and the shadow steps into the light, moving in our direction.

Rell strains to see and whispers, "Jazz?"

Within a few feet, Jasmine lifts the hoodie covering her face with a frown. Her hair cornrowed back, just like Steph used to do. She stops in front of us, glancing over both her shoulders.

"What? What y'all looking at?

"Shit," I gasp with a laugh.

Jarrell clutches his heart, screaming out a breath.

"Merciful! I thought you were a duppy," he says, making a cross over his chest. "Father God, I was ready to run to mi mummy and throw salt on our doormat."

"What are you talking about?"

"Deadass, you scared the shit out of us, Jazz!"

Jarrell claps my shoulder. "Son, I almost peed on myself. It would've been a wrap for these silk boxers."

Jasmine huffs. "What the hell is wrong with y'all?"

Rell catches his breath. "Aight, not for nothing Jazz, I ain't really see it before, and don't take this the wrong way, but you look *just* like your brother."

Still in shock, I nod.

"I thought you were the Ghost of Christmas Past coming through six weeks early," he laughs. "What you out here all late, looking like a dude for anyways?"

"Shut up. I snuck out and I ain't want anyone recognizing me." She stuffs her hands in the front pocket of her hoodie. "This used to be Steph's."

"What you got to sneak for?" I ask.

Jasmine slicks back her edges, avoiding my eyes. "Um, no . . . reason."

This definitely ain't her first time. Where she have to sneak to?

Jarrell takes a long, hard look at Jasmine again, rubbing his chin.

"Hmm . . . you really do look *just* like him." He nods to himself. "Yeah . . . yeah."

A grin spreads fast across his face and he got that look in his eye. I ping-pong from Jazz to Jarrell, smelling the crazy plan cooking up in his head.

"Nah, don't even think about it. Nah, son. Hell no! No!"

*   *   *

The Tunnel is on Twenty-Seventh and Twelfth Avenue in the city. Except the line for the club starts at Eleventh Avenue, a whole long city block away. We huddle up around the corner behind a U-Haul truck to regroup.

"Aight, y'all. How I look?" Under his butter leather jacket, Jarrell has on a black-and-gold silk button-up shirt, black slacks, and some alligator loafers.

"Who cares how you look? What about her?"

I readjust the loose fitted hat and stunner sunglasses on Jasmine, pulling the hoodie farther up to cover her round face.

Jarrell shrugs. "She looks soft . . . but funny-looking enough to pass for a brotha."

Jasmine inhales deep, her chin trembling, then sucks her teeth. "Shut up, Rell!"

I slap his arm. "Yo, that shit ain't cool."

"I'm only playing," he laughs, bumping elbows with her. "You know that, right?"

Squirming, she pats her cornrows under the black durag I let her borrow. She doesn't have to say it, but I know that comment bothered her. I wish I could tell her, even with her breasts wrapped down and her clothes way baggy, she still looks like a girl to me. A beautiful girl.

I pull her hoodie down some more, and she waves away my hands.

"Stop, Quady," she snaps. "I'm fine."

"Sorry. I'm just—"

"Well, I'm good! I got this."

"Just remember, you can't walk with no switch in ya hips," Rell warns. "Put a bop in your step. Hold your arms loose. And when you sit down, spread your legs wide."

"Other than teaching her how to be a boy, what's the plan?"

"Okay, so boom: Pierce said he's gonna be chilling by the stage. We gonna roll through, show face, have a drink, ask to use the bathroom, and by that time, the club should be closing down, and we'll dip before anyone notice we gone."

"What if they ask her a question?"

"Just grunt, nod, and shrug."

"That's it? That's your plan? Have her act like a monkey up in VIP? Yo, deadass, we should bounce."

"Would you relax? This is gonna work. I heard the Tunnel be mad dark. It's three in the morning. Pierce probably drunk, so she won't have to do much talking."

"What if something pops off in there? You expect her to fight like a dude too?"

Jasmine folds her arms. "I like how y'all talking about me like I'm not even standing here!"

"And don't be rolling your neck like that either," Rell says, pointing. "That's a dead giveaway you a chick."

Jasmine chuckles but I can't shake the feeling that this is a bad idea.

"Just . . . stay close to me, aight?"

"Dag, Quady. For the last time, I ain't no baby!"

"This ain't about you being a baby or not! Shit gets crazy up in there! I know you heard what happened to Lil' Rocko."

Lil' Rocko used to live on the second floor of Steph and Rell's building. When he turned eighteen, he made a big deal about going to the Tunnel for his birthday. The Lox was performing; it was a whole Bad Boy Entertainment night. He waited on line for two hours, and as soon as he made it through security, some dude Mike-Tysoned his ass and knocked him the hell out. Case of mistaken identity, but within ten minutes, Rocko lost his wallet, chain, Timbs, leather jacket, and woke up in the hospital with a wired jaw.

The Tunnel has been closed down a few times for fighting. And not no small fights neither. I'm talking full-on brawls with cats snatching whatever's not stapled to your body right on the dance floor. The security stay confiscating all kinds of weapons at the door and it's still crazy.

"Yo, I'm with Quady. For real, Jazz, it's mad gully up in there."

She sniffs the air and shrugs. "I hear you, aight? But I can handle myself."

Jasmine ain't the type of girl you can just tell what to do. She has to see for herself, always.

"Besides," she says. "If we pull this off, get a deal for Steph, then we'll have the funds to find out what really happened."

"Um right," Rell mumbles. "Aight, let's do this."

We head to the front of the club, walking past the line that starts almost two blocks away, metal barricades keeping people flush against the building wall.

"Shouldn't we be in line too?"

"Pierce said ask for Jessica at the door. She has our names down on a list."

At the entrance, the line turns into a hurricane.

"Ladies to the left, men to right. Single-file line," a bouncer yells from the steps. There's dozens of them at the door, looking like the Giants' starting lineup.

"Shoes, jackets, belts . . . off!" Another one yells.

"What line should I get into?" Jasmine whispers.

Three bouncers drag a guy out by the collar, launching him into the street. He falls like a brick, his face lumped up and bleeding. One even rips the chain off his neck.

"If I catch your ass in here again, I'll break your fucking jaw!"

The guy passes out and two girls step over him.

"Girls!" Rell and I say together.

"Just wait for us by the door until we inside," Rell whispers. "Keep your sunglasses on, and don't say nothing."

We each walk through the metal detectors and get patted down by a team of bouncers. I don't even think they do this type of thorough search at the airport. They turn all my pockets inside out, bang my shoes together, feel up every square inch of me. Satisfied I'm clean, they let me through.

"Hey, where's Jazz?"

"I don't know," Rell says. "I lost sight of her."

I double back to the door but it's swarming with people. Shit, what if they looked too close at that ID we gave her? What if they take her to some back room? What if . . .

Jazz walks out, adjusting her glasses, smiling, and I resist snatching her up in my arms.

The club looks exactly like its name, a long, narrow

straightaway with old train tracks. There's one bar almost the length of the entire club, packed with people damn near climbing over the counter for drinks. The crowd is mad thick, barely room to breathe, but everyone is dancing like they have all the space in the world. In the back, there's a small platform for the DJ booth. Funkmaster Flex is on the turntables, light shining around him. That's when it hits me: we're really up in here.

It takes us almost forty-five minutes to walk through the crowd to the stage. Pierce is posted up with a gold bottle in his hands, ladies surrounding him. But he ain't his regular smooth self. He got a bop in his shoulders and a giddy smile, slurring the lyrics to Biggie's "One More Chance" loud as hell. Rell was right; duke's sloshed, and behind the stage is dark enough that he may not even notice Jasmine's thick lips.

Not that I was paying attention to them like that or nothing.

"Well, damn, it's about fucking time," Pierce shouts, spotting us. "What took you so damn long?"

Jarrell steps right up. "You know how that door be!"

"Yeah, that door is crazy," Pierce laughs. "Heard they even turned Tupac away once." He looks at Jasmine. "What up, kid! Beginning to think you weren't real or something!"

He daps and pulls her up into a hug. She freezes, her back stiffening. Jarrell grabs my wrist, stopping me from yanking her out of his grasp.

"Son, LONG time! Glad to finally meet you," he says, all proud, staring at her with dollar bills in his eyes. "Yo, you have a drink yet?"

Jasmine shakes her head, keeping mute.

"Oh nah, son, we can't have that. Here you go. Got some Cristal on ice." Pierce pours two champagne flutes. "To a new partnership. Now, let's get this money!"

They clink and he takes his glass to the head. Jasmine hesitates, drinking slow.

"Oh nah, you need more than that. Here, have another glass. So like I was telling y'all over the phone, I got some big plans for you. Once I run this past the big dawgs, we gonna get that contract drafted, cut you a check, and you'll be good money. The world's about to know your name."

Jarrell and I share a stupid silly grin, giving each other a pound. Yo, I'm so happy I could jump twenty feet.

We did it, Steph. We did it.

"Got a surprise for you. I—"

"Here you go, boss!" One of Pierce's goons pushes through the crowd with two drinks in his hand.

"Finally! In fact, here." He passes the glass with light-green liquor to Jasmine. "Don't know if y'all up on that Incredible Hulk yet."

Jasmine readies herself and I catch the glass midway to her lips. "Actually, he's already pretty done. He's had a lot already."

Pierce sucks his teeth. "Who you? His momma?"

Jasmine glares over her glasses and grabs the drink from my hand, knocking it back like a shot. She gasps and chokes as Pierce pats her on the back.

"Damn, son," he laughs. "You from Bed-Stuy and you can't

handle your liquor? Here, have mine. Drink it slow."

"What's an Incredible Hulk?" I whisper to a chick strutting by.

"Hypnotiq and Hennessy," she whispers back with a wink.

Jarrell makes an "oh shit" with his lips as Jasmine coughs harder, her shades falling on the floor. Jarrell jumps in front of us.

"Oh yo, isn't that . . . ummm . . . Halle Berry?" he yells.

Pierce spins around. "Oh word? Where she at with her fine ass?"

I scoop up the glasses and pass them to Jasmine. "Jazz, you okay?"

She nods, scrambling to fix herself but coughing like she about to pop out a lung. That Incredible Hulk must've burned the hell out of her throat. I glance up at Jarrell and shake my head. This ain't going well.

"Come on, Jazz," I whisper. "Follow me."

I grab Jasmine's arm, pulling her toward the stairs leading back to the dance floor.

31
JARRELL

I ain't gonna lie: I knew this plan was trash from the start. Still, I figured, what we got to lose? This night could either go right or wayyyy left. But I damn sure wasn't gonna miss out on a chance of going to the Tunnel and seeing all the fly honies. Picture that with a Kodak!

But I never expected to play defense *this* heavy.

I push Quady and Jazz out of the way, side-stepping in Pierce's line of sight.

"Man, your ass need some glasses," he barks with a slur, turning back to me. "That ain't Halle Berry! Just some . . . hey! Where those two going?"

"Um . . . think Arch wanted to check out the ladies. He'll be right back."

"Huh. Aight. Anyways, thirsty?"

"Yeah! Hey, thanks."

"Thanks? Nah, little homie, I was talking to myself. Asking if *I'm* thirsty," he snickers, taking a huge swig from the bottle. "If you don't treat yourself well no one will, right?"

Damn, he's an asshole for real. Surprised he ain't ask us to pick him up a pork fried rice from Chinatown on the way here. But I ain't gonna let him ruin my night. Not when I can see Funk Flex up close and in person. This is his party, his night. And I'm here to witness him take over the city.

"Aye yo," Pierce coughs, tapping my arm. "What the fuck is homeboy doing now?"

I spin around, hoping my eyes are playing tricks on me. Hoping I ain't seeing Jazz all up in Quady's face on the dance floor, two-stepping like some old lovebirds at the cookout.

"You gotta be fucking kidding me," I mumble, and straighten up before facing Pierce. "Yeah, um, Arch is just trying to show . . . Quady this new dance everyone been on!"

Pierce eyes them with the screw face. "That don't look like no dance moves I've ever seen."

"Nah, it's just something we do in the hood. It'll catch on soon—you know we always starting the fly shit in Bed-Stuy. Aye, where you say you from again in Harlem?"

"Wh-at? Oh, yeah, I'm from 135th and St. Nick. Born and raised." Pierce is distracted by the question like I knew he would be. Cats like him love talking about themselves heavy. "In fact, I was just like your homeboy. Living in the projects, trying to get into this music thang. For real, son, I was nice with it. Used to call me P Smooth."

"Oh word?"

"Yeah. Brothas were paying two stacks just to battle me, and I'd rip them to shreds, bars straight off the dome!"

"Ha! Just like Steph."

"Who?"

"I mean, Arch!" I choke out a laugh. "My bad, son, I ain't mean to call out his government like that."

Pierce doesn't look confused enough and starts searching the crowd again.

"Uh . . . SO . . . why you stop?"

He smirks, stretching his arms out like he's the king of world. "Stop what? What you mean? I'm out here, running this ish! Half the music you vibing to is from one of my artists."

"But you behind the scenes. I thought you wanted to be up front, on the mic."

Pierce sets his bottle down on the table by the stage with a laugh.

"You a cocky little mutherfucker, but I like you so I'mma teach you something 'cause I could tell from day one you about your paper, while your other homie is all about the 'love of the game.'"

Damn, duke read us like the Sunday funnies.

"Not everyone was made for center stage. Some people are

better at moving the puppet strings around, you feel me? Yeah, I could've signed a record deal, made some hits, but that ain't where the real money's at, kid."

"You bugging. Who wouldn't want to be out here pushing a Benz, flossing in Versace and Gucci shades?"

"Let me ask you, do you want a fly-ass car or do you want a driver? Do you want to drop stacks in the mall or do you want a stylist? Do you want to be in first class or do you want your own private jet? There's a difference between being rich and being wealthy. The rich get paid, but the wealthy . . . they own the fucking bank!"

Whoa. I ain't never really thought about it like that.

"Is that why you started working at Red Starr?"

He smiles and finally pours me a glass. "Best job in the world!"

"And you working for Steve Dunn, right? He's, like, your boss at Red Starr?

His grin falls a little. "Been my mentor since college."

"Wait, hold up. YOU went to college? What for?"

Pierce looks dead serious. "Like I said, you wanna be rich or you wanna be wealthy?"

"Bet," I laugh with a nod. "So when you gonna, you know, start your own thing?"

"My own thing?" he asks, with a chuckle.

I shrug. "My Old G says you should always start your own thing. Can't grow under a rock, y'knowwhatumsayin?"

The side of Pierce mouth twitches, and he has this weird look in his eyes. Maybe he didn't hear me right. I mean, it's mad loud in here, and duke has had a lot to drink.

"Hmm. Maybe your Old G is right," he mumbles.

One of Pierce's goons come over and whisper in his ear.

I ain't gonna front, he got my mind spinning with all this rich vs. wealthy talk. So does that mean cats on the block hustling major weight . . . they just rich? That sounds mad corny now. I wonder what category Mack falls under.

Jazz and Quady are still chilling in the middle of the dance floor, the crowd crazy thick. I ain't never seen so many people trying to fit in one spot before. Quady is standing mad tense and Jazz is waving her hands in the air like she don't care. I'm up in here sweating bullets, and they living it up.

Pierce and his goons are arguing over something, so I help myself to some more of his Cristal, and the room goes silent for a split second when I hear his voice.

"Yo, you look mad familiar, b."

Fast Pace ain't as tall as I remember. Duke about my height, wearing Timbs, a long white tee, and dark denim, surrounded by a crew of cats either fresh off the block or out the pen. Same homies that rolled with him to Ronnie's birthday party.

"Don't I know you from somewhere?" he asks.

"Who, me?" I say, playing stupid. "Nah, son, you got the wrong brotha."

He squints at me, mouth opening before Pierce rolls up on us.

"What up, playboy! Glad you made it!"

"Well, you said I gotta meet this Architect cat that's coming for my neck or whatever. So where he at?"

There ain't no humor in his voice. His face is stone cold.

"Chill, son," Pierce laughs, clapping his shoulder. "Ain't nobody coming for your spot. I was just saying, some friendly competition never hurts. Beef sell records!"

Fast Pace grills me again, like he's still debating where he knows me from, and I slide behind a shorty in a blue velvet dress, dancing like I ain't got my ear cocked up, listening.

"Been asking around," he barks. "Ain't nobody in Brooklyn ever heard of homeboy. No one's even seen him. He either a ghost or a fucking fraud."

"And I told you," Pierce says, hard. "He keeps a low profile and stays in the studio. That's why I asked you to roll through. So you can meet him!"

I shift away, creeping toward the stairs. We gotta bounce. No way Fast Pace came up in here with all these brothas just to *talk*.

Just as I scan the crowd for Quady, someone screams, and everybody scatters in a thousand directions. A group of bouncers descends down onto a mosh pit in the middle of the floor like an army. People bum-rush the stairs as a shorty yells.

"Yo, they fighting! Run!"

32
Jasmine

It's like a scene straight out of a music video on BET. All these black and brown bodies dancing under red lights. Skins glistening, white teeth shining, laughing, drinking . . . this is what our people were always supposed to look like. Filled with joy, love, and happiness.

While I sit in my room, listening to Lauryn, sneaking into underground spots, watching brothas spit poetry about the movement . . . this is how the other side has been living. Rocking the latest hairstyles and designer clothes. Sexy open-back tops, skirts with slits, heels, expensive bags. In here, I'm just a regular girl (well, boy). Not some girl being teased about my natural hair, my headwraps, baggy clothes, or my African medallion. In here, I'm one of *them*.

Is this what I've been missing out on all this time? Maybe it's the drinks pumping through my system that has me seeing the room so different. They make it look so easy.

Or maybe it's because I'm here with Quadir.

"Jazz, you okay?" he whispers in my ear, his chest pressed against my back as he tries moving me through the crowd but can't push more than an inch. Folks going crazy over Jay-Z and Jermaine Dupri's "Money Ain't a Thang" blasting through the speakers.

I turn to face him, but he holds my shoulders, his fingers grazing my neck.

"Nah, he may be looking."

He maneuvers in front of me, holding both my elbows. Why does it feels like his hands have been all over me all night? It's the drinks. It has to be.

"What d'we do now?" I ask.

Quadir searches for the fastest way to the exit. But Funk Flex is on the turntables, and the whole club is waiting for him to drop the latest banger. Nobody's trying to leave. It would be like pushing against a tidal wave to reach the front door. More people push up toward the stage, squeezing us closer together, until he's almost kissing my forehead.

He shakes his head. "This was dumb. I should've never brought you up in here."

"Brought me here? You act like I didn't have a say in it. I knew what was up."

"You know what I mean."

"Nah, I don't. You act like I don't have my own mind and can't make my own decisions. I told you, I could handle this."

"Handle this? You almost choked to death on a damn drink! You too young to be—"

"Yo, stop trying to treat me like some kid . . ."

"I'm not! But this ain't no game, though, Jazz. This shit is dangerous."

Dag, why is he ruining this night for me? For a change, I can see the allure of this lifestyle and just want to let down my armor. Why won't he let me enjoy myself? Why can't I be like everyone else who pretends not to see all the problems in the world, not see how our community is hurting, and just . . . BE?

"You know what? I think you too damn serious."

"What?"

I laugh. "I mean, you heard the man, right? He's drawing up paperwork. That means we did it! We got Steph a deal! And now, we up in the Tunnel! People would kill to be in our kicks."

Quadir's face loosens out of its tight scowl, and without us realizing it, we're swaying with the crowd. Flex is in a whole Jay-Z set. He scratches out to "Money, Cash, Hoes" featuring DMX and there's a "Ohhhhhh" from the crowd. The strobe lights flicker with the drums. A few fellas beside us scoop up some ladies, dancing on their backs.

"So?"

"So, let's just enjoy it!" I laugh. "Please?"

Everybody got their hands up, singing along at the top of their lungs. A girl next to me is sweating like crazy, hair matted to her face, dancing with her eyes closed. Quadir glances back at the VIP area, a black hole near the stage.

"Aight. We can chill for a second. It's dark enough. But once I see a break in the crowd, we out."

Flex runs the song back again. And again. And again.

Quadir still standing all stiff, and I ignore him to vibe with my peoples. You can't help but rock to it, the bass is bananas. My hands are up, the beat pumping through my system. I close my eyes and let it take over. I don't know if it's on purpose, but that magnetic pulse pulls me closer to Quadir. I mean, we were already close, but now I'm melting into his chest.

His eyes flare. "Jasmine . . . I can't," he says gently. "We can't."

I should listen to him, that's what my mind says, but the liquor is making me brave. I turn my back to him, pushing my butt against him. This time, he doesn't push me away, his hands are gripping my hips, arms wrapping around my waist, lips on my hoodie.

"Jazz . . ." he breathes in my ear, clenching me tighter, desperately. "We . . . can't."

Feels like he's talking more to himself than me, so I don't let go. Not of him or the moment. We ease into a slow whine to our own rhythm as the club parties around us.

I peep a couple of brothas staring at us. I would have paid them no mind, except I notice one guy with a white durag and a black bubble coat staring mad hard. My trance is broken as I watch him make his way toward us.

"Quady," I whimper, too quiet for him to hear just as Black Bubble reaches us.

"AYE! GET OFF MY GIRL!"

A fist swings in our direction.

"Shit!" Quadir shouts, and pushes us forward. The fist connects with the brotha dancing behind Sweaty Girl. The entire crowd leans away as the two brothas start fighting. More jump in. Black Leather loses his balance and falls to the floor.

"STOP! STOP!" Sweaty Girl screams, trying to pull them off. An elbow connects with her nose, and she tumbles back, blood spitting out on my hoodie.

"GUN!" Someone screams.

Like a rock thrown in a lake, the fight ripples outward, everyone running. Quady and I slam into the brick wall behind us. He stands in front of me before more people stampede into him.

"Quady," I cough out as we're squeezed into the wall. He tries to push back, but his arms are pinned. I gasp for air, trying to fight with him.

"Yo, hold up! Let us up!" Quadir begs. "She can't breathe! Wait!"

"Aye yo, calm down," I hear Flex say on the mic.

More frantic screams and cries. My head is crunched between the wall and Quadir. The room starts spinning. My muscles slip down to the floor and I bury my face into his back.

Don't faint. Don't faint. Don't . . .

Flashlights shine in our faces and a defense line of burly football players appear, arms linked, and like a long broom, they sweep the floor clean of anyone fighting.

Including us.

In a merciless wave of people, lights, and screams, we're caught in the riptide and wash up outside.

I land on my knees, hands in a nasty puddle. Quadir stumbles on his back.

"Now get the fuck outta here!" one of the bouncers screams over us. "Before we stomp y'all little asses out!"

Quadir scrambles to help me to my feet. "Come on, Jazz! Come on!"

He grabs my hand and we take off running, passing the endless line of people still trying to get inside.

Quadir and I pooled our money together for a cab ride home. After what we survived, a late-night train ride wasn't an option. I take down my hoodie and durag, brushing down my edges with my hand. Now alone, I could at least try to look cute . . . for him.

"What about Rell," I ask as we speed over the Brooklyn Bridge, the city skyline twinkling behind us.

"Me, Rell, and Steph got one rule—whenever something pops off, we meet up at the spot." Quadir winces and stares out the window. "I mean . . . I guess . . . well, me and Rell."

My stomach clenches, and I'm instantly carsick as we approach downtown, the Big Ben clock reading three forty-five a.m.

"That was . . . fun," I say, trying to change the air.

Quadir head snaps. "Fun? You trippin'. We almost got trampled to death!"

My shoulder blades are sore, and there's a cut on my knee,

but overall, I'm okay. More than okay.

"Yeah, but before all that . . . the music, the people, the dancing . . ."

I reach across the seat, slipping my fingers between his. Maybe we needed to touch again, so he could remember the moment. Deep down, I know he felt something the same way I did.

He glances down and snatches his hand away before peering back out the window.

"Yeah, I guess," he mumbles.

There ain't words to describe what it's like to lose your brother or words to describe what it's like to lose your best friend. But if I had to compare it to anything, it would be the heart-crushing disappointment of having the boy you're feeling, the boy who's helped plug up the holes in your heart, snatch his hand away from you and then you realize you never had and never will have a chance with him. I can almost feel my muscles hardening and the memory of our moment passing with a blink.

We ride in silence up Fulton Street, reminding me of all the blocks we marched up, hustling Steph's CD on every corner. And all for what? To get him a deal? Is that really as important as getting him justice? I've been playing games, wasting time . . . while his killer still walks around breathing and free.

The cab pulls up to the corner, and I hop out while Quadir pays the driver. I wrap my arms around my sweatshirt, the late night air almost freezing. Glancing around at the empty corner, I wish more than ever that Steph was here to welcome us home.

"You thirsty?" Quadir asks as the cab pulls off.

I ignore him. Only reason I'm even standing here and not heading home is to make sure Rell makes it back safe. I couldn't face his moms if he didn't.

"Jazz? You okay?"

He touches my shoulder, and I swat him away with a glare. He backs off, crushed.

"Jazz, I'm sorry," he says, flustering. "I ain't mean to confuse you. I just . . . we can't do . . . this. You Steph's sister. It ain't right. And it's not that . . . I just . . . we can't."

I notice he doesn't bring up Ronnie, only Steph stopping him. But I refuse to let his pleading eyes soften me.

"Are you going to help me find out what happened to my brother or what?"

Quadir blinks. "Jasmine . . . I told you . . . it's too dangerous."

A yellow cab pulls up to the corner and Rell hops out, a huge grin on his face.

"Yooooo! Boy, am I glad to see y'all!" He holds his belly with an exhale and daps up Quadir. "I ain't even gonna front, y'all had me mad worried when I couldn't find you outside. I thought it was Reynolds for you kid."

"Reynolds?"

"Yeah, Reynolds Wrap. Like, it's a wrap. Get it?"

Quady shakes his head. "Did you just make that up?"

"Nah, but it's the truth, right?"

Rell heads toward me, arms spread open wide for a hug.

"Don't touch me."

Rell's smile drops and he glances at Quadir. "Yo, what's up with her?"

Quadir stuffs his hands in his pockets.

I don't know where all the rage came from, maybe I've been holding it in since Steph died, but it erupts right on time.

"I want the money you made off my brother," I snap. "All of it."

Their mouths hang open, looking at each other as if wondering if they heard the same thing.

"What?" Rell asks, scratching his head. "All of it?"

"You heard me. We had a deal. And y'all ain't keeping up with your end of the bargain."

Quadir begins with a heavy sigh. "Jazz—"

"You said you would help me find out who killed my brother! But all y'all done is make money off him and party up in the club."

"Party?" Rell says as if the words stank. "Yo, we ain't partying. This all been about business! You even saw—"

"If it's all about business, then you understand the concept of a deal being a deal, right?"

Rell looks plain stuck, and Quadir can't even look me in the eye.

"So looks like you have three options," I say, crossing my arms. "One, you give me my brother's money. Two, you help find his killer. Three, I tell Pierce AND my mom everything, including how y'all swindled a grieving young sister into this bullshit plan of yours."

"Yo, how could you even say that?" Quadir gasps. "Don't front like you don't want this for Steph just as bad as we do. Come on, Jazz, this ain't you."

I don't even feel the cold anymore as I narrow my eyes at him. "You don't even know me."

Rell glances between us and rolls his eyes. "Damn," he mumbles, shaking his head.

Quadir is staring, and it's like looking back at a stranger. Almost as if he's hurt.

Hurt? He has some damn nerve.

He sighs. "Aight. I'll help you."

Rell's mouth drops. "Yo, son, I don't think you . . ."

"A deal's a deal, Rell," he says to him, his voice cold. "You handle the business, and I'll take care of this. Keeping our word to Jazz is keeping our word to Steph." He pointedly looks at me, making it known this is more about my brother than about me. He sure knows how to keep his knives sharp.

Rell rubs his face. "Aight. Just . . . I don't know. Be careful!"

Quadir nods at him and looks at me again.

"Aight, Jazz. Where you wanna start?"

Less than three hours later, I'm dressing for school half sleep when Mom busts in my room.

"Jasmine," she says, standing in her robe, ready for bed

after her overnight shift. "Your bag."

Bag inspection. Ever since she found them CDs she's been checking my book bag like she works for airport security. I sigh, careful not to roll my eyes, and hand it to her.

As she digs through, she says, "This week, I want you to start collecting empty boxes."

"Why?"

"'Cause we need to start packing. We're moving."

"Moving? Moving where?"

"To Mt. Vernon, up in Westchester. We're going to stay with Cousin Karen while I look for a place of our own. She says they'll be an opening at her hospital around Christmas, so we'll move then."

"What? That's only a month away. "I can't leave yet!"

"Why not?"

I think of Steph but hold my tongue.

"Um, school," I hesitate. "Mt. Vernon's like two hours away. How am I supposed to—"

"You'll start school there after the holiday break. Karen's already registered you."

She hands me my bag with a stoic expression. I know what she's doing. This isn't about our safety or starting fresh. This is about Steph and those CDs.

I slip on my bag, holding in my rage, and rush out the door, a timer ticking in my head.

If I don't find out what happened to Steph before we move, will anyone else seek justice or will he just be forgotten?

33
JARRELL

Yo, word to my mummy, I'mma kill Quady if he gets himself murked chasing after ghosts. Ain't no way of knowing what the hell happened to Steph! Not saying I don't want his killer lit up, but . . . damn, son . . . it's risky as fuck.

Jazz is hurting. People don't think straight when they hurting. And when you ain't thinking straight, you bound to make mistakes, y'knowwhatumsayin?

But just in case Jazz try to pull the ole' okeydoke on us, I'm counting all the bread we got so far against our sales numbers. I've been keeping a ledger in the back of one of Steph's notebooks. Yes, a ledger, son! This is a legit business. We making that good money so we gotta keep our shit tight. I keep all the money in Timb boxes under my bed. My system is mad sophisticated. Check it:

Dollars go in the black Timbs box.
Fives and tens go in the wheat Timbs box.
Twenties go in the brown leather Timbs box.
Hundreds go in the army green Timbs box.

See? Who needs a bank?

"Jarrell! You're going to be late!"

"Yes, Mummy!"

I yawn, rubbing the sleep out my eye. I'm tired as hell from last night's party. I don't know how people do it. Party on a Sunday night and go to work the next day. I'm nodding off already, and I'm not even at school.

As I slip the box under my bed, taking one last flip through one of Steph's notebooks. Every time I open one up, I read through some of his old rhymes.

Stupid on a track/but still a

Tutor to y'all cats/ I

Exude the gravitas to snatch fools from offa that/

Pedestal, now you should nap/

High schooler, true I act/

Old school like movin' back, to the future 'cause the fact/ I'm

Not new, I'm two years past,

Use an almanac/
What's my name?
I just spelled it out for you, now do the math!

Damn, I miss him. I know he's up in heaven looking down at us. Wonder if we're doing things the way he wants or is he wild disappointed? Some days, I question if we should be doing this at all. But then I open up his book, and it reminds me how dope he was. Makes no sense for the world not to experience him like we do.

A business card slips out from between the pages of his notebook and falls on the floor near my kicks. I can't bring myself to pick it up, like my brain forgot how to tell the rest of my body to move. All I could do is stare at the NYPD logo in the corner.

"Jarrell! The boys are ready to go to school!"

"Um . . . ye-yes, Mummy. Soon come."

I can't leave it on the floor. If Mummy or the boys find it, they'll have all kinds of questions. Even having it in my house has me shook. Any association with police . . . ain't a good look. But I stick it under my heavy computer monitor, where no one will find it.

"Rell, you ready?" The boys come in, coats, hats, and book bags on. They pile on to me, latching themselves to my legs.

"Uh, yeah. Yeah. Come on, we out."

The boys bust through the front door of the building, racing up the pathway to the first corner, where they'll wait for me to help them cross the street to school. I always drop them off first before heading to the bus. Even if I wasn't running on two hours of sleep, I'm still gonna have a hard time concentrating on anything else but that card.

Detective Paul Vasquez. Of the 79th Precinct.

The card looked worn, faded yellow, like he'd had it for some time. But why? Why would Steph have some cop's business card? What was he doing talking to 5-0? He knew better than to trust cops about anything. What if someone found out he had been talking to one? Maybe that's why he . . .

"Aye yo, J-Money!"

I look up at Mack, pulling up in a sleek black Range Rover.

"Where your head at, playboy? I called your name like ten times!"

"Oh. I, uh, just got a lot on my mind. That's all. What's up?"

"You taking the boys to school?"

"Yeah."

"Hop in, I'll give y'all a ride."

I look at the boys on the corner playing tag with each other and gulp.

"Uh . . . nah, you ain't got to do that."

"No problem. I gotta talk to you anyways. Get in."

I've known Mack my whole life. I trust him. But I ain't stupid. I know what he do to make his bread. And I don't want my little brothers anywhere near that. Not even his car.

"Mack, let me drop my brothers off first," I say, hard so he know I mean business. "It ain't nothing but a block and a half up. And then I'll go with you wherever."

His face changes, like a shadow crosses it, as he nods. Quickly, I hustle over to the boys.

"Come on, y'all. Let's roll!"

I grab both their hands and rush them across Patchen Ave, up to the elementary school, then run back, halfway expecting Mack to be gone. But he's there, sitting where I left him.

"Thanks, man," I say as I hop into the passenger seat.

He gives me a long look then starts the engine. We ride in silence up Fulton, blasting Big's "Ten Crack Commandments." One of my favorite tracks on *Life After Death*. 'Cause it spells out the rules of law for the streets so perfect . . .

Number 9 shoulda been Number 1 to me,
If you ain't gettin' bagged stay the fuck from police

Steph knew these rules as much as I did. So why did he have that card?

"Surprise you got time to grace me with your presence and shit. Heard you been busy in these streets and hanging out in nightclubs."

I swallow my shock and play it cool with a laugh. "Nah, nothing like that."

He glares at me. "Then what is it, then?"

"Just . . . chilling. Making some moves."

He grabs a dutch from the center console, lights up, and offers me a smoke.

"Nah, I'm good," I say. "Can't be walking into school flying high. I can barely concentrate as it is."

Detective Paul Vasquez. Of the 79th Precinct.

"So, looks like you ain't thinking about what we talked about before."

I crack the window and gulp. "I have. Been on my mind heavy, for real."

"How, if you out here hustling?"

"Yo, I ain't moving no weight!"

"You don't think I know that?" he barks. "You think you still be walking if you was? I'd break both of your fucking legs. What I tell you? I know everything, kid!"

The words come out the side of my neck before I could stop them. "If you know everything, then do you know who shot Steph?"

The question pops him upside the head and he blinks twice.

"Man, I told you before, I don't know what happened to duke. Wasn't anybody in B-Voort. And I told you, when I find out, I'll handle that shit myself, word to my mother."

Word to my mother . . . that used to mean something. Mack used to say never say that unless you dead serious. But nowadays, I can't tell. If he knows everything, then why hasn't he called me out about selling Steph's music? If he knows everything, does he know Steph been talking to the 5-0? Who else knows?

"Well, if it's been on your mind heavy," he says, changing topics. "Then what you thinking?"

He pulls up Jay Street, parking a block from school.

I shrug. "I don't know. College . . . just ain't my thang. I don't even like school now. You want me to go do more school? It's just a piece of paper."

He puts the car in park. "Son, I ain't trying to tell you what to do. You a man, you make your own decisions. All I'm saying is . . . you got potential, always have. Don't waste it on stupid shit. That piece of paper gonna get you in the right rooms. And if you need the bread, I got you."

I hesitate at the offer. Nothing comes for free. Everything has a price. I've learned this from Mack.

"How you expect me to pay you back? You know that college shit is wild expensive and ain't like I'mma make the bread back quick."

"Nah, man, it ain't nothing. When you get your business degree, I'mma have you working for me. Legit, though."

"Doing what?"

He shrugs. "Accountant. Lawyer. Maybe run one of my businesses. Who knows? Whatever it is, you got the brains for it. Saw that shit from day one. You the closest thing I got to a brother, and I don't want you letting all that potential go to waste."

I nod, checking the time. "I . . . I gotta get to class."

Mack laughs. "Good. Keep getting them good grades in school and everything. I'll holla at you later. Aye yo, about Steph. I'm serious, don't go trying to handle that shit yourself. You find out anything you come holla at me first. Aight?"

We dap up and I climb out the car. Mack's been pushing this college thing for the past few months. But that one little talk I had with Pierce got me looking at everything different.

You wanna be rich or you wanna be wealthy?

"Here! Take this!"

Ronnie comes out of nowhere, shoving a brown paper shopping bag into my hands.

"What the hell?" I stutter, trying to balance it before everything tumbles out.

"Tell *your* friend I don't want any of his shit no more."

A dusty Valentine's Day teddy bear falls by my kicks. "Why?"

Ronnie cocks her head to the side and chuckles. "He didn't tell you? Quady and I broke up. Nah, let me step back, I dumped his wack ass!"

"Wait, y'all broke up?" I can feel the smile take up my whole face. Why didn't he tell me? This is the best news I've heard in forever.

She narrows her eyes. "Don't get too happy about it. Surprised you don't know. I thought y'all talked about everything."

I dodge her jab with a shrug. "Man, I don't know. Maybe he thought y'all were gonna get back together and didn't want to say something too fast."

Ronnie seems a little surprised by this but then shakes her head. "Nah, Rell . . . I'm . . . we through, that's all. Probably seeing somebody already."

I think of Jasmine and my jaw tightens. Looks like Ronnie's been crying. Face all puffy, eyes swollen. Now I feel bad, maybe she really did care about Quady.

"Aight, look, Ronnie. I'm sorry y'all two are beefing.

But . . . I ain't trying to get between it! Why can't you give this to him yourself?"

"'Cause I hate him! And he ain't here today. He over at that new school, Bishop or whatever."

I blink hard.

"Wh-what?" I say.

Ronnie don't miss a thing.

"Ha! You didn't know about that either, did you?" She laughs. "Says he gonna use the money from y'all little business to go school, then college. He trying to get away from you *and* me."

Now normally, I'm the cool, calm, collected type. Not too much really ruffles my feathers, y'knowwhatumsayin? But this chick right here . . . even her voice irks me. I drop the bag on the ground and brush past Ronnie, heading into school, her laugh echoing behind me.

Breaking up with chicks like Ronnie, that's one thing. But nah, no way Quady would just up and change schools without telling me. And how she know about our business? I know he wouldn't tell that blabber-mouth broad what we up to. Nah, he ain't that stupid.

But love makes you do stupid things. Like ditch your girl-friend and best friend for a different school, talking about college, talking about leaving Brooklyn. Plans that have nothing to do with me or making Steph famous when we supposed to be in this together. Love makes you dumb.

And I know that dumbass better not be falling in love with Steph's sister.

34
Quadir

I hate looking like sheep.

That's the first wack thing I notice about Bishop. Everyone looks the same, dressed in dark-purple polos and khaki pants. I mean, Rell's the flashy fashionable one of our set, but I like having a little swag too. If I go to this school, that'd be impossible.

The hallways are different too. No one's chilling, clowning, spitting bars . . . everyone seems mad pressed to make it to class on time, like some nerds.

Other than that, I really can't find nothing wrong, as hard as I try.

The coach wanted me to do a day visit, shadow one of the other players' schedules and practice with the team so I could get a feel for the school. Everyone's real cool and friendly, even the teachers. All the kids talk about colleges, taking the SAT, scholarships, stuff I don't talk about with anyone back around the way. But they also talk about music, videos, and TV shows. One girl's locker was wallpapered with magazine covers.

After practice, I dap everyone up as we leave the gym and spot her puffs from the door, chilling by the gate. Jasmine grips the straps of her book bag, eyeing each student as if they're about to rob her.

"Hey," I mumble. I told her to meet me here after school.

"Pierce called," she says, her voice mad hard. Guess she's not over last night.

"Oh, word? What he want now?"

She swallows. "He wants Architect and Fast Pace to do a song together."

Feels like someone chucked a basketball right into my stomach. "Shit."

"Yeah. Shit."

I slump against the gate next to her. This game we've been playing has me worn out. The late-night partying, running all over Brooklyn, the pretending, the lying . . .

"I don't know how long we're gonna be able to keep this going. Maybe it's time."

Jasmine nods, seesawing on her heels. "What'd you think Pierce will do?"

"You mean after he throws us out the window?" I chuckle. "Probably come and spray the whole block just to get to anyone we know."

"Guess that's the worst-case scenario."

"Or . . . maybe he'll still fuck with us. Maybe he'll even understand why we did it."

Jasmine looks up at the school and chuckles. "Why did *we* do it, Quadir?"

"Jasmine . . ." I sigh. "You know why."

She stares at me with stone cold eyes. "You ready?"

I didn't want to answer her. I didn't want to go anywhere she had in mind. I wanted to be back in her living room listening to music, hear her sing again. If she only knew how many times I've listened to her track with Steph, just to hear her voice. But a promise is a promise.

"Where are we going?"

She zips up her coat. "Just follow me."

We head toward DeKalb Avenue in silence, Jasmine stomping fast. We're a few blocks from school when she finally opens up.

"How was Bishop?" she asks, her voice still hard.

"It was . . . cool," I admit with a smile. "I kinda like it."

"That's good. You, um, deserve to be happy. Is Ronnie gonna come with you? You know her pops got the money to send her anywhere."

"Nah. It ain't really her . . . thing. Plus . . . we ain't together no more."

Jasmine keeps straight, the corner of her lip twitching as she clears her throat.

"Oh. Really? What happened?"

I shrug. "Things change. So do people."

We walk in silence for a while. I don't know what to say, if anything. I kind of want to talk about us, but the timing don't seem right. Ain't never been this nervous around a girl before. Maybe 'cause she ain't just some girl. She's a whole other level.

"You ever hear of Weeksville?" she asks as we approach a corner.

"You mean that place over by Buffalo Ave, where they give tours of all them old houses from like the 1800s or something? Yeah. Never been, though."

Jasmine smiles at me. "Weeksville Village was made up of seven hundred freed slaves. It was one of the country's first free black communities where blacks owned property and ran businesses. I mean, they had their own schools, churches, newspaper, even an old-folks home."

"Is that where we going?"

"Nah, I just like talking about black history. Anyways, ain't that fly, though? All these black people living together like one big tribe, working in unity, keeping each other safe. That's what my daddy wished B-Voort could be for us. A village, helping one another."

"Maybe we already are."

"If so, then someone would know what happened to my brother. We turning left up here."

We head down a block I don't recognize. I'm not even sure we're in Bed-Stuy. The sun has already faded. If we blink for two seconds it'll be dark.

"Jasmine, where we going? I promised I'd help you, but I ain't about to walk into the valley of the shadow of death, willingly."

"It's just up here, come on."

She walks ahead a bit, and I'm looking over my shoulder when she stops in front of an old prewar apartment in the middle of the block. To the right of it, an abandoned lot, prepping for construction. I wasn't paying attention, to the street signs or nothing. Where the hell are we?

"Back here," Jasmine says, walking down the narrow path between the building and the lot.

"Jazz, hold up!"

I follow her to the back of the building, where she stops, staring at a patch of grass, trashed with chips of concrete, wet plastic bags, and glass beer bottles, the area shaded by tall weeds.

"This is it."

"This is what?" I ask as a ripped piece of yellow plastic ribbon tied to one corner of the building waves at me. I step closer to read it . . . *POLICE LINE. DO NOT CROSS.*

No. She wouldn't. Nah.

"Jasmine . . ."

She takes a deep breath and meets my eye. "This is where Steph died."

35
Jasmine

It's quiet back here. You can barely hear an ambulance or a car horn. A strangely peaceful place for my brother to die.

But in the distance, Big plays out of someone's open apartment window, "Who Shot Ya?" My stomach tenses; the breeze hitting my neck makes my whole body shiver.

Quadir stares at me, his mouth hanging open. "Nah . . ."

"This spot, right here, is where they found him." I keep my voice level. Don't want him to know about the storm inside me. He won't listen to everything I have to say otherwise.

Quadir paces around, circling the perimeter of the grass patch, his fingers tangled together, holding the back of his head, breathing heavy.

"Shit, shit, shit," he mumbles.

I don't fault him. I threw up the first time I came back here alone.

Quickly, I pull the folder I stole from Mom months ago out of my book bag. So in her own world, I'm surprised she hasn't noticed it's gone.

"I read the police report. But even standing here, none of it makes sense."

"Where'd you get that from?"

"Not important. What's important is the details. They said they found Steph behind this building, shot point blank in the chest."

"Jazz . . . I really can't hear this," he says, waving his hands by his ears as if swatting away a fly.

"I mean, the person shot him so close that it couldn't have been no robbery or a random accident. It means he was facing his killer, even to the very end."

Quadir is still pacing, biting his nails. "We shouldn't be here, Jazz. We shouldn't."

"You know how they say, when kids are kidnapped without a struggle, it sometimes means that the kid might've known his capturer? What if that's the same with Steph? What if he knew who the killer was, and that's why he was over here? Steph wouldn't come around here otherwise. We don't have no family over here. No friends . . . technically."

"What you mean by that 'technically'?"

"Remember at the funeral, you said, he was at the studio before he died?"

"Yeah. Funky Slice Studio, downtown."

"I went by there and checked. Steph's never been up in that studio."

His face is a question mark. You could see the wheels turning.

"But . . . you heard that last CD. He had to record it in a studio. The quality was too good!"

I rip one of Steph's old notebooks out my bag and turn to the first page.

"You see this little drawing? That three lines with the snake down the middle, you've seen Steph draw this all the time, right?"

"Yeah."

"I saw this *same* drawing in the booth at Kaven's studio. It was Steph. I know it. And Kaven's studio is only . . ." I turn in the opposite direction and point. "Three blocks that way. It's mad close! If Steph was leaving the studio and heading home, he would've walked this way."

Quadir studies the page. "So . . . what do you think happened?"

I inhale deep. "I think . . . Steph owed whoever he was supposed to sell drugs for money. I think the brotha saw him leaving Kaven's studio and followed him. I think they reached the corner and he approached Steph. Maybe told him he wanted to talk in private. They walked around back here, and then . . . that dude we saw on Coney Island shot him."

It feels good to lay out the story to someone, all the pieces of the puzzle that have been locked inside my head for days.

Quadir sighs, pinching the bridge of his nose with his eyes closed.

"He wasn't selling drugs, Jazz."

"I know, I know! I didn't want to believe it either," I say, walking around him. "But that box under his bed tells another story. Mom was mad stressed about money since Daddy died. He probably was doing it to help us out. Or maybe to pay for time at Kaven's studio to work on his demo. And that's why . . . we have to go to Kaven's studio."

He frowns, scoffing. "What for?"

"Them security cameras . . . one of them must've captured Steph leaving, maybe even catch his killer. I swear Quady, this is gonna work! We'll finally be able to know who killed Steph."

Quady stares at the spot, his eyes filled with sadness. He holds his breath, shaking his head.

"Jazz . . . I have to tell you something."

"What?"

"That bag of jacks we found. They weren't Steph's. They were mine."

He says it so fast I didn't think I heard him right.

"Huh?"

"The crack . . . it was mine," he coughs out, tears in his eyes. "Steph . . . he took them from me I think . . . 'cause he didn't want me getting caught up."

"Took them . . . from you . . . how?"

He doesn't answer. He can't even look at me. That chill I felt before is gone, and I'm on fire. I put so much trust in him. How could he lie to me like this?

"All this time . . . you had me thinking my brother was a fucking hustler, selling that poison . . . and it was you!"

"Jazz, I swear, I was gonna tell you." He reaches for my hands and I snatch them away.

"You got him killed," I whimper.

"What? Nah."

"All that weight, Quady . . . No one gives drugs away for free. You don't get something for nothing. Someone definitely was trying to get paid. Did you . . . tell someone you gave it to Steph?"

"Yo, word on my moms . . . I didn't. And I don't owe nobody nothing."

"Who'd you get them from?"

Quadir straightens. "Come on, Jazz . . . you know I can't tell you that, you know what's up."

"But I tell you everything!"

Quadir flinches, his hands held up in prayer.

"I'm sorry. But I promise, I swear I'll help you find out what happened. 'Cause maybe you right. Maybe he was at Kaven's and he walked this way."

"But . . . if he wasn't selling drugs, why would anyone *want* to kill him?"

"Maybe something else was going on. He had so many secrets." He looks me square in the eye. "Don't we all?"

Something shatters inside me. That protective shell that stopped the thoughts in the back of my head from creeping to the front. The space feels tight, the buildings caving in around us, and I'm suffocating. I gag before I take off running.

"Jasmine! Jasmine!"

"Leave me alone, Quady! Just leave me alone!"

I run. Running from that one dark thought coating my eyes . . .

That maybe it really was my fault he was killed after all.

36
JULY 20, 1998

Jarrell beatboxed on a bench, a slow lazy rhythm, as he observed the scene. They weren't at the B-Voort courts or the nearby park. They were at a different park, deep in the crook of Bed-Stuy.

"Yo, why are we here?" he asked in a low voice. "This place is mad corny."

Quadir set his book bag down on the bench gently as if planting an explosive. He unzipped it, grabbing his water bottle, and rubbed his sweaty hands dry on his new hunter-green basketball shorts with a shrug.

"I'm saying, we always hang at the same spots. Figured we try someplace different."

Steph sets down his identical book bag next to Quady's and bends to retie his sneaker, surveying the perimeter. His pops always taught him to take in his new surroundings no matter if he's in the hood or the boardroom. A car parked nearby provided the day's sound track, a demo by a new artist named Fast Pace. Steph knew he was from around this part of Bed-Stuy, so no surprise he would be played heavy. Picnic tables by the gates were set up for a summer family reunion, the grills smoking, sweet honey sauce filling their noses.

Jarrell snickered. "Yo, you think I can pass as family and cop me a plate of BBQ spare ribs and some rice?"

"They Puerto Rican. You ain't gonna fit in."

"So what? I can salsa! Watch, I'mma do like Tupac did in *Poetic Justice*." He stretched his arms out wide, grinning and with a pitched voice says, "COUSIN!"

Steph laughed from his belly, looking at Quadir to join in. But Quadir was razor-sharp focused on the game being played on the court.

"Quady? You good?"

Quadir didn't smile as sweat ran down his sideburns. They hadn't even been outside an hour yet.

"Yeah," he stuttered. "Why you ask?"

"Um, aight," Steph said, though his gut told him to push further. "You ready to play? Who you know up here? Can't just be rolling up on someone else's turf."

Quadir froze, his eyes widening. "What you mean, someone else's turf?"

Steph chuckled, but the hairs on his neck prickled. "I mean, imagine if some random cats came to B-Voort, trying to jump in. They'd look mad suspect. So . . . you know somebody here, right?"

Quadir gulped. "Um, nah. But, we could just make friends. It's cool."

Jarrell straightened and sucked his teeth. "What? You mean you don't know nobody? Aw, hell nah, we out!"

"Wait, hold up! We just got here."

"You bugging! Got us out here looking scrambling, plotting on people's food and shit."

Steph shook his head. "Rell's right. I ain't with this."

Quadir's heart raced, his hands drenched again. He hadn't thought his plan through fully. He expected his friends to go along with it like they went along with all his ideas. He knew it was selfish, but what he had to do . . . he felt better having them near.

"Just a few more minutes. Or . . . maybe we can ask to play?"

"Yeah, and get *played*," Rell said, hopping off the bench. "Let's bounce. We can play at the courts back home. With OUR peoples."

Quadir glanced over his shoulder, focused on a shirtless brown-skinned brotha in red shorts taking it to the hoop, girls on the bleachers cheering him on.

"Man, forget y'all, then. Never wanting to try nothing new. You go on home if y'all want."

Jarrell shrugged with a laugh, chucking the deuces, and headed for the gate. But Steph noticed the desperation in

Quadir's eyes and the way he kept clocking that one kid on the court.

Following Jarrell, Steph gave the court another once-over, and that's when he saw it. Red Shorts duke giving Quadir a subtle head nod.

But he said he didn't know anyone out here, Steph pondered. Unless he was supposed to find someone. Or they were supposed to find him.

Steph stopped in his tracks, glancing at Quadir's new green shorts. "I know he didn't . . ."

He charged back to the bench, shoving Quadir out of his way.

"Yo, son! What you doing?"

Steph snatched Quadir's bag, ripping it open. Packed at the bottom was a ziplock . . . the crack vials had mini red caps.

He grabbed Quadir by the collar and shouted under his breath. "Son, are you fucking crazy?"

Quadir flustered, his hands up to block a hit. He had never seen Steph so enraged.

"Come on, man," he stuttered. "I ain't doing nothing, just . . . making a delivery."

"Are you stupid? And you bringing me and Rell with you? What if this was a setup? A trap? We could've all gone down!"

"Aight! I'm sorry."

"What the fuck you doing getting wrapped up in this shit?"

Quadir stared at the ground, shame cast upon his face. "It was only supposed to be one time. Just something to make some bread. Son, we *need* it."

Steph could kill Quady. But he knew his friend's heart. He knew he'd sacrifice everything he had for others. Even his innocence.

Steph noticed Red Shorts watching them from the court. He loosened his grip.

"Go home, Quady," he snapped. "Forget this shit. And I'm . . . doing this for your own fucking good."

He grabbed a bag off the bench and stormed off. Once out the gate, Steph passed a cluster of cats chilling by the car with Fast Pace on repeat. That's when he overheard a light-skinned duke in a red tank top and jeans with bad acne say the familiar name that made his heart jump out of his throat.

"Oh yeah, that Rashad kid lived over on Ralph Ave . . ."

Frozen in fear, Quadir watched Steph through the gate, wondering if their friendship could still be salvaged. Would he ever forgive him? Could he even forgive himself? Red Shorts shook his head and kept playing. Too many eyes on him, the dropoff clearly canceled.

Quadir grabbed his bag, noticeably lighter than before, and opened it with a groan.

Steph had switched their book bags.

37
Quadir

All I want to do is dive on the sofa and play *Jeopardy* next to my moms. I'm wrecked. Last person I wanted to hurt was Jasmine. She's been through enough. The look on her face, I swear I'll remember that for the rest of my life.

Rell is on the courts when I make it to B-Voort, and I'm mad happy to see a familiar face.

"What up, son!" I yell from the gate.

He glances over his shoulder and continues shooting his free throw. I must be tripping, 'cause I swear he looks tight. He didn't even crack a smile. Maybe the light just blinded me or something. I'm halfway across the court when I peep his kicks.

"Aye yo, what's that on your feet?"

Rell pivots his foot and grins.

"Oh, these? These are them new Air Jordans XIV."

Those cost a grip, no less than two stacks. How he get the . . .

"Yo son, we're not supposed to be messing with that money yet," I snap. "We agreed—"

"How was your trip to Bishop today?" he asks with a sly grin. "You like it? They treat you right? Team was cool?"

Damn, I didn't have a chance to tell Rell about Bishop yet. Not that I wasn't going to, I just didn't have a chance.

That's a lie, I didn't want to be talked out of it. Deadass, I wanted this decision to be my own.

He rolls his eyes. "Yeah, don't act like you don't have plans for that money too."

"Aight, so I got plans. Ain't like I'm acting on them plans YET! You out here flossing! If Jasmine find out you dipped into that money—"

"Oh yeah, how is Jasmine? I saw her running by here not too long ago, crying. Trouble in paradise?"

I keep my face straight. I don't want him thinking his little game is affecting me.

"Son, I don't know what you talking about."

He bounces the ball. "Man, you out here keeping secrets. Lots of them."

"What's that supposed to mean?"

He chuckles. "Nothing, man. Nothing."

Damn, did Jasmine already tell him about the drugs? He probably hates me too. Seems like everyone does now.

"Anyways, so about this track with Fast Pace," Rell says, throwing another free throw and missing. "They don't have to record 'together.' I'm thinking, how about we let him record first, grab the track, then find some old verse to throw on there. Maybe we could convince them to record at Kaven's. I know it ain't all official like what the celebrities be using, but Pace is from the hood like us. I bet you he'll be down. We can even dress Jasmine up again, take pics of her in the booth. What'd you think?"

The plan sounds . . . mad dumb.

"Rell," I sigh. "I think we need to come clean."

He stops dribbling, shifting the ball under his armpit. "What?"

"Son, the shit is getting too hot! We can't keep this up anymore."

"So after ALL that. All that running up in studios, trekking down Fulton, late nights sneaking, chucking and jiving for some Harlem cat, you just ready to give up? You got the money you need for school, so you good now? Nah, I'm trying to get paid for real! You might be living that good life, but I'm still up in the projects."

It always comes back to this . . . money. "Son, we gonna have to come clean eventually. How long you really think we were gonna be able to keep this up. And Jasmine is—"

"Ohhhh right. Jasmine. Of course," he chuckles, shaking his head. "I knew it had to be some chick. You ain't never been one to think on your own."

I take a step forward, ready to shove the ball down his

damn throat. "Yo, what'd you say?"

"You been creeping on Steph's sister from the moment his body went in the ground, b. You would have never pulled this shit if he was still alive."

Rell's nose is flaring. I've only seen him this mad before once when some kid called him out for wearing fake Tommy Hilfiger shorts to the block party.

"Look, she got nothing to do with this."

"You talking all the hot talk about 'doing this for Steph.' You think this is what Steph would've wanted? Your ass messing with his sister?"

"You think Steph would have wanted you spending HIS money on some fucking sneakers? That's STEPH's money! You didn't make that shit! Steph did. You ain't talented for shit!"

Rell drops the ball, stepping to me, chest puffed out.

"Yeah, well, I'm talented enough to keep this whole operation together while you creeping with my best friend's sister."

"He's my best friend too."

Rell pokes his chin out, straddling his legs, fisting one hand into the other.

"Don't look like it from where I'm standing."

I give him a once-over, my voice reaching a new low. "Oh, word? Well maybe you should take another look."

We stare each other down, inches apart, right in the middle of the courts we played mad games on. My fists tighten. Am I really about to fight my best friend? We already lost Steph, are we about to lose each other too? Rell snorts, shaking his head.

"Yo, this is some fugazi-ass shit," he mumbles. "Got us out here fighting in the cold like some dumb-ass Negros. You running around here like some cocky ass God of Thunder, acting like I'm just some duke in a tin suit."

"What? What the hell you talking about?"

"Thor? Iron Man? The Avengers? Come on, son!" His face loosens up as he glances back at B-Voort. "Yo, when you just gonna come clean and stop lying about what you really want? You wanna be with Steph's sister? Fine. You don't want to be with Ronnie? Fine. You wanna go to some bougie school? Fine. You want to go to college? Fine. But lying about all this shit . . . you ain't keeping it real with anybody."

Too wound up, I swallow, not really knowing what to say.

Rell snatches up his ball and heads for home.

By the time I walk in, *Jeopardy* is over, and Mom has already turned to UPN to watch *Moesha*. She loves singing that theme song: "'Mo to the, E to the . . .'"

"There you are," Mom says, putting a KFC bucket in the fridge. "I thought you were coming home right after school. I've been waiting!"

"My bad, I . . . went for a walk to clear my head."

"You hungry? Want me to heat up the chicken?"

I drop on the sofa, my coat and book bag still on like I have no plans on staying.

"Not really."

Mom is cheesing hard. "So . . . how was it?"

"Huh?"

"Boy, the school . . . Bishop! How was it?"

"Oh. It was aight. I guess."

Mom shuffles across the room, her arms crossed. "Quadir . . . what's wrong?"

There's so much wrong I don't know where to start. "Mom, do you think I'm a liar?"

She doesn't skip a beat. "Yep."

"Damn, Mom. Not you too."

She chuckles. "Quady, you are the king of white lies. Even when you were little and I asked if you wanted seconds, you would say 'no, I'm not hungry,' even though I knew you were. You were always trying to make sure everyone ate first. From your sister to the mice. I mean, do you really think I believe you're sleeping over Jarrell's all the time? I wasn't born yesterday, you know."

Damn, Moms be on it.

She heats up a plate and even though I told her I wasn't hungry, as soon as I see them biscuits, my mouth waters.

"So let me guess, you don't want to go to Bishop. But you going just to make me happy. Am I right?"

I shrug. "Sort of. I mean, it's a good school, and the team is on point. But . . . we ain't got the money."

She sighs and sits beside me. "You always talking this 'we' stuff. I'm the parent here, remember? I'm supposed to take care of you. And if I say don't worry about it, then don't worry about it. Me and your father . . . we always figure something out."

"I know but . . . I ain't blind, though. I can see when we hurting."

Mom sucks in a breath, faking a smile. "I know. And it's one of the things I love best about you. You lie to protect people's feelings, thinking you know what's best for them. But do you ever think that maybe telling the truth works just as well?"

I think about the lies I told Jasmine and stuff my mouth with mashed potatoes.

"So what do I do?"

"You need to start being straight with people. The truth will get you farther and faster than lying. 'Cause every lie gotta be followed up with another lie, and sooner or later you lose count."

38
August 22, 1998

Under the cover of darkness, Jasmine was a shadow among shadows, stealthy with her moves through the back paths of B-Voort. Hair braided down, covered by a thin hoodie, she returned from her evening excursion unscathed, until she reached the front door.

"Where you been?" a deep voice echoed in the courtyard.

"Shit," she screamed, jumping out of her skin.

Steph sat perched on the back of a bench like a black owl, his hands folded.

"I—I went to a concert," she stammered.

Steph twisted his lips. "Really, Jazz? You gonna straight up lie to me?"

She knew she was busted. She could lie to the world, but not to the one person who could see right through her.

"I—I was . . . with a friend."

"A friend got you out at three in the morning?"

"He's not that—"

"He!"

"Nah, Steph. Not like that! He's a part of this . . . group."

Steph measured the weight of the words she used to circle around the truth. "What group?"

She takes a deep breath. "The Guerrillas."

"The Guerrillas? You trying to be one of them? You crazy?"

"Steph, they all about black empowerment and . . ."

"Jazz, no!"

"But they understand me."

"I understand you!" he barked.

"No, you don't! You don't know what it's like . . . to be different than everybody else. To have people tease and call you names, telling you to go back to Africa . . ."

"Man, think about what you saying right now. That's what gangs do! They make you feel like you one of them, that no one understands you but them. That's the mind games they be playing. That's what Dad always said about them."

"Yeah, and then he got killed, and no one did anything about it! Everything he did, he did solo. No one had his back! At least being with them . . . I'll have my peoples. I won't be alone."

Steph snapped his mouth closed, noticing the crack in her

voice. He pressed his hands together as if in prayer.

"Jazz, look me in the eye and tell me you really want to do this."

She crossed her arms, stomping her foot a few times, her chest tight with frustration. "Damn it."

Sinking down on the bench next to him, she leaned her head on his knee, holding in a sob. Steph patted his little sister's head lovingly. She was one of the few people in this world he would take a bullet for.

"They want me to fight . . . this girl. Like, some kind of strength test." She looked up at him. "I can't just . . . drop out. I already started the process."

Steph sighed, looking up at the sky, up at his pops, searching for the star he lived upon.

During a class trip to the Liberty Science Center, Steph learned about light pollution and how all the bright lights in the hood prevented folks from seeing the millions of stars in the sky. He imagined himself running around the hood with a bat, snuffing out streetlights, just for one night, so that everyone could see what they'd been missing.

He would be a hero. Just like his pops.

"Don't worry, Jazz. I'mma fix this."

"How?"

Steph gently wiped one of her tears away. "Don't worry about it. Just . . . just stay away from them for now. Aight?"

He stretched up to the sky and climbed off the bench.

"Where you going?

"I'mma have a talk with them. Set them straight."

"Steph . . . don't . . ."

"You trust me, right? Then trust me. Everything's gonna be okay."

Steph marched off, passing the bodega, palming the business card in his pocket.

39
Jasmine

Sometimes I stare at the corner by the bodega, squint, and can see Steph standing there, the same spot he always chilled at. I exhale, thinking, it was all a dream! Then I wake up to the nightmare that he's really gone.

The hood is quiet on Black Friday night. Everyone's still out buying up the stores. I hope folks are supporting some local black businesses. We shouldn't even be celebrating Thanksgiving, some holiday to commemorate the Indians saving white people from starvation and in turn they "thanked" them by slaughtering their tribes, stealing their land, and poisoning the earth.

"Don't be a hard rock, Jazz. Let them have their fun."

That's what Steph would say. I would give anything to hear him say those words to me now. Maybe I'd listen and stop taking life so seriously. Everybody's human; we all make mistakes. We all want to let loose and have fun.

Even me.

Quadir walks out his apartment in his bubble coat and knit hat, crossing the street toward my direction. I hold my breath as he stops a few feet away.

"Hey," he mumbles, hands stuffed in his pockets.

"Hey."

"Been watching you for a while out here by yourself. My mom is working a double, and if I eat any more leftovers, I'mma bust. Can I . . . keep you company?"

I wipe my face and stay silent.

"Please, Jazz, please. I . . . really need to talk to you. I *miss* talking to you. You the only one I really wanna talk to, all the time."

There's a sadness in his voice that I can't fight. I shrug and scoot over. He sits on the back of the bench, staring at the bodega with me in silence.

"I'm sorry I didn't tell you about that weight and had you thinking different about your brother. That was mad foul. I never wanted to hurt you."

I still can't look at him. As much as I want to.

"You were right, though," I say with a sniff. "Steph . . . had a lot of secrets. Secrets he kept from us to keep us safe."

"Always playing 'Captain Save-a-Hoe,' as Rell would say,"

Quadir chuckles, swinging his knees left to right. "Can I be honest with you about something?"

"Sure."

He sighs and rubs his head. "I got that weight from Mack."

"What? Why would you do that?"

"I . . . I don't know. Mom lost her job, Ronnie was breathing down my neck, and well . . . I guess I thought it was the only way."

"But you know what that stuff does to our communities!"

"Yeah, I know. But if I had to pick between helping to feed my family or nah . . . I can't say I wouldn't make the same choice again. It's real out here, Jazz."

I think about the lyrics in so many hip-hop songs and understand why Steph made me listen to them. Life has never been easy for black folks, and survival means doing things you wouldn't normally. Can I really judge someone trying to live?

"Does Rell know?"

"Nah. Only Steph," he sighs. "He tried to talk me out of it, and I guess he took matters into his own hands. But I swear, Jazz, I swear on everything, I squared up my debt . . . with Ronnie's help. She's the one who gave me the bread. No one knew Steph took that weight from me, so it couldn't have been no retaliation. Deadass, I thought Steph flushed that shit down the toilet. That's why I was so shocked when we found it under his bed. I started thinking, maybe he stole it to start selling it himself. But nah, Steph ain't like that." He shakes his head. "Still, I would never be able to live with myself . . . if he got hurt because of me."

The tears come up so fast I can't stop them and I sob into my coat sleeve.

"Jazz, what's wrong?"

"It's my fault. It's all my fault!"

Quadir hops off the back of the bench to sit beside me, rubbing my arm. "Hey, stop crying. It's aight!"

"Steph found out I was trying to join the Guerrillas. He said it was too dangerous and that Daddy would never approve of me being in a gang. I told him they wouldn't let me go so easily, and Steph said he would handle it. Now . . . he's dead and I'm afraid I had something to do with it."

"Nah, Jazz. The Guerrillas ain't about killing black people. Even I know that."

"But what if he went to talk to them and things went bad?" I whimper, my body feeling heavy. "I'm sorry, Quady. I'm sorry I got my brother and your best friend killed. My mom is a mess . . . everything's all fucked up, and I don't know what to do."

He wraps an arm around my shoulders and I sob into his chest.

"Shhhh . . . it's not your fault, Jazz. For real, it ain't. None of it. Who knows how it all really went down?"

I'm shaking, and he wraps another arm around me, pulling me closer.

"It's gonna be alright, Jazz. I'm gonna get us out of this shit with Pierce . . . so we can just get our lives back to normal.

Then, we're gonna find out who killed Steph. I promise."

I look up at his bright brown eyes, staring down at me, flickering over my face, and a calm melts over me, remembering how safe I feel in his arms.

"Okay."

He leans his forehead against mine and exhales through his nose as if he had been holding his breath for years. His hands are fire through my coat, palming my back as my legs slide over his thighs. When our lips touch, I grasp his neck to pull him closer. I didn't want some gentle peck. I want to re-create the pulse that scorched all my nerves back at the Tunnel. Hot, ragged breath, sweet tongues, and sweat.

He pulls away slowly, mouthing "wow," and I'm dizzy. We look around, relieved we're still alone.

"Can I be honest with you about something else?"

"Sure."

He squeezes me a little harder. "I've been wanting to kiss you for mad long!"

I laugh. "Dag, someone's on an honesty kick tonight."

He blushes. "Nah, you just gotta keep it real with the real ones."

"Yeah, I know what you mean."

We stare at each other, everything feeling different and the same.

"Yo, is your mom home?" he asks.

"No."

"Can we . . . go up to your place?"

My stomach sinks and I wiggle in his arms. "Um . . . Quady . . . I'm not ready for . . . all that."

He jumps, eyes going wide. "Oh, nah! Nah, only when you're ready. I mean, you know, that's if we . . . I mean . . . it's just . . . it's brick out here, and I kinda wanna listen to some Lauryn."

40
JARRELL

That Monday after Thanksgiving break is when everybody comes to school in the new outfits they copped during those crazy Black Friday sales. Fresh Timbs, bubblegoose, ski goggles, Pelle Pelle, and FUBU sweatshirts.

But all this fighting with Quady has my stomach leaning. I ain't even want to shop. Picture that? Me? Not hitting them stores with the crazy half-off stickers. I couldn't even roll out of bed that morning.

It's been six days, the longest we've gone without speaking.

I sit in the back of the library 'cause I don't want them teachers beating me in the head about eating around the books, but snacks are the only things keeping me calm.

Quady and I usually spend fourth period study hall chilling in the hallways, but I heard he's been meeting with guidance counselors, trying to get his transcripts and stuff ready for his transfer. Duke is really about to up and leave me with no warning.

Like Steph.

Steph is different, though. Steph was taken from us on some thief-in-the-night-type ish. Quady still among the living. He's still my boy, no matter how stupid he's acting right now.

"But did you listen to track number seven? Son is ill with it!"

My ears perk up at two kids talking at the table in front of me. I recognize one from my English class. His name is Jabari. I've seen him carry around Nas tapes, so I trust his taste.

"Which track seven? On volume one or two?" the other kids asks. He's holding Steph's demo, popping the CD into his Discman.

"Two. One got them bangers, but two . . . he puts in that work."

He stares at the CD cover. "Son is like a lyrical genius, b."

"Word."

Wow, they calling Steph a genius? Giving him five mics in *The Source* magazine and he don't even have a real album out yet?

"I mean, I ain't never heard anything like him," Jabari says, with that type of smile that makes it hard to stay angry. "No disrespect to Biggie, but this kid is really from the projects like me, he understands. I can't wait to seem him live. I'mma break the bank!"

"Even got my pops listening to him," the other kid says. "My pops mad old school but says he sounds like a young Melle Mel, from Grandmaster Flash and the Furious Five, the way he be talking about the hood and stuff."

I slowly put away my second Twinkie. Besides me, Jazz, and Quady, I've never really heard anyone talk about Steph's music like this before. Yeah, Pierce be talking, but he be gassing us up, just so he can make a dollar. This talk is different. This is what the streets are saying about him. It's like, they really feeling him. The same way we always have.

"And that line about snitching . . . I can't even front, son has a point. 'If you keep being quiet, you only a chain on the neck of violence with your silence.' Yo, he talking about being an accessory to murder, son."

"Son is the truth."

"You think he's gonna get signed soon?"

"No doubt. He could be on any label he wants right now. Bad Boy, Def Jam, Interscope, even Red Starr."

"Anyone know who he is yet?"

"Nope, definitely from Brooklyn, though. He talks about Brevoort all over the tracks. But no one knows who he is."

He chuckles. "He's on his Clark Kent, Superman ish."

Jabari laughs. "Or Spider-Man."

"Nah, Batman," I say.

They both turn to me, shocked by my eavesdropping.

"Huh?" Jabari says while the other kid grills me.

"See, Superman, he's an alien," I explain while packing up my bag. "And Spider-Man got them silly strings. Plus, Spider-Man's from Queens—don't disrespect homie like that. But Batman, he's just a regular-shmegular everyday brotha doing extraordinary things for Gotham. He proves that you don't need no special powers to save the city. You just gotta have heart. Y'knowwhatumsayin?"

Jabari and the kid glance at each other as if I'm speaking Spanish.

"Uhhh . . . yeah. Aight."

They turn back like I said nothing, never knowing they just changed the game for the kid.

Quady shoots from the free-throw line. His bubble coat is so bulky he can barely lift his arms.

"Yo son, you look like the black marshmallow man out here," I call from the gate.

He gives me a cold stare. "That's not what your momma called me last night."

"Damn, son," I laugh. "We going for 'yo momma jokes' now? What are we, nine?"

He shrugs, holding back a laugh. "Sometimes you gotta keep it old school."

We meet in the middle, standing like two dukes who don't know each other. Noses dripping, hands ashy, ice blowing down our necks.

"Winter didn't waste no time."

"Nah, not at all," he says, stuffing his hands in his pockets. "Thanks for coming. So . . . yo, my bad about . . . everything."

"Nah," I say. "My bad, son. I was letting the bread get to my head."

"No, it was on me. I wasn't being real with you. About a lot of things. We better than that."

I pause. "So we just gonna keep apologizing to each other all night or what?"

Quady cracks a smile and daps me up. "Man, shut up."

We stroll over to a bench with the best view of B-Voort. Folks already started stringing Christmas lights in their windows. The projects can dress up nice when it wants to.

"I ain't gonna front: I never thought we'd make it this far," Quady says. "I mean, I thought we'd sell a few CDs, make a few dollars . . . but this? Steph in *Vibe*, on the radio, people at Red Starr trying to sign him . . . this shit is wild, b. I never imagined dreams really coming true for kids like us. Made me start looking at things different, you know. Like actually going to college, becoming a writer, moving out of B-Voort."

"Oh, word? That's what you want to be? A writer?"

He nods, like he just came to grips with it. "Yeah. Yeah, I do."

"That's what's up, man."

"What about you?"

"Me? I'm actually thinking about getting into the music business. Not on the mic, though. Nah, I want to be one of the big wigs calling the shots in the boardrooms."

"That's what's up, Rell! I think you'd be good with that."

"Really?"

"Yeah. You called it. You the one who kept the whole operation together. We wouldn't be here without you."

"The appreciation is appreciated," I say with a head nod. "So what we do now?"

Quady sighs. "I meant what I said, though. We ain't gonna be able to keep this up for much longer. I think we should come clean."

"Yeah. And if they don't like us . . . well, fuck it. We'll keep it going. Not for the bread, but for Steph. The world needs our man's music."

Quady smiles so bright it looks like another light in the hood. "Word."

"You hungry? Mummy made some curry goat. You probably know already since you were with her *last* night."

41
Quadir

In the morning, Jarrell drops off the twins and cops us two bacon-egg-and-cheeses on a roll from the bodega as we head to the subway, hopping on an express train to Manhattan.

"So what's the plan?" I ask, holding on to the pole as the train sways.

Rell squirts some ketchup on his sandwich and stuffs his face. "Ain't no plan. Just gonna tell him the truth. Straight up."

"You a brave man."

"Nah, I'm shooker than a mutherfucker."

We rush out the subway, through Times Square, and enter the lobby of Red Starr Entertainment.

Rell presses the elevator as I mentally ready myself. This is it. We're finally gonna tell him the truth. Maybe it won't be too bad. I can live without my legs. I think.

Fletch leads us into Pierce's office, where it's a full house, and my feet turn into bricks as soon as I see who's sitting on the sofa.

"Um, Mr. Williams . . ."

Pierce glance up at us from behind his desk.

"Ah! Right on time, just how I like it. Y'all didn't get a chance to meet at the party the other night. Fast Pace, meet Beavis, Butthead, and . . ." He searches behind us. "Aye. Where's Architect?"

Fast Pace smirks at us, turning to the two brothas on his right. Something's real unsettling about the way they measuring us up.

"Um, that's what we're here about," Rell stutters. "We got something to tell you . . . in private."

Pierce closes his eyes, pointing at the ceiling. "Yo, don't even try to tell me you comin' up in here without my artist. Fletch, call 911. Somebody's gotta die!"

Rell starts to panic. "Yo hold up, if you—"

"Relax, boss. Ain't nothing," Fast Pace says, his voice real smooth, like he just finished smoking some lah. "I'm good. I ain't gonna do the song with homeboy anyways."

"What?" Pierce snaps, pissed as hell. "Why the hell not?"

He stands up and stretches as if he's rolling out of bed. "I got a reputation to keep, and word on the street is . . . this nigga Architect is a snitch."

Rell shakes the water out his ears. "Aye, what'd you just say?"

Fast Pace grins, only facing Pierce, his hands behind his back.

"Yo, the brotha's been on the Feds' payroll for a grip. A lot of cats in jail because of this mutherfucker. I ain't trying to be next."

Rell charges, and I have to push my full body weight against his chest to stop him.

"Wah di rass!" Rell screams. "Yo, bredren. Meh nah no infahmah!"

Everyone stares blankly.

"Wh . . . what did he just say?" Pierce asks the room.

"I believe he said he's not an informant, meaning not a snitch," Fletch says proudly. "It's Jamaican Patois."

"Good looking out, b," Rell says, slapping Fletch on the back. "My bad, got a little carried away."

"Not for nothing," Fast Pace says to Pierce. "If I was you, I wouldn't sign homeboy. Not on no hip-hop label. He'd probably have your whole roster in the pen."

What's his problem? Where's all this coming from?

"Mr. Pierce," I say, jumping in. "I don't know where duke is getting his information from, but he's wrong. Step . . . I mean, Arch . . . he wouldn't do nothing like that. There's some codes you just don't break."

"Snitches get stitches where we from. Everybody knows that," Rell spits, turning to Fast Pace. "And we don't snitch for nobody, word up!"

Fast Pace chuckles, amused by something unknown.

Pierce bounces from me to Fast Pace then Rell and Fletch before sucking his teeth.

"Well, where this mutherfucker at to defend himself? All this talk and he ain't even here!"

Fast Pace glances at us, crossing his arms with a smirk. "Aye yo, I'mma take it a step further," he says. "I'm not sure if I wanna be down with a label that rocks with snitches!"

Fletch mouths an "oh shit" as Pierce grabs his chest. Either he's having a heart attack or trying to keep the Hulk from busting out.

"Son, you gonna do me like that? You gonna do RED STARR. . . like that?"

Fast Pace laughs. "Nah, it's all good, boss man. Word on the block is the kid is good as dead . . ." He gives us a hard look. "If he ain't dead already. But if he ain't . . . there may be some things I have to reconsider. That's all."

The room turns cold, and I'm having a hard time keeping my mouth closed. I turn to Rell, looking just as stunned.

He knows? But how?

"Shit," Pierce mumbles, pacing around his office. Fast Pace and his boys don't take their eyes off us, and I'm wondering how we're going to make it back to Brooklyn without getting killed.

"Um, sir," Fletch starts off timid. "I'm sorry, but you have a meeting in the next five minutes."

Pierce ignores him, fixated on his television, still set to MTV, playing DMX's "Get at Me Dog" video, shot in the

Tunnel. It was the first time people really saw how popping the spot could be. Everyone was trying to go after that.

Pierce nods, a thought coming to him as he rubs his chin. "Yeah . . . that can work. Word."

He turns to the room, smiling. "We gonna have a battle!"

"A what?"

"A Brooklyn emcee battle. Fast Pace vs. the Architect. At the Tunnel, TONIGHT!"

Fletch drops his clipboard. "Um, sir. Opening the club up on a weekday, paying the DJs, the bouncers, the promoters . . . that's . . . that's going to cost a lot of money."

"Put it on Red Starr's tab. I ain't worried, what we'll make at the door, the night will pay for itself."

Fletch nibbles on the top of his pen.

Fast Pace sucks his teeth. "Man, I ain't gonna do a song and dance to prove myself."

"Pace, you haven't done the Tunnel yet, right?" he says, reasoning with him. "Well, neither has Arch. We'll put you both on, boxing-match style. Whoever wins, wins it all."

"What you mean?"

"If you win, I won't sign him. If Arch win, I keep you both on . . . and there won't be no problems. Right?"

Fast Pace cocks his head to the side to look at us and laughs. "Yeah, aight."

"Cool. Now, I'mma get to this meeting. Fletch, get Funk Flex on the phone, tell him the plan. Then call all the promoters around the city. This shit is going to be popping! Y'all can see y'all way out."

"Wait, but—"

Rell grabs my arm, eyes shooting over to Fast Pace. He's right—we can't play ourselves in front of him.

Pierce rushes out the room with Fletch close on his tail. I'm ready to sprint back to Brooklyn when Fast Pace and his boys step in front of us, his lips curled up.

"So how long y'all gonna keep up with this little game you got going on?"

Rell glances at me quick but keeps up the act.

"What game? Man, I don't know what you talking about. And I don't appreciate you calling my homeboy a snitch!"

Fast Pace smirks then digs into his pocket, pulling out a tape recorder. He holds it in the air and presses play. Steph's voice fills the room, his raw vocals from the song we mixed with Jasmine. But it's a verse we never heard before . . .

OK, OK
Single me out
'Cause I say what they don't say
This single be out
But watch all day they play
On the radio
'Cause Holmes, hate don't pay—

My stomach smacks the concrete forty floors below. Rell's eyes almost drop out of his head. He has the original recording. But . . . how?

"Where did you . . . where . . ."

"I wouldn't worry about that, playboy," Fast Pace says, stuffing the tape back in his pocket.

Out of nowhere, Rell charges full speed into Pace, knocking him to the floor, and the room explodes.

"What the fuck!"

"Aye yo, chill! Easy!"

"Get off!"

"I got him! I got him!"

Two quick jabs to the gut by his boy and Rell slumps, rolling up into a ball.

"Rell, you good?" I whisper, and he moans back as Fast Pace's boys help him to his feet.

"You fucking dummy!" Fast Pace barks with a swift kick to his ass. "You lucky we up in here with all these cameras and not on the block." He turns to me. "Yo, I don't know what kind of game y'all playing but if your boy *is* still alive, he better watch his back. Word is, people from the strangest places are looking for him as we speak. Ain't no place safe. Not even home."

He nods and calls over his shoulder with a laugh as he leaves. "See y'all tonight!"

My ears pop as I walk through the revolving door. My whole brain feels like it's ready to pop, too. Even outside I can't seem to breathe right. Back and forth, back and forth . . . I'm pacing, my heart power-drilling against my chest.

"Yo, what the fuck was that?" Rell cries, leaning up against the wall on the corner, recovering.

"I don't know. But Fast Pace knows *everything*!"

"How? We were careful! Did you tell anyone?"

"Nah, you?"

"Hell no! What do we do? Fast Pace probably running his mouth and I ain't with going back to Brooklyn not knowing what we about to walk into."

So much happened in a matter of a few minutes . . . I need to think.

I pace in a circle as Rell stares up at the clouds. Snitching, the original tape . . . it all has to be connected somehow.

"Yo, where you think he got all that snitching stuff from?" I ask.

"Beats me." Rell leans against a car parked nearby. "Wait . . . in one of Steph's notebooks. He had a business card. For a detective."

I snap my fingers. "And those cops that hemmed us up, they were asking about him!"

"So you think . . . you think he really was a snitch?" Rell is hurt just by the thought.

"I don't know," I say honestly. "We should start there. Call that cop and find out what he knows."

Rell nods, cursing under his breath. "Aight."

We head for the train, dragging. Feels like we failed and I don't even know how. I knew eventually folks would find out about Steph . . . but not like this.

"Not for nothing, but a rap battle competition . . . at the Tunnel," Rell says, grinning. "Steph would've smashed that shit."

"No doubt. Easily would've come home the champion." I laugh. "Aye yo, why you attack Pace like that? Were you trying to get us killed?"

Rell shrugs with a smirk, slipping the tape out his pocket. "How else was I gonna cop this?"

"Son! You a genius!"

"Man, I didn't think that'd work, for real, for real! Can't believe they didn't cap my ass for . . ." Rell stops short, grabbing my arm. "Wait . . . if cats think Steph's still alive like Fast Pace was saying, and they looking for him . . . then they'd go to the one place they'd know where to find him." He looks at me. "B-Voort."

I stare at him until it hits me. "Oh shit, Jasmine!"

42

Jasmine

The best part about going to school so close to home is in less than ten minutes, I can be inside my warm room, listening to that new Brand Nubian album. And in this cold, you don't want much more than that.

My hair is cornrowed half up and the rest pulled into my regular two puffs. Quadir says he likes my natural hair, thinks it's fly. They should be done with their meeting with Pierce by now. It's over. No more secrets. No more pretending my brother is still alive. And Quadir and I, we're . . . something. Nothing official, no titles or nothing like that yet. But it's the start of something beautiful.

They'll probably come straight to my crib after. Maybe I should pick up their favorite snacks from the corner store. Or maybe . . .

"Hey, Jasmine!"

The voice comes from the passenger seat of a green Dodge Neon with tinted windows, rolling slowly next to me. The brotha's brown locks are twisted into two french braids. He knows my name . . . but why don't I know his? And how long have they've been following me?

"You Jasmine, right?" he says, the crook of his mouth pulled up into a half smirk.

I stare back at him, the car too dark for me to see the driver. Did something just move? Is someone in the back seat?

"What? You don't remember me?" Guy with the brown dreads says, all sweet.

I don't. And I'm pretty good with names and faces. I would've remembered those hazel eyes.

"What you want?" I ask, putting some bass in my voice so I don't sound shaky.

"Yo, come here for a second."

Inside the car, hanging off the rearview mirror is a leather medallion . . . a gift you receive when you join the Guerrillas. The block isn't empty. There's a few pockets of kids around, walking home. But I never felt more cold and alone.

"Nah," I say, walking away, arms pumping. If I run, they may hop out and grab me. And I doubt anyone would help if I scream. I just need to make it closer to B-Voort. Then, I can dip and disappear in one of the buildings.

The car crawls beside me. "Jasmine? Yo, Jasmine? We just wanna talk."

Breathing hard, I'm a few feet from the bodega when the car revs its engine and takes off. It skirts around the corner and stops, cutting me off in the crosswalk. Four brothas hop out.

"Jasmine," Brown Dreads says, all the sweetness in his voice gone, a dark shadow across his face.

I take two steps back into the wall with a gasp, my muscles already sliding down to my feet. Once I faint, I'll be an easy wet noodle to throw in the trunk of their car. Life wasn't flashing before my eyes or nothing, but I did note the last place I would've been seen alive is the same corner my dead brother chilled at.

The bell on the bodega door jingles. Ronnie and her girls come out, sucking on red and green Blow Pops, dressed in bubble jackets. They gather right between me and the brothas, giggling to themselves when Ronnie notices me on the wall. She frowns, eyes ping-ponging between me and the brotha by the car.

"Hold up," she mumbles to her girls. "Yo, Jasmine. You good?"

I don't answer, too afraid to speak or take my eyes off the brothas for one second.

Ronnie measures me before turning to them.

"Y'all lost?" There's a bite in her voice. Her girls straighten, tuning in.

Brown Dreads raises an eyebrow. "Nah, we straight."

"Then what's the problem?"

"Ain't no problem," he snaps. "This ain't none of your business, so step."

Ronnie squares her shoulders, her girls doing the same, rounding on either side of her, forming a wall between us.

"Nah, son," she says. "I'll stay."

Brown Dreads rolls his eyes. "Look, we here to holla at Jasmine. Ain't no problem. We just want to make sure she's making the right decision."

"And you need four grown MEN to do that?" she snaps. "Y'all know how wack y'all look right now? Stepping to a girl like this?"

Brown Dreads takes a deep breath and moves closer to her. "Look, I ain't gonna tell you again. Go on home and mind your fucking business."

Ronnie cups her mouth and makes a distinct birdcall sound. Within a minute, brothas are popping out of cars and hopping off benches in the courtyard . . . walking in our direction, hands tucked in their jacket or behind their backs as if reaching for their gun. The wide circle surrounding us slowly shrinks as they inch closer, like lions creeping in on their prey.

The three brothas by the car watch them approach, fidgeting. Brown Dreads glances over his shoulder and the driver shakes his head at him.

Ronnie crosses her arms, her neck rolling. "Like I said, I'll stay. But my pop's peoples may wanna holla at you."

Brown Dreads smacks his lips, glaring at me. "This is what you really want, then?"

The first of the lions reach us, standing in front of Ronnie. "Ma, is there a problem?"

Ronnie smirks at Brown Dreads. "Nah, I think we good. Right?"

He looks at me again. "Yeah," he mumbles, backing toward the car.

"Don't come around here again."

"We ain't," he says, glaring at me. "And she better not come sniffing around us either."

I clutch my chest, holding Daddy's medallion tight like a lifeline as the brothas hop in their whip and drive off.

Ronnie's room is not that much different than mine. The gold daybed with a white ruffle comforter set sits up against a pink wall layered with posters cut out of *Word Up!*, *Vibe*, and *Right On!* magazines. All women. Lil' Kim, Mary J. Blige, Total, Aaliyah, Foxy Brown, Monica, and Brandy. I notice a Lauryn Hill poster in the corner and smile.

"You want a drink?" she asks, pouring some Alizé into a blue plastic cup.

"No thanks," I say, trying to keep the disgust out of my voice.

She chuckles and pours a cup. "Here."

I hold my breath and take a sip. It doesn't burn like the drink Pierce gave me in the club, but it does sizzle over my fried nerves.

"Thanks," I whisper.

She picks up a see-through neon-blue rotary phone off her

desk and dials a number. The closed door muffles the music playing in the living room.

"Hi, Ms. Gray. It's Ronnie. Good . . . is Quadir there? Oh okay, well, could you just tell him to hit up me AND Jasmine back at my crib? Okay. Thanks." She hangs up and shrugs. "He'll call us back."

"Oh," I mumble, fidgeting with my coat as I stand. "Well, I should probably get home."

She sucks her teeth. "Girl, sit down. You can't be in these streets alone. Whoever those fools were probably know where you live. So you might as well just wait for Quady and Rell."

Wait for Quady . . . here? I rather take my chances outside.

"Uh. Okay. Thanks."

"Yeah, whatever," she mumbles, rolling her eyes. "You know how to play spades?"

"Um . . . no."

"Come on," she huffs up from her chair. "I'll teach you. Pay attention, though."'

In the living room, it's a party. The stereo on HOT 97. A card table set up with four chairs. Girls scattered around, drinking and smoking weed. I recognize some from school and some from around the way, but none of them have ever been cool with me. Ronnie takes a seat, pulling a stool up next to her.

"Watch first, then I'll teach you."

I give her a sharp nod. I have no interest in this game, but I should at least act grateful after she saved my life.

Ronnie looks across the table and nods at Tamika Hawkins,

shuffling a deck before dealing.

"How many books y'all want?" Chanté Williams asks, writing team names on a torn piece of loose-leaf paper.

"Hmmm . . ." she says. "I got five. What you got, Tasha?"

La'Tasha Mayes studies her cards. "I got four, easy."

"Aight. Don't be reneging like last time."

"Damn, I said my bad," she laughs.

I grip the cup and take a longer sip. Not trying to make drinking a habit, but the unfamiliar faces make me nervous.

"So . . . who were them Negros out there?" La'Tasha asks as they start to play.

"I don't know." It ain't a lie but it ain't the whole truth either.

"They knew you. Your face was about to be on the back of a milk carton."

"Tasha, leave her alone," Ronnie says with a smirk.

There she goes again, saving me. She's being really nice. She must not know about me and Quady yet.

"If I didn't say it before, thank you . . ." I offer. "And . . . I'm real sorry about you and Quady."

The rooms goes silent, eyes staring at Ronnie. Shit, why did I say that?

Ronnie doesn't even spare me a glance, tossing out another card.

"Whatever. That fool ain't shit anyways," she mumbles. "And are you paying attention? You better not ask a whole bunch of questions when it's your turn."

The girls whip their heads around.

"Wait, you don't know how to play spades?" Tamika asks, almost dropping her cup.

"Oh snap, we'll teach you," Chanté says. "Aight, ready? First, dealer gives us cards and we each have to write down how many books we think we could win, based on the hand dealt. Dealer goes first, puts down the first card, then we each gotta put down a card from the same suit. Hearts for hearts, diamonds for diamonds, nah mean? Whoever has the highest card wins the book."

Ronnie throws a king of diamonds on the table. Everyone throws out diamond cards, and she collects. King being the highest, the book is won.

"Spades is the highest of all the suits. Jokers are wild," Chanté says. "And if you can't play a card from the suit, you gotta play whatever you got, but if you want to win the hand, you throw out the spade."

"And what's reneging?"

"That's when you play a card from another suit when you could've played the right suit," Ronnie says. "Like playing a heart when you should've played the diamond you had."

"Girl," La'Tasha says, pouring herself another drink, "how you black and don't know how to play spades? That's like . . . the law?"

"Ooo! Y'all hear that?" Ronnie says, her shoulders bopping. "Chanté, turn that up!"

Chanté jumps over to the stereo raising the volume on Lil' Kim's "Crush on You."

The girls sing along hard, like they trying to be rappers.

"Aye yo, Jasmine," Tamika says, throwing out a ten of clubs. "Who's your favorite? Lil' Kim or Foxy Brown?"

I say it extra fast. "Psst. None of them."

The table glares at me.

"You serious?" La'Tasha asks, seeming hurt. "What you got against Kim?"

"Or Foxy?" Tamika snaps.

I shrug, taking another long sip. The alcohol has me talking reckless.

"I mean, they only getting all this attention 'cause they dressing half-naked and rapping about sex. They'd be nothing if they covered themselves up for a change."

Ronnie cocks her head to the side. "So what? You rather them dress in kente cloth, grow dreadlocks, and rap about herbs?"

"Nah, but . . . what kind of message are they sending us women? That the only way to get ahead in the game is to play into man's porn fantasy?"

Ronnie sighs, throwing out an ace of spades. "My daddy taught me that anything a man can do, a woman can do too. So if a man can rap about sex, why can't a woman?"

"Yeah, but . . ."

"But nothing. And if you can't see how you wrong for judging them, then you a hypocrite."

My back straightens. "I ain't no hypocrite."

"Who are you or anyone to judge the way they want to live their lives? No one judging you for living yours." She glances at my medallion. "To me, when they talk about sex, they just sound . . . powerful."

"Powerful? You bugging."

She smirks. "You know how gully you gotta be to break the mold everybody tries to bake you in? How I see it, Kim and Foxy took all the shit that Negros throw at us—calling us bitches, hoes, I pay your bills, blah blah blah—and started using it on themselves. It's like they took men's weapons and used it against them. 'Cause once you let someone know they weak-ass words can't hurt you, that you don't need them, that you got your own, they no longer have any power over you. And you can be, do, say whatever you want."

"And so what they talking about sex?" Tamika says, her neck rolling. "Men talk about sex in songs all damn day! How it makes them *feel* good. So what, chicks can't feel good?"

Ronnie chuckles, throwing down a four of hearts.

"Word. Like, how *dare* ladies enjoy sex, too?"

They dap each other up, laughing. I'll be honest, I never expected they'd have such feminist views. Maybe I really am too . . . judgmental.

"Aight, I feel you," I say with a smile. "Guess I never really looked at it like that. But . . . if taking back your power means you can be whoever you want to be . . . how about be a teacher and help children to read. A doctor and help cure cancer. A humanitarian and help feed the world's poor. A social worker and help kids in the hood. If your only goal is a selfish one . . . if your looks is only thing you care about . . . what does that say about you?"

Ronnie stares up at me, her face unreadable, but something hit her at the right angle.

La'Tasha sucks her teeth. "Damn, Ronnie, you reneged!"

"Wait, hold up, y'all," Chanté says, her hand raised to quiet us. "Yo! That's Pierce Williams on the radio!"

I suck in a breath. Shit, is Pierce about to get on the mic and tell everyone about Steph?

"Shhh," Ronnie says. "Listen!"

"What up, everybody," Pierce says. He doesn't sound angry. Not like a man whose been lied to for weeks.

"I got a special announcement 'cause we got a very special event going down tonight! Now, I know y'all heard of Fast Pace and this new kid the Architect. But tonight . . . we taking it back to the corner, back to the streets! Battle of the Emcees, Brooklyn vs. Brooklyn, Fast Pace vs. the Architect."

My mouth drops. "What . . . ?"

"And only you, ladies and gentlemen, can decide the winner. Tonight, you'll decide these two brothas' fate at the Tunnel, where we'll be coming to you LIVE—"

BOOM BOOM BOOM

We all shriek at the loud knock on the door. Ronnie and Tamika look at each other, something unsaid passing between them before they glance at me. My stomach drops as I jump to my feet.

Ronnie puts a finger to her lips, waving, and the girls spread out, Tamika grabbing the baseball bat in the corner. I don't know what to do. Not like I can climb out the window and jump. My muscles start to mush but I push myself up, fists ready. A tribe of fierce women surrounds me, and I'm not going down without a fight.

Don't faint! Stay strong.

Ronnie tiptoes to the door, inching toward the peephole.

"Shit," she exhales. "It's just Quady."

She clicks the locks and swings the door open. Quady stands in the doorway, eyes scanning the room until they lock on me, chest heaving. He rushes across the room and gathers me in his arms.

"Damn," he whispers. "I was so scared."

I grip him back tight, burying myself in his warmth. Over his shoulder, Ronnie's face changes from a dozen different expressions at once but one that stood out the most is hurt. Tamika stands by her, taking her hand.

Rell stumbles in, sweaty and out of breath. "Whew, thank God!" He leans against the doorway, panting.

"Yeah, she's straight," Ronnie snaps. "Some guys were trying to snatch her up."

"Well, what's up, ladies," Rell says, smoothing down his eyebrows. "Oh, we having a party?"

"No!" the girls say in unison.

Rell grins. "Hey La'Tasha. How you doing?"

Tasha rolls her eyes. "I'm good."

"Oh, I know you good," he chuckles. "I'm just trying to be a part of your *better*."

Ronnie purses her lips. "Y'all wanna tell us what's going on now?"

Quadir turns to her, his arm still around my back. "It's . . . a long story."

She nods, her lip twitching. "Whatever. Well, y'all better go before my pops come home."

Rell straightens. "Welp. Don't gotta shoot at me twice. See y'all at the elevator."

"Can you go with him?" Quadir whispers.

I wince a smile at the girls. "Nice meeting y'all. And, uh, thanks."

The girls don't say nothing. Just stare with hard eyes. I shrink into the hallway after Rell. Quadir follows, stopping at the door to face Ronnie.

"Yo, Ronnie thanks for taking care of . . . Jasmine. You know, she already been through a lot and—"

"Yeah, whatever. I didn't do it for you."

He takes a breath. "Listen, I'm sorry . . . about everything. I know we haven't talked, and there's a lot I want to tell you. But right now . . . I just gotta deal with something. But I promise, I'll tell you everything. I owe you that."

Ronnie doesn't say anything, and I try to ignore the tightness around my neck. Maybe he'd rather be with her. Maybe he's changed his mind.

But once he walks out, the door slams so hard behind him the whole hallway shakes. Quadir and I look at each other and a relieved smile grows across his lips.

"I just heard Pierce on the radio," I say, in a daze. "What the hell happened?"

43
JARRELL

Quady is pacing around my room, which basically mean he's twirling in a circle 'cause they ain't no room in here to pace.

"Yo, I can't believe they went after Jasmine like that," he barks. "She could've been hurt! You think they gone for good?"

"The way the homies tell it, sounds like them Arrested Development hippies went back to Tennessee."

"And then Pierce went on the radio and now the whole city gonna be up in the Tunnel looking for Steph!"

"If it ain't one thing, it's another." I sigh and slip the tape out of my back pocket, loading it into the boom box.

"Son, you really trying to listen to music right now?"

"Yo, did you peep that missing verse Pace was playing? He cut it short. Why?"

The tape hisses as Steph busts out the speakers . . .

'Cause Holmes, hate don't pay
Shout-out to Sport and the whole Brevoort
I heard they killed Rashad in broad daylight on the court
At first thought
Sound a little like BUMPY to me, now the whole hoods jumpy
'cause that bump in streets
But we gon' pave the road
I'm 'bout to take it home
Started this verse OK
End it with a K.O.

"Rashad?" Quady says. "Ain't that that kid that got murked last summer?"

"Yeah! But . . . who the hell is this Bumpy cat Steph talking about?"

"I don't know. But I swear that verse wasn't on anything I listened to in Steph's room."

"And this ain't no bathroom studio track either," I say, popping out the tape. "This shit sounds professional. There's probably more. Where you think Pace got this from?"

Quady slaps his forehead. "Kaven!"

"Kaven? How? He don't know nothing about Steph. We've been careful!"

"Remember that first day in the studio? I swear he made

a face when he played them tapes, like he recognized Steph's voice. Then Jasmine said when she was in the booth, she saw that little doodle Steph always did, right on the wall."

"That three lines and a snake?"

"Yeah!"

"Damn. So Kaven's been playing us from day one."

"But I don't get it. Why cut out this verse?"

I purse my lips. "Son, think about it. Steph was naming names without naming them. If the wrong person heard this, the right person would catch a case."

"So you think Kaven knows Bumpy, and he took the verse out?" Quady shakes his head. "Son, we need that original recording. That'll prove Kaven knew Steph all along!"

"Man, how we gonna prove any of this to anybody?"

Quady snaps his fingers. "The cameras! Jazz called it. Steph gotta be on them security cameras. If we can get the original track and footage, we can prove he was there and Kaven had something to do with Steph's murder. Yo, we gotta do it now before Fast Pace gives him the heads up and he deletes everything!"

"That's if Pace hasn't figured out I swiped his tape. Him and his boys could be looking for us right now."

"Nah, remember, he should already be heading to the Tunnel. Come on, son, we can do this!"

Quady's right, but there's no way Kaven gonna give us the goods without us packing some heat.

I dive under the bed, scooping shoeboxes out from underneath.

"Son, what you doing?" Quady asks, panicking behind me.

"Come on, where is it?" I mumble to myself.

"Rell! What you doing? Come on, we gotta go!"

I grab the last box, way in the back, and throw it on the bed.

"Yo, close that door!"

Quady rolls his eyes and slams the door shut. "Now what?"

I pop the lid and almost shit on myself. Nothing but a pair of brown Lugz I wear when it rains. Maybe I'm tripping.

"It's in one of these," I say, my voice drifting. Boxes are scattered all over. I'm sweating and cursing as I rip off each lid. Quady just stands there watching me search through nothing but sneakers, boots, and money.

"Rell!" Quady barks.

"I swear, I put it right there!"

"Put what where?" Quady says, kicking a box next to him.

If Mummy found it, I would've been kicked out the house by now. Could I have thrown it away by mistake? Nah, I ain't that dumb. Should I ask the twins? Nah, they would've been rat me out to Mummy.

Could've, would've, should've . . .

Who else was in here that would've been messing with my stuff? Who else even comes in here like that except . . .

"Aw shit," I groan as it hits me. "Damn. That fool took it."

"Who? Took what?"

"Steph," I sigh, staring out the window at the courts. "My gun."

44
Jasmine

Detective Paul Vasquez. Of the 79th Precinct.

I pinch the edges of the business card Jarrell dropped off with my thumb and forefinger at the kitchen table, drawing blood.

"Jasmine, can I have some more Kool-Aid?"

Behind the card, Carl's little face stares up at me, mouth covered in cheese sauce. I picked him up early from the baby-sitter and cooked him some dinosaur-shaped chicken nuggets and Kraft macaroni and cheese. So caught up in everything, I haven't paid Carl much attention the past few months, and all I want to do is be close to the ones I love. I mean, he lost a brother too, and I'm his only sister. I need to be there for him, make sure he remembers Steph and Daddy.

"Sure, pook. Let me make you some more."

Outside, night has fallen. And Jarrell and Quadir are heading to the studio, about to charge in like some superheroes and save the day.

Dummies.

I begged them not to, but they wouldn't listen. Instead, they left me with one job to do.

Detective Paul Vasquez. Of the 79th Precinct.

After dinner, we watch some TV, and I tuck Carl into bed with his Hess truck. First time he's tried sleeping on his own since Steph died. Hopefully I won't wake up and find him in my bed again.

I slide the card out my back pocket and stare at it some more. My gut says never trust the police. So what business does Steph have with one? Only one way to find out.

I pick up the phone in kitchen and dial the number before I have chance to change my mind.

RINGGG

Damn, it's already nine thirty. Maybe it's too late to call. Should I leave a message? Who do I even ask for? Is that safe—

"Vasquez!" His voice is sharp and alert, as if he just started his day. "Hello? Helllooo?"

I jump up to close the open kitchen window, afraid of my voice carrying and someone overhear me talking to the police.

"Yes," I whisper. "Is . . . is this Detective Vasquez?"

"Well, it's Sergeant now. Who's speaking?"

His voice sounds real familiar.

"Um . . . J."

"Okay . . . J. How can I help you?"

I squeeze the phone to my ear and clear my throat. "I found your card in my brother's stuff."

"What's your brother's name?"

"Steph."

Silence. He snaps his fingers, muttering at someone and papers ruffle.

"Steph?" he asks eagerly. "Tall, brown skin, braids?"

I slide down the wall, landing on the kitchen stool. "With a scar, yes."

"Young lady," he says with a sigh of relief. "Boy, am I happy to hear from you."

I don't know what to feel about him. "How do you know my brother?"

"Steph reached out to me last August. Said he had some information about a murder."

"He reached out to you? Why? How?"

"Said he got my number from a friend, and I didn't question it."

None of this makes sense. Where would he get this cop's number from?

"After our last meet-up," he says, "it's like he disappeared off the face of the earth. Been trying to contact him for weeks, but we only had a pager number. He called back once . . . but I take it that was you. We heard about his murder from his friends. I'm sorry for your loss."

So that's where I know him from, the pager!

"His friends? How you didn't hear about him being killed before?"

"We only had a first name to work with, and nothing came up in our system. We tried everything. Stefan, Stephon. Stephen. Nothing."

Steph's smile shines bright in the picture of us on the windowsill. The last picture we took as a family—Mommy, Daddy, Steph, Carl, and me. The last time we were whole.

"He goes by Steph," I say slowly. "But his real name Michael Stephon Davis. Junior."

"Wait . . . Steph is Mikey Davis's son? Is this little Jasmine?"

I pop up from the stool. "You know my daddy?"

He chuckles. "Yes, sweetheart. We all know him well around here."

45
JARRELL

We about to bring a knife to a gun fight. Except we don't got no knife. Might as well say we rolling up to Kaven's studio butt naked.

But fake it till you make it has been the motto from the start.

Not for nothing, I should holla at Mack first like he told me. But then I would have to come clean about losing that piece he gave me, and my plate's already full.

But for real, though, what the hell did Steph do with my gun? It wasn't anywhere in his room, we'd checked through all them boxes. So what he end up doing with it?

Quady rings the bell at Kaven's studio, standing in front of the camera, nibbling on his bottom lip.

"You ready?" he whispers without looking at me.

Off to the side, I squat down, hidden. "Yup. Let's do this."

Quady has the mace in his hoodie pocket and I have the size. Between the two of us, we could over overpower this fool, no question. Get what we need and dip.

The door locks click. I take off running, ready to ram it until some brown-skin young cat with short dreads swings it open.

"What the . . . ?" I trip right into him and we fall inside.

"Yo, get off me!" he barks, shoving my chest. "Aye yo, Kaven! Who the hell is this?"

Inside, it's a party. I mean, so many brothas squeezed up in the spot you could barely see the walls. And it ain't them regular around-the-way brothas either. It's that Mobb Deep–loving crew that got the room smoky and Henny flowing, dressed in nothing but black and army green. It's like we interrupting a cypher or something.

Kaven leans back in his chair at the soundboard, poking his head around a few cats standing in his way.

"What y'all doing here?"

Quady grabs my jacket, pulling me up off the floor.

"Nothing. We must've got the days wrong. We leaving."

Dread jumps to his feet, slamming the door shut.

"Nah, bump that, son! They were scheming. Trying to run up in here and stick you!"

Shit. Busted.

The whole room stops to stare at us. The kid in the booth rapping over Big's "Warning" beat takes off his headphones to see what's popping. Kaven's the only one that doesn't seem surprised.

"Really," he says, his voice calm.

Quady's jaw clenches as he surveys the scene. We outnumbered at least nine to two.

"Aight, look. We ain't want no problems. We just here . . . to get our man's music."

Kaven shrugs, all cocky. "I don't know what you talking about."

"Quit playing games," I bark. "You know what we talking about! You knew who Steph was the first time we walked up in this bitch."

"Maybe. Maybe not."

"We just came to get what's his, and that's it," Quady insists.

His face twists up. "Ain't nothing in here belongs to anybody but me."

"Yo, how you gonna lie to our face?" I snap. "We heard the song, the real song, b! Not that shit you gave Steph before you had him killed!"

Kaven slowly rises to his feet. "You coming up in my spot, accusing me of murking some kid?"

The temperature in the room changes, like project heat on full blast as everyone stirs. Quady double-taps my elbow, warning me to chill. But it's too late. Duke is lying, and he has something to do with my best friend being murdered.

"We don't want no beef," Quady says. "We just need his song."

"You hard of hearing?" Dread says behind us, taking a step closer. "There ain't no song!"

"Son, this ain't none of your business," I snap. "And I ain't leaving without my man's shit!"

Kaven chuckles and waves us off, turning back to his board. "Y'all handle that, will you?"

I only manage to throw one punch before the room caves in on us.

46
Jasmine

BOOM BOOM BOOM BOOM

At first, I thought I was dreaming. The banging on the front door sounded like four quick gunshots. I rub my eyes and check the time.

BOOM BOOM BOOM BOOM

Three a.m.? Who the hell is knocking at our door this late? Rolling out of bed, my feet hit the cold floor as it hits me.

Oh shit. The Guerrillas . . . they know where I live!

BOOM BOOM BOOM BOOM

I throw on some sweats and my sneakers and rush out into hall, running right into Mom.

"Ah!" she screams. "Jasmine, you scared me to death!"

"Mom! What are you doing home?"

She throws her hands on her hips. "Girl, I live here!"

BOOM BOOM BOOM BOOM.

We stare at the door and I gulp, breaking into a cold sweat. What if they come in here and something happens to Mom and Carl. I can't let anyone else get hurt because of something I did.

"Mom," I whisper, pushing her back down the hall. "Go in Carl's room and hide!"

She reties her blue house robe. "What? Why?"

"Mom, please just listen to me. You have to hide."

Mom's eyes widen. "Jasmine, what is going on?"

"Nothing, just please, Mom—"

"Aye. Open up this door," a familiar voice yell. "Y'all act like I can't hear you up in there."

"Pierce?" I mumble.

"Who the hell is Pierce?" Mom snaps and charges toward the door.

"No, Mom, don't!"

She swings it open, gazing up. "Can I help y—HEY!"

Pierce bulldozes in with his two goons and I backpedal into the living room with a yelp.

"*Where* is he?" Pierce shouts, stumbling in.

"Hey! You can't just come in my home!" Mom screams.

"Yo, shut the hell up," Pierce slurs and points his finger at me. "You! You must be his little 'assistant' right?"

"How . . . how'd you know where we lived?" I choke, the only thing I could think of to ask.

He sways and hiccups. "Oh please. I got connects all over this city. It wasn't hard tracking you down. Now where is this little mutherfucker? Gonna stand me up? *Me!* Fucking no-show to a club I rented out for *him*! I swear once I get my hands on this little—"

As soon as he turns, Mom lands a slap across his cheek that could be heard in Kenya. I gasp, covering my mouth. The goons only flinch, glancing at each other.

"How *dare* you come up in my house, cursing up a storm, and talk to my daughter crazy like that? Who the hell you think you are?"

Pierce blinks twice, shaking his head, almost losing his balance.

Mom eyes the goons. "You two! Close my door. You letting out all the heat and got the whole building up in our business."

"Yes, ma'am," they say in unison, and do what they're told.

Pierce grabs his chin and plops down on the sofa, staring at the floor.

"I'm sorry, ma'am," he says in a quiet voice. "I meant no disrespect."

The goons and I share a baffled look. I didn't even think he could talk at this level.

Mom folds her arms and turns to the goons. "You two, go in the kitchen and help yourself to some water."

"Yes, ma'am," they say in unison, and hustle to the kitchen. I forgot how Mom could control a room with a snap of her fingers. It's good to have her back!

"Jasmine, who is this fool, and why is he up in my house?"

"I'm Pierce Williams," he says. "I'm looking for the Architect. Is he here?"

"The who?"

"Architect. I am . . . was . . . going to sign him to my label, Red Starr Entertainment."

He pauses for recognition and Mom only shrugs at him.

"What happened?" I ask.

Pierce lets out a long sigh. "Homie didn't come through to the show today. It was a massive L. Cost the company almost a million dollars . . . and I was made a fool of in front the entire music industry. The *whole* city was tuned in. My boss already gave me the heads-up to expect termination papers on Monday."

"They're firing you? For what?"

He shrugs. "Said I was 'too much of a liability.' With my temper, ego, blah blah blah. I ain't tripping off that. I already saw the writing on the wall." He shakes his head. "But . . . damn. I don't know, I saw potential in the kid. That raw hunger I had when I was first starting out. Something I haven't seen in years from anyone. I mean, he could've been something *big*."

Suddenly, my heart breaks for Pierce. We dragged him into this mess, and he really believed in Steph after all.

"Who is this Architect you looking for?" Mom says, more confused than ever.

Pierce wipes his eyes. "Isn't there a Michael Stephon Davis here? That's the only person it could be."

A deep V forms down the middle of Mom's face until she hisses and glares at me.

"Jasmine! Is this about those damn CDs?"

Dag, busted.

My head drops to the floor. "Sorry, Mom."

"Unbelievable," she fusses. "Listen . . . Pierce. Steph? Steph is . . . gone."

"Gone?"

"He died a few months ago."

Pierce almost smirks as he gently corrects her. "No, ma'am, I think you talking about someone else."

"No, you not listening. My son is dead," she says, hard. "He was killed back in August. Them CDs you've been listening to, that's his old music. Stuff he did before he passed."

Pierce blinks slow, holding his hands out as if to block the truth.

"Wait, wait . . . are you saying he's . . ." He slowly rises to his feet, taking a step in my direction. His eyes narrow then widen in shock as he recognizes me.

"Oh shit," he mumbles, falling back into the sofa, holding his face. "Shit. How the hell . . . ?"

Mom shakes her head at me. "Yeah. His so-called friends roped my daughter into this mess, trying to make a dollar off my dead son's music."

"That ain't it," I say, my voice sharp. "Quadir and Jarrell, all they wanted was for the world to hear what Steph could do! Mom, Steph was . . . really good, he could've really been somebody. They wanted everybody to know Steph wasn't just another kid gunned down in the hood. He was special. You saw it too, right, Pierce? You ever lose somebody and wonder what they could've been?"

Mom tears up, wrapping her arms around herself.

"Quadir and Jarrell, they haven't even touched the money we made. And they didn't rope me into nothing. If anything, I tricked them. I only agreed to give them his music if they'd help me find out who killed Steph. And they out there RIGHT NOW doing just that!"

Pierce, still in shock, listens close, rubbing his chin. He nods, as if deciding something.

Softly, he says, "Where them boys at now?"

47
August 23, 1998

Summer decided to cough out one more heat wave before August ended. Brooklyn sweltered, the humidity a thick layer of paint coating skins and suffocating mouths. Most folks retreated indoors to park themselves in front of fans and air conditioners, leaving the block a ghost town.

Quadir and Jarrell took their positions on the corner, Steph noticeably missing. It had been almost twenty-four hours since the boys had seen him. "This ain't like him," Quadir mused.

"Yo, where the hell is dude at?"

Quadir shrugged, itching to pace.

Jarrell downed his third quarter water, wiping his face with a rag he kept in his back pocket.

"Mummy says when it's hot like this, a storm's coming."

"Oh, word?"

"Yeah. All this pressure gotta let out somewhere, y'knowwhatumsayin?"

Quadir's shoulders tensed, looking back at B-Voort as dark clouds crept closer. Maybe they should stop by his crib, call, or something.

A police car rolled up on Patchen Ave, lights flashing but no siren. Probably just patrolling, Quadir figured, but behind it, an unmarked car parked up front. Two white guys in suits stepped out, disappearing into B-Voort.

Dante ran around the corner, biting his fist. He spotted the boys and his eyes widened.

"YO! I came as soon as I heard."

Jarrell frowned. "Heard what?"

"About Steph!"

Both boys pushed off the wall. "What about Steph?"

"Yo, son got murked last night!"

Jarrell lets out a nervous chuckle. "Shit, you had me worried there for a second. I thought you were talking about OUR Steph."

"I am, though!"

"Nah, son, you got the wrong duke."

"Yo, word on my momma, it's Steph!"

Quadir studied Dante, the frantic way he shook his hands and couldn't keep still.

The air changed around them, his belly shrieking at him. Without realizing, he headed for Steph's building, but froze in the crosswalk as a gut-wrenching scream poured out of an open window.

Jarrell backed away, shaking his head, his eyes watering. "Nah. Nahhhh. It ain't him! It ain't fucking him!"

Quadir squeezed his ears, falling to his knees in the middle of Patchen Ave.

In the distance, thunder cracked and the sky opened.

48

QUADIR

The bodega is mad convenient.

Besides having the best bacon-egg-and-cheese in Bed-Stuy, they also sell ice packs, aspirin, and dishcloths. Exactly what we need after our ass-whooping.

I lean against the wall next to Jarrell, spitting blood onto the concrete. My mouth is busted up, left eye swelling. My right arm is turning purple, and my shoulder needs to be popped back in. One thing for sure, I'll be out for the rest of the season.

Goodbye, Bishop.

Jarrell has a devil's horn growing out of his forehead and right cheekbone. Holding an ice pack against the back of his head, he winces every time he raises an arm, and hops on one foot.

"Yo," he moans. "I haven't had my ass beat this bad since . . . never."

"You think we should go to the hospital?"

"Son, Tweety Bird's flying around my head. Of course we need to take our asses to the hospital. Which means I'mma have to wake up Mummy and get my ass beat twice tonight."

The first laugh comes up like a cough. Then a hiccup, until I'm giggling like some little baby.

"What? What you laughing for? This shit ain't funny."

"Yo, remember that episode of *Martin* when he got his ass whooped by Tommy Hearns?"

Rell chuckles. "Ha! Son came out his room lumped up! Big old bobblehead looked like an anthill. A burnt pizza. Planet Pluto."

We fall over each other, howling.

"Yo, chill," I cackle, tears in my eyes. "I think they cracked my ribs. I can't be laughing like this."

Rell shakes his head, thinking back. "That was one of Steph's favorite episodes."

The mention of Steph brings the mood right back down as we glance at his spot just as Dante rounds the corner, a blunt lit in his hand.

"Aye yo, what . . . DAMN! What in the hell happened to y'all!"

Rell sucks his teeth. "Nothing, man."

"For real, you—"

"Drop it, Dante," I snap. I ain't in the mood to entertain his questions.

Smoke swirls around his head as he throws his hands up.

"Yo, my bad, son," he says, and leans against the wall next to Rell. He takes a hit, passing the dutch across. I ain't smoke in a grip, but tonight, I need . . . something.

"Damn, y'all look fucked up."

"We know, son," Rell snaps, taking a hit. "We ain't blind."

"Was it them cops again? They did this to you? You know how they be messing with black folks."

"Just got jumped by some kids, ain't nothing. Misunderstanding, that's all."

"Psshh! You lucky you still breathing."

"We know," I say, and spit more blood on the ground.

"These streets be crazy," he mumbles, shaking his head. "Y'all gotta be careful. Can't be caught slipping." He takes another hit from the L, blowing smoke out slow. "Maybe if Steph wasn't caught slipping with them Feds, he'd still be breathing."

I don't know if it was the weed, or being knocked upside the head, but everything in that moment seem to happen in slow motion . . .

Dante passes the dutch to Rell.

Rell holds it to his lips and freezes, standing like some type of statue. His eyes narrow as he snarls, turning to him.

"Yo . . . what did you just say?"

The words come out so low and cold. I immediately sober up.

Dante pauses, eyes growing twice their size. In an instant, he knows he messed up.

"I—I . . . um . . ." he stutters then takes off running, hat flying off his head. He doesn't even bother to grab it. Only one reason a person runs like that: they did something foul.

Rell hobbles to the middle of the sidewalk, watching him ghost. He flicks the blunt in the street, spitting where Dante once stood. For a long while, he's quiet, fist balled up, huffing through his nose.

I'm sick to my stomach. "What d'we do now?"

"Quady!"

Jasmine is running out her building, frantic, voice echoing through the empty streets. Behind her, Pierce and his two henchmen slowly follow.

"Oh shit," I gasp.

"Damn, I take that back," Jarrell grumbles. "We don't need a hospital. We might as well just go straight to the funeral home."

"Oh my God," Jasmine screams, running across the street, right to me. "What happened?"

"I'm aight."

She cradles my face, inspecting my injuries in the light of the bodega sign. I ain't gonna front: her soft hands feel mad good on me right now, so I'm definitely not pushing her away. She's that slice of comfort I'm always craving.

"Yo, Jazz," Rell mumbles, slipping off his coat, wincing with every move, watching Pierce cross the street. "Make sure they play 'Juicy' at my homegoing service. And make sure I look fly, aight? Don't let Mummy put me in the ground in some busted corduroy pants or them itchy Cosby sweaters she loves so much."

"Son, what you doing?"

"I ain't going down without a fight," he huffs, raises his fists to his face. "They can snack on you, but I'mma make these two woolly mammoths work for their dinner."

"Rell," Jasmine says, like some mom scolding a child. "They ain't here to fight."

He purses his lips. "They sell you the Manhattan Bridge along with Prospect Park, too?"

"I'm serious! They . . ."

"WELL! If it isn't my two favorite 'managers,'" Pierce says with a slow clap. "Bravo, you two deserve an Oscar. Oh, my bad . . . rough night?"

He throws his head back and busts out laughing. I mean, he can't even stand up straight, he's cracking up so hard.

"Yo, I don't see anything funny here," I bark. "Do you, Rell?"

Jasmine slips under my shoulder, holding me back.

"Nope," he says, fists up, flexing. "So let's go!"

Pierce waves us off, still snickering. "Man, put your Mickey Mouse guns away. Far as I'm concerned, you deserve it, after all the shit you put me through."

"Yeah? Well, we done with all that now."

"What?" Jasmine says.

"Jazz, I can't do this no more. I'm sick of all this lying. It's over anyways."

"Over?" Pierce asks, his eyebrow raising.

"Yeah," Rell says, hopping closer to him. "This duke Kaven won't give us Steph's original music track. Fast Pace about to blow up our spot and now you up in our hood, ready to feed us to your two overgrown rottweilers."

Pierce smirks, pointing a thumb behind him. "Who, these two? They teddy bears!"

"Now who's lying?"

"So what, that's it? You just gonna quit?"

Rell sucks his teeth. "Man, what do you care? Worried we won't be around to pick up your laundry?"

"Nah, y'all, listen," Jasmine urges. "Pierce got fired tonight because of us."

My neck snaps. "For real?"

Pierce nods, his lips in a straight line.

"Oh, word?" Rell says. "Damn, my bad, son. We weren't trying to make you lose your J-O-B. Bet you had those good benefits, too."

He shrugs. "Ain't nothing. About time I did my own thing. What'd you say the other day? Can't grow under a rock, right? But what about you two? I thought y'all were doing this for your boy."

"Well, yeah, but . . ."

"If I let every little hiccup stop me from chasing my dream, my ass would still be slicing honey-roast turkey in my pops's store. Your girl said something . . . that really hit me. So I'mma help y'all finish what you started."

I can't believe it. Even after learning about Steph, we got the hottest producer on our team. I don't know whether to thank him or Jasmine, smiling up at me.

"But Kaven . . ."

"Yo, this Kaven cat ain't nothing but a roadblock." He smirks. "And sometimes . . . you gotta get creative to work your way around them."

49

JARRELL

It's six against one this time: Pierce, the goons, Fletch, Quady, and me. I'm surprised Kaven even let us in. Shoo, I wouldn't.

"Do you know who I am?"

Kaven slouches in his chair, glaring at me, a toothpick hanging out the side of his mouth, his hat pulled down low.

"I said, do you know who I am?" Pierce asks again, hard.

"I do," he says like he's amused.

Pierce is flossing in a white turtleneck sweater and slacks, with a black leather trench coat. He raises an eyebrow.

"Then you know what I'm capable of."

"Or what you *used* to be capable of," Kaven says with a smirk. "Last I heard, you no longer with Red Starr."

Pierce chuckles as Fletch pulls up a stool for him while Quady and I stay close to the goons.

"Oh, so I see someone got the juice. Well, you right. I'm not with Red Starr Entertainment anymore. But I said, do you know who I AM? Not who I be with. So allow me to reintroduce myself . . . and my associates. I'm Pierce Williams, a free agent. This is my lawyer, Fletcher."

Fletch eyes bulge before he puts on a fake smile, clutching some old brown leather briefcase.

Kaven eyes him, sitting up a little straighter. "Lawyer?"

Fletch clears his throat. "Um, yup, Gordon Fletcher, Esquire."

Kaven rolls his eyes, growing impatient. "What y'all want?"

"Come on, Kaven. You know what's up and why we here."

He juts his lips out at Fletch. "And the lawyer?"

"I'll save you the legalese but he's here to represent the young man's estate. He was smart enough to draft himself up a will before his untimely passing."

He nods at Fletch, who passes him a contract out his briefcase.

Kaven scans over the contract, nodding, then lightly tosses it on the floor.

"You think I'm stupid? You expect me to fall for this?"

Pierce shrugs. "That's on you. I got no problem letting this play out in court."

Kaven's jaw tightens.

"But hey! I'm sure you could afford a lawyer. Sitting here in your state-of-the-art studio in the middle of the hood. How long this place been open again? Could be used for collateral, considering all the expected profit losses I plan to sue you for."

Kaven tenses, his shoulders sitting up by his ears. They hold a stare-off. He still don't believe him.

"Or we can just do this old-school style," Pierce says, hands clapping as he talks. "You wake up one day, and your baby here will be mad empty. I'll make sure they don't even leave a light-switch cover up in this bitch."

Damn. That's cold-blooded.

"Or we could get REAL personal, Kaven Stewart Brown. Surprised you still working in this business, Old G. Didn't you used to be at Flavor Studios in South Jamaica, Queens? But you dipped, or they ran you out. Something about missing money. And you already haven't paid taxes in a few years, so I can make a few calls and—"

"Aight, aight," Kaven barks, sucking his teeth. "What y'all want?"

Pierce smirks and looks to us. "It's on y'all."

Quady doesn't hesitate. "Tell us what happened to Steph. From the top."

Kaven rubs his temples and sighs.

"The young brotha came through last summer. Think he got my number from Dante, this runner from around the way. The kid was . . . dope. Knew it from the very first time he stepped in the booth. He had this pure, raw talent I haven't seen in years. Word is bond, he gave me chills. I sent one of the singles we worked on over to Fast Pace, hoping he could help put him on. Pace used to record here back in the day, and he owed me a few favors. Put in front of the right people, the kid could've been signed on the spot. But when Pace called, he was heated. Told me to delete the single, that the young man is calling out one of his peoples on the track. I thought, maybe if we just lose that last verse it could still be, you know, usable. So I gave Steph an edited cut.

"When Steph came for his next session, he stepped to me about his song being different. I warned him that if he keeps playing with fire, he's gonna end up burned. He insisted it was the right thing to do. 'Silence keeps folks ignorant of the truth.' We argued for a grip before he left. He was scheduled for a session the following week but never showed. I figured it was a wrap. That is, until you two came in and brought his tapes. I recognized his voice instantly. I reached out to Fast Pace again, hoping he could stop by. But Pace told me he heard the kid was 'handled.' That's all somebody gotta say to know what's up."

I'm real blown right now. Kaven was digging Steph from the start.

"You think Pace got anything to do with what happened to Steph?" Quady asks. "Had him killed 'cause he was jealous?"

"I've known Pace for a while. He's a gossiper, but he ain't no killer. He was just trying to protect his man."

"Must be Bumpy," I mumble.

Quady shook his head. "Why . . . didn't you say nothing?"

Kaven folds his hands. "After you've seen it all, and done it all, you learn to stop asking questions and mind your business so you don't get caught up. I knew what y'all two were doing and kept working with y'all 'cause I fucks with what that young brotha had to say. But I wasn't trying to be involved any further."

"You gotta talk to the cops," Quady says. "Tell them what you told us."

Kaven stares at the floor, shaking his head, and I can't even believe the words coming out my mouth.

"Come on, it ain't snitching, man. It's doing the right thing so no one else gets hurt."

"Or . . . maybe you don't have to say nothing," Pierce offers, a small smile growing.

"What d'you mean?"

"Give us the song and your security cam footage. We won't say how we got it. You play dumb if anyone asks. Give us what we need, and no one will know."

"What? So we gotta bargain with this chump now?" I turn to Kaven. "You really gonna be a punk ass for the rest of your life? My boy walked out here and wasn't seen alive since, and you still won't help us?"

"Relax," Pierce warns. "And respect your elders. There ain't nothing wrong with a man wanting to protect himself."

He shrugs. "Some codes you don't break."

"You a grown-ass man," Quady says, his voice cracking. "Steph . . . he was just *sixteen*."

Kaven eyes soften, his hands opening up. "I . . . I can give you the rest of Steph's music. So y'all can keep doing what y'all doing."

The record scratches, and the whole room freezes.

"What'd you mean 'the rest?'" Quady asks, wincing like he's trying to compute.

"Steph recorded a bunch of tracks. Not just one. Never seen a kid work like him. Reminded me of Tupac, walking into a studio, recording ten songs in a few short hours. One-and-done type of takes."

Pierce is on his feet. "What?"

I grab my chin up off the floor. "Hold up. You saying . . . Steph had more music?"

A soft, satisfied look crosses Kaven's face.

"Brotha, he got a whole album you haven't even heard yet."

After Jasmine handed Kaven's security footage to the police, we bring her with us back to the studio to pick up Steph's final album. I mean, we started this together, so we should end it together too, y'knowwhatumsayin?

Pierce worked with Kaven two days straight, putting finishing touches on the tracks. Strange, but they kinda make a good team, Pierce's passion mixed with Kaven's ear. Old-school-meets-new-school tends to clash, but them two have one thing in common—love of good music.

Pierce comes out the studio, his clothes wrinkled, eyes bloodshot, flickering the CD between his fingers.

"Here it is," he says with a smirk. "Steph's official EP."

The three of us stand there, trapped by some invisible wall. Out of nowhere, sadness kicks in. Jasmine's eyes water up and Quady wraps an arm around her, taking a deep breath.

"What? What's up?" Pierce asks anxiously.

Pierce is holding Steph's very last breaths. The last time we'll hear him crack a joke, spit a bar, or sing a song. Music was life to Steph and ain't nothing sadder than the sound of someone's last heartbeat.

"Um, nothing," I mutter and clear my throat. "Yo, thanks, man . . . for everything. You didn't have to come through for us like you did."

"Don't thank me yet. We ain't done."

"We ain't?"

"Nah," he laughs. "We just getting started."

50
Jasmine

Detective, I mean Sergeant, Vasquez has a smooth caramel complexion, salt-and-pepper hair, and cool demeanor. Not what I'd expect from a cop. Still, it makes me uneasy . . . him being in our home, sitting on our orange sofa, drinking Kool-Aid out of our purple cup. But I'm giving him a chance and not rushing to judgment.

Because he wants to find out what happened to Steph just as much as we do.

Jarrell leans on the wall by the kitchen while Mom and I sit in chairs facing him. Quadir stands behind me, a hand on my shoulder, rubbing circles in my back with his thumb, telling me I'm safe.

"After Jasmine and I spoke, I did some digging. Wanted to get all of our facts straight, so we could get to the bottom of what happened to Steph."

"I still don't quite understand," Mom says. "Where did he get your number from?"

"This card," Vasquez says, pulling out the business card. "I gave it to your late husband years ago. He was an informant for our department and had given grand jury testimony for two of our biggest cases. He truly wanted the best for his community. Even if that meant doing things . . . some people may not agree with."

"Like snitching," Jarrell says, hard.

He shrugs. "You can say that. Although we prefer to call it being a responsible citizen."

Jarrell rolls his eyes. "Yeah, aight."

"Son, really?" Quadir groans.

Mom waves them off. "Shhh . . . go on."

"First time I met Steph was on the Promenade. He told me he was with some friends at a nearby basketball park on Bedford when he overheard a light-skinned male with braids and bad acne talking about killing Rashad Johnson."

"Yoooo," Jarrell says. "I remember that day! Quady, you were the one who wanted to go to that park, remember?"

Quadir tenses behind me, and I touch his hand. "Um, yeah. I remember."

That must have been the same guy we saw on Coney Island.

Vasquez notes the interaction but presses on. "I gave Steph a pager and paid him to be an informant while we worked the case. Such a strong lead, I didn't want him to get lost in the shuffle."

"So, that's where he was getting his money for the studio," I say, looking at Mom. "Not at the shipping company."

"Over the weeks, he was very helpful in closing the loop on a few outstanding cases. Then, early August, he called, wanting to meet up. Asked if I knew anything about something called the Guerrillas, and I honestly didn't know much."

Quadir gives me a small squeeze as my heart sinks.

"Then Steph told me he saw the man who shot Rashad over by a park near the studio he recorded at. Went by the nickname Bumpy. I told him next time he sees him to give us a call immediately, then gave him a ride back, dropping him off a few blocks from here. And that was the last time I heard from him."

"That's probably when Dante saw him," Jarrell exclaims. "Punk ass."

"Chill, b," Quadir warns.

"Few months later, we arrested Fernando Ramirez, aka Bumpy, in connection to several incidents and needed Steph to come in to make a positive identification. So you could understand our . . . desperation to find him."

"You mean, why you hemmed us up on the corner that day?" Rell sucks his teeth. "Should I send my dry-cleaning bill to you or the city?"

"Anyways, without that ID, we had to let him go. Bumpy is nothing but a henchman, meaning he answers to somebody." He grabs a VHS tape out of his bag, pointing at the VCR.

"And there may be a clue on this security footage. You mind?"

Jarrell grabs the tape, rewiring the VCR to the TV. He slips it in and presses play. As soon as the screen pops up, Mom gasps, her hands clutching her face.

There's Steph. Walking up to Kaven's door. It's only been a few months, but seeing him moving around and not just a picture in a frame . . . my whole body goes numb, lips trembling.

"Oh my God," I whisper. Quadir presses both his hands on my shoulders, leaning into the chair.

The screens cuts to footage of Steph in the booth.

"Yo, there he is!" Jarrell says, sliding on the floor in front of us. "Ha! My man!"

"Is there any sound?" Quadir begs.

"Unfortunately, no."

Steph is pressed up on the mic, his hands doing that thing he always did when he rhymed, a smile on his face. He's having the time of his life, doing what he loves.

"Look how happy he is," Mom whispers, holding both my hands, tears in her eyes. "Oh, my baby."

The screen goes black, cutting to the outside footage.

"Now, this is the second time he goes to the studio," Vasquez says. "I want you all to pay close attention to him leaving."

We all lean in, eyes glued. Steph is in the studio, back in the booth for hours. He draws his symbol on the wall. He comes out the booth and is talking to Kaven. They're arguing. Steph looks upset as he leaves. Outside, the camera is cut off slightly by a large bush in the front, but you can see Steph standing on the sidewalk, right by the gate. There's a black car parked out front. A door opens, someone gets out. He's talking to some-one we can't see. The bush is blocking our view.

"Now, does anyone recognize that car?" Vasquez asks, hitting pause. "We were only able to zoom in on a partial on the plate . . . but does it look familiar to anyone?"

Jarrell is up on his feet, tears in his eyes. He stands in front of the TV, shoulders sagging.

"That's not a car," he sighs. "That's a black Range Rover."

51
Quadir

Rell wipes sweat off his brow for the third time in five minutes and stuffs one of the cinnamon rolls he picked up from the corner store in his mouth. I want to crack on him for being so shook, but deadass, my right leg won't stop shaking. Not when there's a huge HOT 97 logo staring back at me.

"Would y'all relax?" Pierce grumbles at us in the waiting area. "Y'all making me look stupid out here."

"Son, I can't believe we up in here," Rell whispers to me.

Jasmine gently places a hand on my bouncing knee.

"You ain't nervous?" I ask.

"Nah, I'm cool," she says, her voice calm and sweet.

That's hard to believe, but she's at ease, taking in all the people walking in and out, as if we're chilling on a bench in B-Voort. Like we ain't sitting in the most famous hip-hop radio station in the world.

"You bugging," Rell mumbles, finishing off his last roll.

A young white lady with long brown hair walks in with a clipboard.

"Hi, Mr. Williams," she says, all cheery. "We're ready for you now!"

Pierce nods at us, and we follow. The radio is playing on some type of surround sound through the hallways. Everyone looks real official in their office but dressed mad regular in jeans and kicks, not all uptight in suits and hard-bottoms. Working up here must be sick. You get to listen to tight music, meet all the fly celebrities, and attend the illest album release parties.

The lady opens the door to a low-lit studio, and the Puerto Rican woman behind the mic stands, her gold hair in a high bun, smile blinding.

"P-Money! What's up, baby," she says.

I blink a few times to make sure I'm not imagining who I'm seeing but her voice is unmistakable.

"Angie! What's up, girl? Thanks for having us."

Pierce gives her a hug like they're old friends.

"Nah, thanks for coming!" She turns to us and smiles. "Hey, what's up, everybody? I'm Angie."

The three of us look stuck on stupid.

"Angie . . ." Rell gasps.

"Oh my God," Jasmine mumbles.

"Mar . . . tin . . . ez."

"Oh my God," Jasmine says again, her mouth hanging open.

Angie Martinez. She's no regular disc jockey. She's the official voice of New York, always with the exclusive hits and interviews. She's friends with some of the biggest names in hip-hop—Jay-Z, Mary J. Blige, Lil' Kim, Puff Daddy. The whole city tunes in from three to seven to hear her show.

"Aight, y'all," Pierce says, "have a seat."

The producer and board operator give us headphones and set us up in front of mics, across the table from Angie.

"Yo, I'm mad excited about this," Angie says to Pierce. "You gave me a little bit of background, but I'm ready to really get into this story."

Pierce chuckles. "Yeah . . . and I got a few more surprises up my sleeve."

The board operator gives her the signal, and Angie leans into the mic.

"HOT 97! Representing hip-hop and R&B Flavor, yuh heard! What up, everybody, it's your girl Angie Martinez up in the place and I got a few special guests today. First . . . Pierce Williams is in the building!"

Pierce leans up on the mic. "What up, what up!"

"Good to have you here, baby," she says. "And you brought some young friends along. Say what up, guys!"

Rell jumps at the chance. "Yo yo yo! It's your boy Rell, representing the Stuy! B-Voort, getting this money! Big ups to Brooklyn!"

"Son, really?" I shout under my breath.

Angie laughs. "You got some characters up in here today, Pierce."

Pierce narrows his eyes at Rell. "Yeah, regular piece of work. That's Jarrell. And this is Quadir and Jasmine."

"Aight, now let's get into the fun stuff. You mentioned that you're signing this up-and-coming artist, the Architect, to your new label."

Rell whips his head around, mouthing the words, "New label?"

"Yup," Pierce says with a smirk. "The Architect will be the first artist signed to Home Court Records."

"Aight, so I've heard some of his stuff, and I'm impressed! Repping BK to the fullest."

Wow, even Angie's feeling Steph's music! My chest swells with pride as Jasmine grins.

Headline: NY's Angie Martinez Cosigns New Brooklyn Artist

"BUT," Pierce says. "There's a catch."

"A catch? Uh-oh," Angie chuckles.

"The Architect . . . is deceased."

Angie frowns, glancing at her producer. "Uhhh . . . what?"

"You heard it here first. The rapper the Architect is Brooklyn's own Michael "Steph" Davis. Born, March 18, 1982. Murdered, August 23, 1998."

Angie, the voice of New York, is speechless. "So . . . the mixes everyone's been listening to . . . ?"

"All previously recorded tracks. Produced by these knucklehead kids. They've been pretending he's still alive, hustling like his street team."

"Wowww!" She turns to us. "Now how the hell y'all pull this off?"

Pierce laughs. "How they pulled it off isn't as important as *why* they pulled it off."

"Aight, I feel you. So tell us . . . why!"

Rell and Jasmine turn to me, waiting.

I clear my throat. "Well, um, I guess we just wanted our boy . . . to be somebody. There's mad kids from the hood who could've been famous rappers, singers, poets, basketball stars . . . but their life got cut short. We just . . . we just wanted our boy to have a life after death. Steph shouldn't be just another name on a list."

"I'm saying," Rell adds. "We . . . Brooklyn . . . are more than what they say about us on the news. We family, we good people. Plus, Big and Tupac blew up after they died. Why not our boy?"

"You shouldn't have to be famous first for brothas and sistas to recognize your shine," Jasmine says softly.

Angie nods. "Wow. That's really . . . beautiful. So now that everybody knows . . . what's next?"

"Everybody in New York knows," Pierce corrects her. "But we want the world to know! We want to send a message that you may kill the man, but you can never kill his dream. So Brooklyn, stand up for your boy! Meet us on Fulton and Utica, in front of the train station! Tomorrow at four p.m.!"

. . .

And then it happened. Bed-Stuy turned into Weeksville again.

On Fulton and Utica, in front of the supermarket, we set up our own table, with over a thousand copies of Steph's demos. Rell played salesman as Fletch and I assisted. DJ Cash brought his turntables and speakers, blasting Steph's music. Everyone from the hood came and then some. It was like a huge summer block party in the winter.

Pierce hired a street team of fine-looking ladies to pass out posters of Steph with the name of his new company. Rell's pops sold T-shirts while his moms sold beef patties and coco bread. My mom helped the guys from the corner store hand out free cups of hot chocolate and cookies. The HOT 97 street team rolled up in their truck and handed out swag. Reporters from every network and newspaper came with their cameras, talking to anyone who ever knew Steph, which seemed like everyone.

"It's time we stop the street violence, once and for all," the Brooklyn Borough President Howard Golden says to News Channel 4. "This young man had a bright future ahead of him. One of many who have died tragically. But it's amazing to see his family and friends turn this tragedy into hope for the community."

Busta Rhymes, Lil' Cease, AZ, Foxy Brown, the Lox . . . all friends of Pierce, came through. They signed autographs, took pictures with fans, and helped pass out swag. We sold out within an hour.

"Steph was just like us," some girl says to a reporter. "You know, he was talking about life here in the Stuy. Stuff people don't understand but need to."

"He was B-Voort. We gotta show him some love!" another duke says.

Ronnie and her girls start dancing, hyping up the crowd to join them. Ms. Davis and Jasmine walk around hugging and thanking everyone for coming. The party spills out into the street. People dancing on top of cars, shouting his lyrics, bringing traffic to a halt.

Ms. Davis is stunned. You could see it in her eyes as she cried on every shoulder. She never expected to see so many people show love for her baby. But that's what we do. We spread love.

It's the Brooklyn way.

52
JARRELL

E. Rocque's basement is rocking so hard the walls are sweating. DJ Cash ain't playing nothing but Steph's music. Everybody's holding posters, pictures, wearing RIP T-shirts, screaming the lyrics loud enough for Steph to hear in heaven.

And he ain't just at E. Rocque's either. He's up in the Tunnel, Club Lima, Speed, on HOT 97, from Brooklyn to Compton, from hood spots to cookouts—Steph is everywhere. It's the type of homegoing service he would've wanted.

Okay so boom, I got a story to tell . . . of how it all went down:

- Dante told Mack that Rashad was selling weight on Mack's turf.
- Bumpy worked for Mack and took out Rashad.
- Steph overheard Bumpy bragging, went to the Feds, and blew up his spot on the track.
- Fast Pace was friends with Bumpy and word got back to him.
- Mack didn't want the heat, so Mack had Bumpy take out Steph.

Crazy how they say no snitching but cats getting murked 'cause of a bunch of lip smacking anyways.

The air is nice and crisp outside. I pour a little liquor out for my homie. Steph risked his life for everybody, but he died for me, and that's something I have to live with. That's why I can't let a day go by wasting it on just being a regular everyday duke in these streets. Nah, I gotta make him proud and do all the things he wanted me to.

I pour a little liquor out for Mack. He ain't dead, but he's dead to me.

All that time he was pretending like he cared, when really he was just distracting me from his dirt. Feeding everybody ice cream so no one would notice the permanent stains he made around the whole hood. He stays teaching me something about life, even when he's dead wrong.

Inside, DJ Cash switches it up and plays Big's "Hypnotize." It's crazy that it's been over a year and they still don't know who killed him. They don't even know who killed Tupac yet! Wonder how long it'll take for someone to step up and say something.

One thing's for sure, losing them changed the hip-hop game forever.

Losing Steph . . . changed us forever.

Death got a way of moving you. Whether you ready or not. Y'knowwhatumsayin?

53
Jasmine

In a makeshift conference room up in Harlem, Carl and I stand on either side of Mom, sitting at the head of large table. A temp sign—"Home Court Records"—is taped on the bare walls behind us.

With her hair and makeup done up nice, she grips the ink pen and signs the contract laid before her. My heart is beating a million miles an hour. I glance up at Quadir and Jarrell next to me, holding their breath. Quadir's eyes flicker over to me. When she's done, Mom sets down the pen and exhales.

The room full of people burst into cheers as cameras flash.

We did it, Steph. We did it for you.

"With this," Pierce says, addressing the room. "Steph

Davis, aka the Architect, is the first of many artists who will be signed to Home Court!"

Mom hugs and kisses Carl and me. The color has returned to her face. She's our mom again. And with the money we've made, we won't have to move and she won't have to work so hard. She can rest. She can mourn. She can heal.

Fletch pops some champagne for the adults and sparkling apple cider for us.

"Yo, Jazzy Jazz," Jarrell says, squeezing me in a bear hug. "We did it!"

"Rell, I can't breathe!"

"You don't need to breathe, girl, quit playing."

"Yo, man," Quadir says, pushing him off, wrapping an arm around my back. "You crushing my girl."

No matter how many times he says it, I still feel a tingle when he calls me his girl.

"Wait, hold up, hold up! Almost forgot," Pierce says. "We have one more thing to sign."

Fletch pulls a contract out of his bag and slides it across the table. Pierce shifts it in front of me, offering me a pen.

"Can't be a label without a first lady."

54
Quadir

Headline: Three Kids from Brooklyn Pull Off the Biggest Heist in Hip-Hop History

Chilling on the corner, I keep thinking about how one crazy idea turned our lives upside down. I mean, maybe it wasn't so crazy after all. Maybe just thinking outside the box is how you get further than you ever could dream of.

A car drives by, blasting Steph's music. You can hear him echo through the streets of Brooklyn.

On my right is Jasmine, her Afro puffs shimmering in the sun. I grip her hand and she smiles up at me. Like she's proud of me. I'm mad proud of her too.

On my left is Jarrell, beatboxing, flossing in one of those crazy-color Iceberg sweaters Big used to wear. He lost his best friend and his Old G, but still managed to find himself and not kill his little brothers in the process.

Up ahead is Brevoort. Up ahead is my future. Up ahead will always be home no matter how far I go.

55
June 22, 1998

On the corner, Steph faced the sun with his eyes closed, letting it bake his skin. A car drove by blasting Big's "You're Nobody (Til Somebody Kills You)." School was out and the sky was the limit.

"Aye yo, son. What you doing? Trying to go blind?"

Quadir palmed his basketball, spinning it on one finger. Jarrell snatched the ball and dribbled it through his legs.

"Yeah, come on, son! Let me hear a rhyme or something."

Steph smirked at his two friends then laughed.

"Bet. Check it . . ."

They keep sayin'

Let me hear a rhyme, let me hear a rhyme

I'm 'bout to start chargin' pennies, dimes, nickels, maybe

fives

Haha!

I stay sonnin', kids

That means ain't no daughters

Like Jamaican spots at eight o'clock

I take no orders

My style is like curry,

First name kinda the same but got more handle than

Marbury!

But I'm from Brevoort

Breathe or die

Send you to Bed with a sty

Before I,

Finish this,

Remember me for my penmanship, I'm all work, no play

My new name is business trip!! (**oohs and aahs**)

In other words, I'm no joke!

But it ain't no sequel when I make you *Scream 2*

And go ghost! (**oohs and aahs**)

That means I'll disappear into thin air

Maybe then I'll be a legend

When you hear me everywhere!

GLOSSARY OF '90S NEW YORK TERMS

BRICK: Extremely cold

BROLIC: Chiseled, buff, muscular, built man or woman

DEADASS: To be dead serious about a matter; telling the truth

DEUCE DEUCE: A .22 caliber handgun

FUGAZI: Artificial, fake; something that has no substance

GULLY: Rough, raw, street, real

JACKS: Vials of crack cocaine

JAKES: Cops, feds, FBI, or anyone who can arrest

MURK: To kill or severely beat up someone

WORD IS BOND: Truth be told, or the truth is spoken

WORD TO/ON MY MOMS: Swearing to your mother that you didn't do what you're accused of

ACKNOWLEDGMENTS

I was fifteen years old when Notorious B.I.G. was murdered.

On March 9, 1997, I woke up to a screaming call from a friend and turned the radio to HOT 97, where the host sniffled as she broke the news. Callers were hysterical—the entire city of New York was in mourning. Only then did I start to cry. I didn't know B.I.G. personally, but as with many music icons, you felt like they knew you. Biggie was a beacon of hope for the people of Brooklyn. He was one of us, a black kid from the hood who "made it" and represented our borough with so much loving pride. Thus, the raw emotions were akin to those you'd feel losing a family member.

What started as a script in graduate school became the novel *Let Me Hear a Rhyme*. It's a love letter to hip-hop, to Brooklyn, to my childhood, and to everyone we lost before they had their time to shine. Writing this wasn't like writing my previous novels. It involved going back to 1998, arguably one of the greatest years in hip-hop history, reliving those moments, and creating one of my most personal works to date, so you saw a lot of "young Tiffany" within the pages. . . .

The scene involving an ice-cream truck . . .

I'm Tamika.

The scene at the Tunnel nightclub . . .

I'm the girl on the dance floor. (Yes, Mom, I snuck out with a fake ID!)

The scene at Biggie's funeral . . .

I'm one of the girls confused that the police won't just let us have this moment.

Readers, THANK YOU! For trusting me with your time, your minds, and your emotions. The love I've received for *Allegedly* and *Monday's Not Coming* has been overwhelming. I know this particular book is different, but it's also so much of who I am and where I came from. Thank you for allowing me to share that with you.

I could not have written this without my best friend, Malik-16. Malik, you loved this idea from the very beginning and stepped up to the challenge when I couldn't. It was so much fun going down memory lane and arguing over '90s lingo. Thank you for always being my person and seeing my greatness when I refuse to.

To Benjamin Rosenthal, thanks for being so passionate about this project. All those years of loving hip-hop made you the perfect editor to bring this to life! To Samona and Erin, thank you for the dopest cover EVER!! To Natalie Lakosil, as always, thank you for your fierce positivity and planning for a future that is beyond my expectations. To Sam Bernard, thank you for continuing to fight for my dreams.

To Akil Kamau, Shanelle Gabriel, Lamar Giles, and Starr Rocque (and E. Rocque!): thank you for reading the early versions of this book as honorary hip-hop fact-checkers.

Big ups to Brooklyn, my family, my friends, and my writer community. Ya'll made me and keep me humble. Thanks for helping me find my way back after losing my beloved pup, Oscar De La Jackson.

And, God, thank you for raining down blessings and continuing to work on me.

FROM MALIK-16

To my parents, for never throwing away my millions of spiral notebooks full of lyrics.

To Sha-Sha, for waiting for this book.

To every single Brownsville summer spent in the Seth-Low projects at my Aunt Rosey's with my cousins Omar, Rainy, and Leemi introducing me to hip-hop and comic books amid a backdrop of crack-era insanity.